DAY OF VENGEANCE

*The Dorothy Martin Mysteries
from Jeanne M. Dams*

THE BODY IN THE TRANSEPT
TROUBLE IN THE TOWN HALL
HOLY TERROR IN THE HEBRIDES
MALICE IN MINIATURE
THE VICTIM IN VICTORIA STATION
KILLING CASSIDY
TO PERISH IN PENZANCE
SINS OUT OF SCHOOL
WINTER OF DISCONTENT
A DARK AND STORMY NIGHT *
THE EVIL THAT MEN DO *
THE CORPSE OF ST JAMES'S *
MURDER AT THE CASTLE *
SHADOWS OF DEATH *
DAY OF VENGEANCE *

* available from Severn House

DAY OF VENGEANCE

A Dorothy Martin Mystery

Jeanne M. Dams

Severn House Large Print
London & New York

This first large print edition published 2015
in Great Britain and the USA by
SEVERN HOUSE PUBLISHERS LTD of
19 Cedar Road, Sutton, Surrey, England, SM2 5DA.
First world regular print edition published 2014 by
Severn House Publishers Ltd., London and New York.

British Library Cataloguing in Publication Data

Dams, Jeanne M. author.
   Day of vengeance. – (A Dorothy Martin mystery)
   1. Martin, Dorothy (Fictitious character)–Fiction.
   2. Murder–Investigation–Fiction. 3. Women private
   investigators–England–Fiction. 4. Americans–England–
   Fiction. 5. Detective and mystery stories. 6. Large type
   books.
   I. Title II. Series
   813.5'4-dc23

ISBN-13: 9780727872524

Severn House Publishers support the Forest Stewardship Council™
[FSC™], the leading international forest certification organisation. All
our titles that are printed on FSC certified paper carry the FSC logo.

MIX
Paper from
responsible sources
FSC® C013056

Typeset by Palimpsest Book Production Ltd.,
Falkirk, Stirlingshire, Scotland.
Printed and bound in Great Britain by
T J International, Padstow, Cornwall.

Foreword

The selection of a new bishop in the Church of England is a complex procedure, and although I have done a good deal of research, with the help of several clergy in both England and America, I may have made mistakes, and may indeed have contravened canon law in some instances. I can say only that the mistakes are mine alone, and (in mitigation) plead that I am, after all, writing fiction. I owe great thanks especially to two bishops: the Very Reverend Edward S. Little in my own diocese of Northern Indiana, and the Very Reverend Stephen Venner, who has retired but is still serving as an honorary Assistant Bishop in the Diocese of St Alban's, England. Both have been generous with their time and have answered innumerable foolish questions.

All of the churches mentioned in the book are of my own invention, as are all of the characters, with the obvious exceptions of the Archbishops of Canterbury and York, their secretary, and the Prime Minister's secretary, all of whose roles are minor and offstage. There may be clergy with the same names as those I have given my characters; if so, I apologize, and stress that I did not have them in mind.

The title is taken from a passage in the book of Isaiah, used as part of the ordination service in the Church of England: 'The Lord hath sent me . . . to proclaim the acceptable year of the Lord, and the day of vengeance of our God.'

At the time this book was written, there were no female Anglican bishops in England, though there was at least one in both Scotland and Wales. The situation was changing rapidly, however, and by the time you read this there may well be women wearing the mitre in England.

Author's Note

A group of churches led and served by a *bishop* is called a *diocese*. The bishop's home church, called a *cathedral*, houses the 'cathedra', or bishop's seat. The principal clergyman in a cathedral is the *dean*, who is also the senior priest in the diocese. A cathedral will also have on its staff a number of priests called *canons*. A parish church (any church other than a cathedral) is served and led by a priest who may be called a *rector* or a *vicar*, and who may have an assistant called a *curate*.

The terms *High Church* and *Low Church* refer to diverse traditions within the Church of England, High Churchmen preferring practices that are more similar to those used in the Roman Catholic Church, and Low Churchmen being more Protestant and less ritualistic in their customs.

PRINCIPAL CHARACTERS

The Very Reverend Andrew Brading, *deceased, late Dean of Chelton Cathedral*

Dorothy Martin, *ex-pat American living in the cathedral city of Sherebury, in the county of Belleshire, somewhere in the southeast of England*

Alan Nesbitt, *her husband, retired Chief Constable of Belleshire*

Kenneth Allenby, *Dean of Sherebury Cathedral*

Margaret Allenby, *his wife*

Jane Langland, *Dorothy's oldest friend in England and her next-door neighbour*

Lynn and Tom Anderson, *Americans living in London, friends of Dorothy and Alan*

Walter Tubbs, *Jane's grandson*

Sue, *Walter's fiancée*

The Reverend Geoffrey Lovelace, *Rector of St Barnabas', London*

Mrs Steele, *his secretary*

Akbar and **Saida**, *his parishioners*

Jed, *his sexton*

The Reverend William Robinson, *Rector of St Matthias', Birmingham*

Jenny, *his wife*

Becca Bradley and **Brian Rawles**, *his parishioners*

The Very Reverend James Smith, *Dean of Rotherford Cathedral*
Emily, *his wife*
Mr and Mrs Stewart, **Mr Cho** and **Mrs Loften**, *his parishioners*
Jonathan Quinn, *friend of Dorothy and Alan, policeman-turned-private-detective*
Ahmed, *friend of Walter Tubbs, employee of British Museum*
Jack Everidge, *acquaintance of Walter and Ahmed*
Jeremy Sayers, *organist at Sherebury Cathedral*
Christopher Lewis, *his partner*
Ruth Stevens, **Martha Rudge**, **Archie Pringle**, **Caroline White**, *communicants at Chelton Cathedral*

One

'Oh, *no*!'

My cry brought Alan from the kitchen, where he was tidying up after breakfast. Mutely, I handed him the *Telegraph*.

> The Very Rev. Andrew Stephen Owen Brading, dean of Chelton Cathedral, was found dead late Wednesday night in the cathedral, victim of an apparent assault. His wife, concerned that he had not returned from a meeting in London, asked a neighbour, one of the cathedral staff, to accompany her to the church to look for him when he did not answer his mobile phone. They found a side door open, and when lights were turned on, found the dean lying on the floor of one of the side chapels, dead of an apparent blunt trauma injury to the head. There is a possibility of foul play, and police are investigating.
>
> Dean Brading was named on Tuesday as one of four men on the shortlist for the episcopate of the diocese of Sherebury (see p. 3).

The peace of the gorgeous spring day was shattered. Alan sat down abruptly. The phone shrilled; I went to answer it.

Dean Allenby's secretary was on the line. 'You've heard the news.'

'Just this minute. Alan's still reading the paper.'

'Then will you give him a message? The dean has asked that no one speak to the media, not just yet. The diocesan information officer will issue a brief statement, and he would like everyone from the diocese who's on the Appointments Commission to meet in his office this afternoon. Two o'clock, unless someone simply can't make it then. I'll let you know. Thank you, Dorothy.'

'That was Allison,' I said to Alan. 'Nobody's to talk to the press, and you're to go to a meeting at two this afternoon. Dean's office. She said the information officer will put out a statement.'

Alan sighed. 'Yes, the usual thing, I suppose. Shock and sorrow, no one knows anything, cooperating with the police, et cetera. And speaking of the police, they'll want to interview every one of us on the commission, sooner or later. I'd better put in a call to Derek.'

Detective Chief Inspector Derek Morrison had been Alan's right-hand man when he was in the Sherebury constabulary, and later, as chief constable, Alan had relied greatly on Derek's talents and good sense. He was a good friend and would, I was sure, help all he could.

'Won't he call you?'

'I don't think we'll be answering the phone, love.'

Two of them began ringing at that point. Alan turned his mobile off. I waited until the home phone stopped ringing and then took it off the hook, and turned off my own mobile.

2

I took a deep breath. 'We knew this bishop business would be a terrible strain, with all the contention, but this . . .'

'No. Vicious as church politics can be, one doesn't expect murder.'

We had been embroiled for months in the wearisome business of selecting a new bishop to replace Bishop Hardie, who was retiring. First, the dormant Vacancy in See Committee, on which Alan had sat for years, was called into action. After weeks of surveys and consultations, of contention over hot-button issues such as High versus Low Church, gay marriage, women as bishops – whatever concerns had exercised any individual or group – they had come up with a document detailing the needs of the diocese and spelling out what kind of bishop they were looking for. Then several members of the committee, including Alan and Dean Allenby, were elected to serve on the formidably named Crown Appointments Commission, which would actually choose the bishop. That body had met for a day and a half of confidential discussions at Lambeth Palace at the beginning of the week and had come up with a list of four candidates for the job.

One of them was now out of the running.

'Murders have been committed in the name of religion before now.' I looked at the headline again. MURDER IN THE CATHEDRAL. '"Will no one rid me of this troublesome priest?" Alan, this is frightful!'

He sighed heavily. 'It is. You have realized, haven't you, that every member of the commission, with the probable exception of the two

Archbishops and the two secretaries, is a potential suspect in Brading's murder? Not to mention a rich source of information about the man. We've been looking into the candidates' backgrounds and qualifications for weeks, and everyone and his aunt has been lobbying us. We probably know more about Brading, and who loved and hated him, than anyone else in the kingdom.'

I rolled my eyes to heaven. 'I think I need some more coffee.'

Alan followed me into the kitchen. We sat brooding while the coffeemaker did its thing. When we had sat down at the kitchen table, I said, 'All right. Remind me again of who's on the commission. I know their names were published, but I didn't pay much attention.'

'The dean and I and four others, two lay, two clergy, represent the diocese. There are six representatives from the General Synod, three clergy and three lay persons. One of the latter, incidentally, is our MP.'

I groaned. Our Member of Parliament, Archibald Newsome, is an extremely conservative Tory whom I have always disliked. As an expat American, I can't vote, of course, but if I could, it wouldn't be for him. He is a very wealthy and influential man who has been re-elected for years because so many of his constituents owe him favours. Whenever an election comes up, I always think of Chicago, and Tammany Hall, and reflect that politics all over the world are very much the same. Even in the Church. 'I suppose he's been throwing his weight around.'

'What would you expect? As a matter of

interest, Dean Brading is – was – a close friend of Newsome's.'

'Then that takes him off the suspect list.' I must have sounded disappointed, because Alan uttered what was almost a laugh.

'Not necessarily. I'd like to see him left on, if only because he's an almighty nuisance. I don't know any of the rest well. The other four diocesan representatives are from far-flung parishes, and as they never happened to be involved in a crime I investigated, I'd never met them until we all assembled at Lambeth.'

'Well, they're involved in one now, aren't they? Is that everybody, then? Six from the diocese, six from the Church at large, and the Archbishops of Canterbury and York?'

'And the Archbishops' appointments secretary, and the Prime Minister's appointments secretary.'

'Oh, I always forget about the Prime Minister getting in on the act. That seems so odd to an American.'

'It must do. Dorothy, why are we talking about the bureaucratic details?'

'To keep from thinking about what's going to happen. At least, that's *my* reason. Are you serious about the whole commission being under suspicion?'

'If I were in charge of the case, which I am not, praise God, that's where I'd direct my attention.'

'Who will be in charge? What's the drill?'

'The crime happened in Chelton, so it falls to the Gloucestershire chaps. However, a dean is a major national figure, not to mention the fact that this one was a potential bishop. This is high-profile stuff, Dorothy. The Met will get involved, since the commission met in London. Then Church lawyers will be heavily involved, perhaps even the ecclesiastical courts, though that's highly uncertain.'

'In short, it's going to be a huge mess. With you right in the middle.'

That produced a slight smile. 'Slightly off to one side – at least at the moment. I wish I were out of it altogether. Give me your phone for a moment, will you? It's slightly less likely to ring before I can get in a call to Derek.'

It didn't ring, but the doorbell did. Already in siege mode, I peeked nervously around the curtain before opening the door to the dean and his wife, Margaret. 'Come in quick before some journalist spots you,' I said.

'I'm afraid we did rather slink on our way here,' said Margaret. 'Dorothy, this is a dreadful thing!'

'It certainly is, for all concerned,' I agreed. 'But come into the kitchen and let me get you some coffee.' The English often think tea is the cure for all ills. I enjoy tea, but in a real crisis I feel the strength of coffee is required.

'We may not have much time before the authorities arrive,' said Alan when he had finished his quick call to Derek, and we had sat down with steaming cups of comfort. 'We need to compare notes and work out how much we can tell them, given our vows of secrecy.'

6

'So soon?' asked the dean. 'I'd have thought they'd have other people to talk to first.'

'They'll want to interview everyone who might be concerned, as soon as possible.'

'But why?' asked Margaret.

'So that we won't have time to compare notes and work out what we're going to say,' I said. 'Has neither of you ever read a detective novel nor watched a cop show?'

'Of course we have,' said Margaret, 'but it's always the suspects who want to get their story straight before the police get there.'

'Precisely,' said Alan, and paused to let that sink in.

The dean was the first to speak. 'Oh, dear. I hadn't quite realized . . . that is, I was thinking of the vast damage this could do to the Church at large, and never thought about the danger to us – you and me, Alan. But, of course, they'll have to question us, won't they? There's been enough publicity about the controversies that they might think . . .'

'They certainly might. So, Dean, they'll ask where you were and what you did between the end of the meeting on Tuesday and last evening.'

'I . . . Really, I haven't the slightest idea. That is, I came home after the meeting. The train was very slow, owing to the construction delays. I missed Evensong, I know. Then . . . Margaret, did we do anything in the evening?'

'We'd planned to have dinner with Peggy and Howard and the children, but you were too tired and upset. I scrambled some eggs and sent you to bed with a hot toddy.'

7

'Ah, yes, so you did. I felt badly about it. We don't see our grandchildren often enough. But I was too tired to be good company. What did you do, Alan? I looked for you on the train, but didn't see you. We'd got separated at Lambeth.'

'I had driven in. The last time Dorothy and I went to London the delays were infuriating, so I decided to drive, expensive as that is. Then, after the meeting – well, you know how contentious it was. I was feeling fury and exhaustion in equal parts, and decided I was far too tired to drive home. In any case, the traffic was horrendous. So I phoned Dorothy and told her I was having dinner in town. I didn't get home until quite late. Dorothy was asleep when I came up to bed.'

'I was not,' I retorted. 'I pretended to be, so you wouldn't fret about my staying up for you. I knew you were upset, so I worried. Margaret understands.' She nodded and raised her hands in the classic 'But what can you do?' gesture.

Alan shook his head and continued. 'And yesterday I pottered about the house, cleared out the garden shed, worked on my memoirs for a bit – that sort of thing. Dorothy went shopping in the morning and lunched with friends at Alderney's, so she can't vouch for my presence here for a good many hours. Not that her testimony would be worth much in any case.'

'I suppose not.' The dean looked troubled. 'A devoted wife would lie for her husband, presumably.'

'And I,' said Margaret, 'am *your* only alibi.

8

You had no services to take yesterday, and you were looking a bit white about the gills. I made you stay home and rest.'

'I wonder just when Dean Brading actually died,' I said into a dismal little silence, and just then the doorbell rang.

Again I did the curtain routine at the window. 'Gird your loins,' I said. 'It's Derek and a couple of other people who look awfully official.'

'I'll get it,' said Alan, and went to the door. The rest of us stayed in the kitchen.

'Come in, please,' we heard him say. 'I've been expecting you.'

'We apologize for disturbing you so early in the day, Chief Constable,' said a deep voice, 'but, as you'll appreciate, sir, we've a grave matter to investigate.'

'I do understand, and there's no need to use my former title. I've been retired for quite some time now. "Nesbitt" will do nicely. And you would be?'

'Chief Constable Michael Armstrong, Gloucestershire. And you may remember my assistant, Superintendent Frances Davids. I believe you met over a rather nasty case in the Cotswolds a little time back.'

'Of course I remember you, Superintendent Davids! I didn't recognize you at first. Something about your hair . . . well, never mind. Won't you all sit down? May we offer coffee?'

That was my cue. Alan had, effortlessly, taken control of the situation and indicated that the rest of us were to take part in the interview. I assembled coffee things on a tray, along with

9

a plate of biscuits. 'You carry the pot, Margaret,' I said softly. 'We're treating this as a pleasant social occasion. Here we go.' Watson, who had been waiting in the kitchen for something nice to fall on the floor, followed us into the parlour. Both the cats had vanished. They love visitors they know, who can probably be conned into a cat-appreciation session, but they don't care for strangers.

I greeted Superintendent Davids with an effusiveness that probably surprised her, since we'd met only once or twice over the Cotswold mess. I intended to keep the social atmosphere going as long as possible. I poured coffee for everyone, let Alan make the introductions with Margaret and Kenneth, and then sat back and tried to make myself invisible.

Actually, I felt a little sorry for the Gloucestershire contingent. It was an embarrassing situation for them. Here they were in the middle of a high-profile murder, and two of the possible suspects in the room were a retired chief constable and a senior clergyman! They had to conduct the investigation strictly according to the book, but without stepping on important ecclesiastical and constabulary toes. I sat back to watch the fun.

Alan maintained his firm hold of the initiative. 'Now then, Chief Constable. I'm sure you'll want to know, first of all, where I was after the meeting and all day yesterday. You know, of course, that I'd been in London at a meeting of the Appointments Commission. My alibi until the middle of the afternoon is, therefore, impeccable. Two archbishops, among other people, can vouch for me. Unfortunately, my schedule becomes murkier after that. The meeting broke up at a little after three, and as it was not the most comfortable I've ever attended, I was not in the best of moods when I left. I'm sorry I can't give you details, as we're all sworn to secrecy. I can, later and in private, tell you what I said and did, if you wish, but I can't speak for anyone else. At any rate, I felt it was unjust to take out my bad temper on my wife, so I walked about for quite a little time before deciding to have dinner in town. After dinner – at Simpson's-in-the-Strand, if you want to check – I retrieved my car and drove home. The traffic was still miserable – there was a smash-up on the M20 – so it was quite late before I finally got home. And I fear I spent all day yesterday at home, without anyone at all to vouch for my whereabouts most of the day, as Dorothy was out.' He sat back with a bland smile.

Armstrong, who seemed to be nobody's fool, smiled back. 'Indeed, sir. We appreciate your candour, though at this stage there is no question of suspicion resting on anyone. It is possible I may need to speak with you later – privately, as you suggest – about the commission meeting. For now, may I ask why you did not take the train to London and back?'

'The service has been abysmal of late. You know, of course, that there are works on the line at several points along the way. I don't enjoy driving in London, but I anticipated a difficult meeting and did not want to arrive already annoyed by transport delays.'

'Quite understandable, sir. And just to clear the decks, so to speak, you, Mr Dean, were . . . ?'

'I took the train to London and did in fact encounter delays. I was very nearly late to the commission meeting in consequence, but fortunately not quite. As you know, the meeting took up all of one day and part of the next. I spent the intervening night at a small hotel in Vincent Square. On the Tuesday, I left immediately upon adjournment, but missed the next train home by a minute or two. At that time of day they run every thirty minutes, but there were, again, delays, so it was nearly eight when I arrived at Shrewsbury station. My wife met me in the car, and we had intended to eat dinner with our daughter and her family, but I was so tired we simply went home instead. My wife felt I needed some rest, and kept me under her wing all day yesterday.'

'And when did you hear about the death of Dean Brading?'

'This morning over breakfast, when my wife turned on the television. I was horrified, of course, and began at once making phone calls to attempt damage control.'

Oh, Kenneth! I didn't say it aloud, but I rolled my eyes and looked at Alan. He looked grim.

'Damage control, sir?' There was nothing but bland courtesy in Armstrong's voice, but

12

his eyes had taken on a steely look. Watson, sitting between Alan and me, stirred uneasily.

'I am the dean of a cathedral, Chief Constable. The well-being of its clergy and people are my responsibility. Since the man who died was one of our candidates for the episcopacy of this diocese, his murder may cause untold harm, not only to this diocese but to the Church as a whole. My staff and I are trying to limit the adverse publicity, though I fear it is a vain effort.'

Worse and worse. Alan and I know Kenneth Allenby well, and know he has a hard time killing so much as a spider. He grieves over every death in the parish, and indeed in England. But to Chief Constable Armstrong, who didn't know him from Adam, he sounded callous, as if his only concern was the fall-out from this man's death and how it might affect Sherebury Cathedral.

Kenneth really should stop talking until Cathedral counsel was around to advise him.

I opened my mouth to say something bright and breezy, change the tone of the conversation, but Armstrong forestalled me.

'Thank you very much, Mr Dean, Mr Nesbitt. I think those are all the questions I have for now. I appreciate your cooperation. And may I offer my condolences on your loss.'

I didn't miss his quick glance at all of us after that barbed remark.

Two

After they had left, we were silent, contemplating what came next. Alan was thoroughly accustomed to murder, of course, after his long career with the police. I had poked my nose into enough mysterious deaths that I, too, had acquired a certain patina of acceptance. But this one came too close to home. I doubt that Alan had ever before been asked to 'assist the police in their enquiries'.

And as for the dean, I wondered if he was completely out of his depth. With spiritual malaise he was totally familiar, and he knew how to deal with it, kindly, competently, compassionately. He was a good administrator for the Cathedral, whose business affairs were, as far as I knew, in excellent condition. But murder?

I thought back to the first murder case I'd ever been involved with, when I first moved to Sherebury from my life-long home in Indiana. That, too, had involved the Cathedral – the murder of one of the canons. Alan had still been chief constable then, and a friend of the dean's, and had investigated discreetly but thoroughly. The dean had handled the situation with dignity and quiet faith.

Perhaps I was underestimating him.

He was the first to speak. 'Alan, I did not kill Andrew Brading. Nor did you. But you and I may well know the person who did. Given our knowledge of the tensions within the commission, we may be in a better position than most to have insights that the police will not. I think it is our duty to put all our energies into helping the police discover the murderer.'

'You do realize that we are both bound to be under suspicion.'

'Of course. But as we are innocent, we need have no fear.'

Alan looked – as I felt – just a trifle exasperated. 'I'm afraid, Kenneth, that your little speech about damage control didn't do you any good. If you'll accept my advice, you'll have one of the Cathedral counsel with you the next time you speak with the police.'

'My dear Alan.' The dean smiled. 'You think I'm too open, too forthcoming? But again I say, the innocent need fear nothing.'

'Not from the final judgement, no. I accept that. But there are a good many steps before we get to that judgement seat, and some of them are in charge of fallible humans.'

'I never,' said the dean with the hint of a twinkle, 'thought the day would come that I would hear you describe the police as fallible.'

'Oh, I can attest to the fact that they are,' I said, 'and really, Kenneth, you need to listen to Alan. If they start suspecting you – well, once the police get an idea in their heads, it can be awfully hard to dislodge. But you're quite right, of course. We're going to have to do all we can to figure out who killed this man. For a start, who hated him enough to do this terrible thing?'

15

Alan looked at the dean. The dean looked at Alan. Both sighed. Watson was once again disturbed. He whined softly, and Alan reached down to pat him on the head. 'Don't worry, mutt. Everything's all right with your world. The trouble with your question, my dear, is that so many people disliked the man.'

'Dislike and hatred are two different things.'

'Of course they are. And the one isn't simply an intensification of the other. It takes, typically, either a series of increasing grievances boiling up or a single action intolerable to the – the disliker, if I may coin a word – for dislike to develop into hatred. Kenneth, how did you read the commission meeting? Among those opposing Brading, did you sense anyone harbouring real hatred?'

The dean shook his head slowly. 'I wish I had a definitive answer. There was so much ill feeling in the room, so many opposing views about all the candidates, that I couldn't sort out who was feeling what.'

'And you're good at discerning emotions,' I said thoughtfully.

'Well, when one has been a priest for over forty years, one does learn a little about human nature.' The dean spread his hands self-deprecatingly.

'A policeman learns to sort out emotions, too.' I turned to Alan. 'What did you sense?'

'You know I can't go into specifics, even to you. Political interests were overt, of course,' he said. 'Church politics, I mean. Jostling for position. Then there was a good deal of self-interest – less obvious, but certainly present. Several of

16

the members thought they stood to lose something if one or another candidate became bishop.'

'It wasn't all personal, though,' said Kenneth. 'Some of the clergy, especially, were agonizing over the impact on the Church as a whole, or on the diocese in particular.'

'That sort of thing can get awfully heated,' I pointed out. 'Look at the wars that have been fought over religion. All religions.'

'Yes . . .' said Alan thoughtfully. 'But that kind of feeling isn't usually directed against one individual, but against a group. You get terrorist activity, you get massacres like the World Trade Center and, most horrendous of all, the Holocaust. Killing one cleric doesn't seem to fit the pattern.'

I nodded. 'I agree. So, what other kinds of nastiness surfaced at your meeting yesterday? Anything specific about this particular man?'

Neither man replied for a moment, then Alan said slowly, 'I had a sense, which may have been completely mistaken, of a suppressed fury directed against Brading. Or it may have been aimed at Brading's supporters, who were, as you might guess, the ultra-conservatives in the group. It wasn't so much anything that was said as something that was left unsaid but was quivering in the air. I'm sorry. I know that's not much help.'

'I felt something of the same,' said the dean, 'but I have no idea who was projecting such distress. Of course, I'm not a trained observer.'

Alan groaned. 'And I am. I know, I know. If I had been paying attention to body language, I might have seen a clenched fist, rapid breathing, pinched lips – but I wasn't and I didn't. I was

17

too busy trying to keep my own reactions within the bounds of civilized behaviour.'

I sighed. 'So I suppose it's going to come down to a background check of Brading, interviews with anyone who knew him well, his cathedral staff, and so on. All the routine stuff, which obviously the police can do much better than we can.'

'Routine background checks have already been done on anyone who might be nominated for the position,' said Alan. 'That's an obvious necessity these days. No one with a criminal background, no one with a suggestion of sexually predatory tendencies, no one with any scandal of any kind in his past could be considered. The checks, however, weren't anything like as complete and rigorous as the ones that will need to be done now. I didn't always, as a policeman, agree with a great deal in your beloved detective stories, Dorothy. But, in one thing, Hercule Poirot was absolutely right: The key to solving a murder is often a thorough knowledge of the victim.'

'And,' I went on, 'of his potential murderers. Now, in trying to limit that roster, it would certainly be useful to know when the man died. I know when he was found, but when did he actually die?'

'I'm not sure the police know that yet, and the Gloucestershire people may not tell me when they do. Derek probably will. But you know as well as I do, Dorothy, the medical examiners can often only determine a range, sometimes rather a wide range, especially when the body is found some little time after death, as would appear to be the

18

case here. So the time of death may not be particularly helpful.'

I took a deep breath. 'Well, then, I think we need to work out where we can be most useful. There's no point in trying to duplicate the efforts of the police. The things they do – the routine procedures – they can do far more efficiently than any amateur. Saving your presence, Alan.'

'I'm an amateur now, love. I don't have the might of the force behind me, though I can still call in a few favours now and again. But, essentially, I'm part of your posse. What did you have in mind?'

'Nothing yet. We don't know enough. We need to create an approach to the problem. What we need is to know everything we can about Dean Brading, and who might have hated him enough to prevent his ever coming to Sherebury. And since we have to start somewhere, I suggest we start with the members of the commission. What's the most likely source of information about them?'

The four of us said, together, 'Jane!'

Jane Langland, my next-door neighbour and oldest friend in Sherebury, was a mine of information about people. She wasn't a gossip, but she was active in almost every women's activity in Sherebury. She had been a teacher for many, many years, and scores of her former pupils visited her often. She looked a great deal like the bulldogs she loved, and behind a gruff manner she hid a heart of custard. We gathered in her kitchen and sat around the table, surrounded by the bulldogs.

We weren't eating anything, but they lived in hope. Jane had made a pitcher of lemonade, apparently anticipating our visit. She knew we'd come seeking information sooner or later.

'Can eliminate the archbishops, for a start,' said Jane. 'They've better ways of dealing with an undesirable dean.'

'Yes, we'll give you the archbishops,' said the dean, smiling. 'And I think we can eliminate the two secretaries. They're on the commission as functionaries, and took no part in the discussions. That leaves ten people, besides Alan and me.'

'Nine,' I interjected. 'We know our MP, Newsome, was a friend of Brading's'

'Friends have been known to fall out, but you may be right,' the dean went on. 'We can leave him till last, at any rate. Now, I know the other four from our diocese reasonably well, but you, Jane, probably know more *about* them than I.'

Jane shrugged. 'Bits here and there. Nothing startling, nothing much you don't know, Kenneth. Some sorrows here and there. Vicar of Ledingham lost her baby years ago, born dead. Couldn't have another.'

The dean nodded sadly. 'She is an amazingly strong woman. I admire her greatly, and was very glad when she was elected to the committee, but I think we can wash her out as a suspect. The strength I refer to is moral, not physical. She's quite small and delicate.'

Alan nodded in agreement.

'And, of course, poor Tompkins' mind is as strong as ever, but I doubt he could harm a flea, considering the palsy.' The dean turned to

20

Dorothy. 'Ben Tompkins is the other diocesan cleric on the committee, vicar of Padston.'

'So that disposes of the clergy, at least from this diocese. What about our other two lay members?'

'I know very little about them, except that they expressed rather conservative views in the meeting,' said Alan.

'So they might have liked Brading,' I suggested. 'I know he was almost reactionary.'

I looked at the dean, who shook his head. 'They don't frequent the Cathedral. I never met them before the meeting, and know nothing about them.'

We turned again to Jane, who spread her hands. 'Don't know them well. Another tragedy in one of the families, the Lesters. Nephew bullied at school, killed himself. The mother never got over it, in and out of mental institutions. Years ago,' she said to the dean. 'You mightn't have known. Don't know anything about the other – Hathaway – except there's some talk that he's on dicey ground financially. Don't know if there's any truth to it.'

Alan had been taking notes. 'All right, from this diocese we have one clergyman who could not physically have committed the crime, and one clergywoman who is unlikely. I'm going to leave her on the list, though, because it isn't absolutely impossible that she could have done it. Until we know more about the actual cause of death, we're speculating. We know almost nothing of the lay diocesan members, except for the tragedy in Lester's family long ago, and a nasty rumour about Hathaway. That sort of thing, whether true or not, can make a man vulnerable, so at this point I rather like him as a possible suspect.

'Moving on. We think we can eliminate Newsome, from the Synod contingent. I have reservations about that, but for now we can set him aside. What about the others? Kenneth, what do you know about the clergy?'

'Not a great deal. I've met them casually, of course, on various occasions, but Birmingham and Leeds are rather out of my usual orbit. Letitia Morgan, of St Cross, Oxford, I know somewhat better. Admirable woman. Jane?'

She shook her head. 'Out of my range as well.'

'Of the other two lay members, leaving out Newsome, I know only what I gleaned from committee meetings, which wasn't much. You, Alan?'

'Ms Baring – she's a barrister, Dorothy – is smooth and well spoken. Well-off, judging from her clothes and general appearance. She obviously can't abide . . . well, another of the candidates, but I don't recall much of her attitude towards Brading or the other two. Then Hilliard, the other layman, I could scarcely read at all. He seldom spoke, though when he did, his remarks were well argued and to the point. One can see why he's a successful businessman. He didn't seem to favour any of the candidates, particularly. I had the impression he was a trifle bored with the whole business.'

'I agree,' said the dean. 'But that leaves us knowing very little about those two, or the

Birmingham and Leeds clergy – as personalities, I mean.'

'Then that's the obvious place to start, the place where we know the least. Alan, is there any reason why we shouldn't go on a little tour of the Midlands and the North?'

'I can think of several reasons, Dorothy.' Alan frowned. 'The first is that the police will certainly be taking a careful look at the commission members. As you point out, that is the sort of routine at which they excel. And don't forget that I am still under suspicion myself, and it does not behove me to take any action that might interfere with the police. Second, you seem to forget that we're dealing here with a murderer, and there might be considerable danger involved. Third, although we've worked together successfully over several cases, they were far narrower in scope. This is a matter of national importance.'

'"Any man's death diminishes me",' the dean quoted gently. 'But you're right, Alan, on both counts, both as to the danger involved and the scope of this matter. I'm sorry, Dorothy. I know you're pining to exercise your undoubted sleuthing skills. But I do agree with Alan that, as the police will be dealing with the commission members, we'd best leave them for now. There is a different direction that we can take, however; something we can all do – all five of us in this room. It is indeed required of you and me, Alan, and there's no reason at all why our spouses or a member of the parish might not join us on occasion. We will visit the three remaining candidates in their home churches and try to learn as much about them as possible. And if, in the process, we were to learn something about Mr Brading and his associates, it would only prove that God does in fact work in a mysterious way.'

I grinned broadly and said, 'Amen!'

Three

'All right, tell me about all the candidates,' I requested. Kenneth and Margaret had gone home to brave the ladies and gentlemen of the Press, but we still sat in Jane's comfortable kitchen.

'I'll assume you addressed that question to Jane,' said Alan. 'I know only the official bits, and we need the gossip, as well.'

Jane snorted. 'Plenty of that. Starting where?'

'Let's begin with the victim,' I suggested.

'The Very Reverend Andrew Stephen Owen Brading. Leaves out his middle names most of the time.'

'It sounds almost royal, doesn't it?'

'Dorothy.' Alan reproved my flippancy.

'All right, all right. Go on, Jane. Sorry.'

'Dean, Chelton Cathedral. Been there for three or four years. Calls himself a reformer.' She snorted again. 'Arch-conservative is what he is – was. Wanted to reform the church, sweep away all the changes of the past few hundred years.'

'But, Jane,' I objected, 'you're conservative, too, at least when it comes to the liturgy. So are most of our Cathedral congregation.'

'Don't want to go back to the nineteenth century, do I? Women priests, proper vestments, candles, chants – he wanted to do away with them all.'

'I've heard he was something of a protégé of Mrs Thatcher's,' said Alan.

'Mercy! He certainly doesn't sound as if he would have fit very well into this diocese, as High Church as we are. How on earth did he make the shortlist?'

'That was exactly my reaction,' said Alan, 'but you must understand that Mr Brading didn't voice all these sentiments. They were apparent from his actions, but he expressed himself much more moderately. I've read some of his essays in the *Church Times*. "A real need for concentration on the Word of God" was one of his favourite phrases, along with "the danger of elitism in the Church" and "worship that the average man can understand". He was very fond of the average man.'

'There's no such person,' I said.

'No. But he's a useful political construct. Mr Brading, who was a schoolmaster at one time, loved to use the Old Testament to illustrate his sermons. He believed those stories captured the imagination of people of "limited education".'

'All right,' I said wearily. 'Did you have a list of virtues to offset all these idiotic qualities?'

'Well, Chelton is a small city in a small diocese, rather like Sherebury, so he'd have been a good fit in that respect, at least. And certainly the ultra-conservatives in our diocese would have welcomed him.'

25

'How did his own flock regard him?'

'He didn't have a flock, in that sense. Chelton is one of the cathedrals that doesn't have its own parish, so the dean's pastoral cure is somewhat ill-defined. The reports the commission received used cautious language, but the general feel we were able to get was that they respected him for his absolute devotion to his principles, and for his very impressive scholarly background. He was the reigning expert on liturgical history. And he apparently put the cathedral budget in the black for the first time in recent history. So they respected him, but didn't love him.'

Alan picked up his glass and found it empty. Jane raised her eyebrows. 'Yes, please,' said Alan.

'None for me, thanks,' I said.

Alan nodded his thanks for the refill and then continued. 'Actually, Brading seems to have been a hard man to love. No one described him as anything resembling warm and fuzzy. But neither did anyone ever call him wishy-washy. He believed what he believed, and no one ever swayed him. He would, I feel certain, have gone to his death before abandoning one iota of his creed.'

'And apparently he did. Ideal martyr material,' I commented. 'But surely a bishop needs to be flexible enough to meet changing situations.'

'Flexibility was not a word in Mr Brading's vocabulary. Let's do the man justice. If his values had accorded more closely with ours, we would have found his unswerving devotion to them wholly admirable.'

'But they didn't,' I pointed out. 'Which made him a most unlikely person to lead this diocese. So I ask again, why was he under consideration?'

'You've forgotten, Dorothy. Our beloved MP, who sits on the commission, was a close friend of Mr Brading's.'

'Oh, yes. I was trying hard to forget. Very well, we've profiled the victim. Who's next?'

'We could go to the opposite extreme. Jane?'

'Robinson,' she said promptly. 'The Reverend William Robinson, Rector of some church on the fringes of Birmingham.'

'St Matthias',' Alan supplied.

'Socialist,' said Jane morosely. 'Rabble-rouser. Been in gaol more than once.'

'Or, to put it in more diplomatic terms, prominent social activist. He's a member of Eco-watch, Save the Hedges, and a great many more social causes I can't at this moment recall.'

I raised my eyes to the ceiling. 'Okay, I guess I just can't fathom the minds of the commission. Excuse me, Alan, but this guy doesn't sound any better than Brading, at least not for Sherebury.'

'His congregation loves him, though. The parish has been growing by leaps and bounds, and so have their coffers, even though many of the parishioners are young and relatively poor. I think many of the commission members felt he would represent a breath of fresh air, a rejuvenating influence.'

'Which is needed,' said Jane. 'Bishop Hardie's been coasting the past decade or two.'

'Our dear bishop,' said Alan, 'is as useless as

27

Bishop Proudie, without a Mrs Proudie in the background to ginger him up.'

'Well, we can at least be thankful for that small mercy,' I said. I love Anthony Trollope's Barchester novels, and the television series based on them. 'Though, as I recall, Mrs Proudie was usually in the foreground. Unfortunately. Now, look, people. It's nearly lunchtime. I vote we adjourn, cease our catalogue of bishops for the time being, and have some lunch. Do you think we could make it to the Rose and Crown without getting mobbed by the media?'

'Worth a try,' said Jane, pushing back from the table. 'Move, dogs. Mummy'll bring back treats.'

'Don't forget I must go to the dean's meeting at two,' said Alan.

I had, in fact, forgotten all about it. 'What do you suppose he wants of you all?'

'Draft a plan of action to present to the full commission in an emergency meeting, I imagine. If we want lunch, we'd best go now, while most of the media attention is centred on Dean Allenby. Put on a hat, love, and let's go.'

The Rose and Crown, our favourite pub, is also an inn, its earliest parts dating back to about the time the Cathedral was being rebuilt in the fifteenth century, and it's actually in the Cathedral Close. From our house, the shortest way is through the Cathedral, since walking around that huge Gothic pile takes a while. This time it was also the most prudent route. 'Even if a reporter latches on to us, they surely won't dare follow us into church,' I said, thinking aloud.

But it wasn't a reporter who caught us. We had made it into the dim, cool haven of what I consider to be the most beautiful Cathedral in the world and were crossing the nave, lulled by the music the organist was practicing, when the peace was disturbed by angry voices.

'I'll see him, or know the reason why!' The accent was posh. One felt the speaker was in the habit of getting his way.

'Sir, I've told you the dean is not available just now. If you will leave your name—' That was one of the vergers, forced to raise his voice to be heard over the other's roars.

'I will not damn well leave my name! If he's not here, I'll wait until he is.'

The music swelled to a crescendo, and the angry man's voice rose with it. 'Can't anyone do anything about that damned row?'

'I'll ask you to moderate your language, sir. You are in a place of worship.'

'I'm in a bloody great museum, is where I am, and I have no intention of leaving it until I see the dean. Take your hands off me!'

That was when Alan walked over to the combatants. The verger was trying to escort the other man out of the building, and I began to fear that actual blows might follow.

But Alan worked his magic. I don't know exactly how he does it. He's a big man, tall and solidly built, but it isn't just his bulk. Somehow he can stand there and look like a policeman, authority oozing from his very pores, and calm a situation without saying a word.

The voices silenced. The verger removed his

hand from the other man's arm. The angry man settled his impeccably tailored jacket with an irritated shrug.

'Shall we continue this discussion outside, gentlemen?' said Alan firmly. 'I fear the music makes it a bit difficult to converse here.'

Remarkably, they went. Of course, Jane and I followed, at a discreet distance.

The Cathedral Close is dotted with benches here and there, placed where people can sit and look at a particularly striking bit of the building. I found Alan and the other two seated on one of them. They were not looking at the Cathedral.

'. . . to introduce myself. My name is Alan Nesbitt, and this is Mr Mackey, one of our vergers.' He held out his hand and the angry man, after a noticeable hesitation, took it.

'Mellinger,' he said shortly.

'Ah, yes,' said Alan. 'You'd be one of the banking Mellingers, then.'

The man looked at him sharply. 'I am. And precisely who are you?'

Oh, my. Standing just inside the south porch, I caught my breath in a little gasp. The English can be beautifully courteous. They can also be intolerably rude when they want to be.

Alan smiled gently. 'Simply a long-time communicant at this church. Also a retired policeman. Now, what can Mr Mackey and I do for you?'

'You can find the dean! I came here to talk to him.'

'What a pity you didn't phone ahead. The dean is in a meeting and I'm afraid he really can't be disturbed. I hope you haven't come a long way.'

'I couldn't phone ahead. I was in New York until last night. I landed at Heathrow two hours ago, and read in *The Times* about the bishop situation. It is imperative that I discuss it with the dean.' His voice was rising again.

The verger, feeling that the crisis was past, murmured something and went back inside. I don't think Alan and Mellinger even noticed.

'I am conversant with the appointment process. Perhaps I can help you.'

'What do you have to do with it?'

'I sit on the Crown Appointments Commission.'

That did it. Mellinger's complexion turned a bright shade of purple and he sprang to his feet. 'Then I say to you, and you can tell the dean for me, that you're both blithering asses if you let Smith get to be bishop of this diocese! Of all the namby-pamby, milk-and-water priests that ever walked his earth, he's the worst! He'd sell off this Cathedral stone by stone to feed the layabouts he loves so much. And I'll not stand for it! You tell him that for me, the moment you see him. And you tell him I'll be keeping an eye on this!'

He stalked off, and I let out a long, low whistle. 'Good grief, Alan,' I said as he rejoined us, 'is that what it's been like for you, all these weeks?'

He shrugged. 'That was a rather mild example, but yes. Feelings run high. Shall we go and find that lunch?'

Well, okay . . . but I'd try to tackle him later. I wanted to know more about what he'd been

31

having to put up with. I lost my first husband to a sudden heart attack. I couldn't stand by and watch Alan be subjected to stress, and not do anything about it.

We had a pleasant meal at the Rose and Crown, steadfastly refusing to utter the word 'bishop'. Peter and Greta Endicott, the proprietors of the old inn, have been friends ever since I visited Sherebury with my first husband, years ago. Greta, who is an ageless beauty, oversees the hotel part, while Peter is the perfect 'mine host' in the pub. He could have done a good business that day serving the media types, but he has an immense loyalty to his friends, and a subtle way of discouraging unwelcome clientele. Like Alan, he seldom has to resort to any physical demonstration. He just puts on a certain look, and they decide they'd be happier elsewhere.

When we had enjoyed our lunch, and our respite from the cares of the day, Peter glanced outside and then came to speak to us. 'They're out there waiting for you.'

'How did they know we were here?' I asked in exasperation. 'I'll swear no one saw us come in.'

'They have a sixth sense about these things,' said Alan wearily. 'I imagine Peter's manner in fending them off told them there might be someone of interest inside.'

'It was that – let them suspect something – or let them come in and find out for certain,' said Peter apologetically. 'But if you want, you can get out through the cellar and the back door, where the brewers deliver the beer. The door's not very obvious; it opens on the lane that winds round to the High Street. But you can cut straight across at one point to the chapter house door, and then you're nearly home free.'

I was thrilled. I adore the ancient passageways that still exist in modern England. They're useful, so they're still used. No one would think of destroying them just because they're a few hundred years old. In America, they wouldn't last ten minutes.

'It's not so very clean,' said Peter, leading the way. 'But the beer stays in the cellar. Nothing actually comes upstairs that way, so it's not a health hazard or anything like that.'

That, I thought, was for my benefit – the hygienic American. I didn't care, actually, as long as there weren't spider webs. Truth to tell, I felt a little like Catherine Morland in *Northanger Abbey*, delightedly expecting 'something horrid' to pop out as Peter opened the trapdoor behind the bar and showed us down the narrow ladder. 'Mind your head, all, and Dorothy, don't let your hat touch the wall on the way down.

In fact, there was nothing romantic about the cellar at all. It was a trifle dusty, but it was well lit and entirely spider-free, as far as I could see. Bright, shiny beer barrels filled most of the available space; the ones in use had complicated hoses leading up to the pumps in the bar. A door off to one side was closed.

'The wine cellar,' Peter said, gesturing. 'Needs a different temperature to the beer. Here's your exit, ladies and gent.' A gentle ramp led up to a door in the outside wall. 'They roll the kegs down, you see. Had to be really careful when they were made of wood, but that was before my time. All steel or aluminium now. Watch your step.'

No one was lurking outside. We turned into a narrow lane that meandered a bit beside a high hedge and then forked off to the left. To our right, a gap in the hedge led to the massive stone cliff that was the Cathedral, and, sure enough, a door let us into a small corridor and then into the chapter house library.

The librarian was so startled to see us emerge from the stacks that he dropped the pile of books he was carrying.

'Sorry, Colin,' said Jane. 'Came in the back way. Escaping the paparazzi.'

He was still gaping as we made our way into the main body of the Cathedral.

Four

Somehow we managed to make it back to our respective homes without being waylaid.

'I expect Peter is guarding the door of the pub, letting them think we're still there. Poor man – think of the beer he could be selling.'

'We'll have to make it up to him one day. We can't stave them off forever, you know, Dorothy.'

My mobile and the landline rang at the same time. I looked at the displays and turned them off. 'Not for ever, but for now. Because right now I want to know who the Reverend Mr Smith is, and why Mr Mellinger is so dead set against him.'

'I've only a few moments before Kenneth's meeting, but the short answer is that he's the Very Reverend, actually – Dean of Rotherford Cathedral – and I've only a faint notion why a man like Mellinger would hate him so. I must go, Dorothy. I'll have to run the gantlet to get to Kenneth's office, I'm sure.'

'Go, and may the Force be with you.'

I turned my phone back on after he'd left. I always have it with me and turned on when he's away, just because . . . well, just because. Glancing at the long list of messages, I saw that none of them was from anyone I knew, deleted them all, and prepared to ignore calls from anyone except Alan.

Then I turned to my computer. I've come late to the Internet, and I still don't indulge in the social media, but the Web is the greatest source of information ever devised, and I love it.

I'd never heard of Rotherford Cathedral, though I thought I knew most of the notable cathedrals in England, and when I Googled it I was amazed. How could I have missed hearing about this glorious place? Then I read further and understood.

A few years back, the Church of England upgraded some parish churches to cathedrals. Rotherford was one of those, it turned out. Like my beloved Sherebury, it had been an abbey foundation until the dissolution of the monasteries under Henry the Eighth. It seemed to be remarkably well preserved, unlike some of the old abbey churches, many of which had fallen to ruin.

The website didn't say a lot about the dean, so I waited impatiently for Alan to come home and tell me more.

The meeting seemed to last a long time. I was thinking about tea when Alan walked into the house. Watson greeted him as rapturously as if he'd been gone several years instead of a few hours. The cats went as far as to open their eyes to slits before settling back to their afternoon naps.

'Yes, old fellow, yes. You're a fine chap, aren't you? Who's ready for a walk, then?'

Watson trotted off for his leash, and I linked my arm with my husband's. 'Woof,' I said. 'At least – have the media vampires gone away?'

'Having extracted as much blood as any of us had to give, they've folded their wings and gone back to their belfries to wait for the next sensation.'

'I don't think vampires dwell in belfries,' I said. 'Coffins? Anyway, we're free of them.'

'For the moment. *Yes*, Watson, we're going, old boy.'

The Close was relatively free of wanderers, so we turned Watson free to race about as he wished, while we kept a more leisurely pace.

'Tell me about the meeting. It certainly took long enough.'

'We had a lot to discuss. The first item on the agenda was to find a date for an extraordinary emergency meeting of the full commission. Such a thing has never happened before, so there are no protocols in place. The secretary's in something of a dither about the whole thing, and if you'd ever met him, you'd understand how remarkable that is. His usual demeanour runs from calm to phlegmatic.'

'The gamut from A to B, as a reviewer once said of a Katharine Hepburn performance. So the secretaries were at this meeting?'

'The Archbishops' secretary was, and he was badly shaken. He simply could not get over the horror of a clergyman being murdered in his own church.'

'He should read some history. It's happened before. It happened here. Yes, it's perfectly awful, but dithering isn't going to help. Did you fix a date for the emergency meeting?'

'A range. We're hoping for next week, but everyone has other commitments; it may be longer. Meanwhile, all of us in the diocesan contingent are to get cracking about visiting the three remaining candidates. The secretary doled out assignments for the first visit, and Kenneth and I drew the Reverend Mr Lovelace, of St Barnabas', London.'

'He's one I know nothing about, though I think I've seen his name in the news now and then.'

'Undoubtedly. You should hear Jane on the subject.'

'On what subject?'

I hadn't heard Jane approaching across the grass, which softened her solid tread.

'Hear me on what subject?' she repeated.

'The Reverend Mr Lovelace,' said Alan, trying

37

not to grin. 'I was telling Dorothy he's often in the news.'

'Pah!' (Jane's the only person I've ever heard actually say 'pah'.) '"Often in the news" indeed! Photo ops, smiling at some urchin. Child wouldn't know him from Adam. Assistants do all the work. Volunteers, most of them. He poses for pictures, makes speeches. Thinks he'll be at Canterbury one day.'

Watson had lolloped over to greet Jane, one of his favourite people, and now whined at the tone of her voice. Alan soothed him.

'You know someone in his congregation,' I said. It was not a question.

'Walter.' Walter is Jane's grandson. 'Not at that church anymore. Couldn't bear the man. Doesn't like hypocrites.'

'And what does he think about the whole contentious matter of our bishop search?' asked Alan. 'Does he have a point of view?'

Jane grinned. 'Thinking of getting married, isn't he? Worrying more about getting a better job than mouldy old church fights. What about yours?'

Our only grandchildren are, in fact, Alan's, since my first husband and I never had children. 'Hmm,' replied Alan. 'It never occurred to me to ask them. They probably haven't much interest in church politics, either. Football's more their speed.'

'Yes. Old ones and young don't care. In-betweens are the ones that'll cause trouble. And the vested interests.'

I raised my hands to the sky. 'It's all wrong!

This should be about choosing the best man for the job, not pushing agendas! Where's any hint of the Gospel in all this, where's even a whiff of Christianity?' This time Watson's concern was for me. He came and sat on my feet.

Jane jerked her head at Alan. 'Where Alan comes in. Deals in principles, not schemes. Sound man.'

Alan shuffled his feet and looked away, embarrassed. I winked at Jane and changed the subject. 'You say that grandson of yours is getting married? When did this happen? Last I heard, he was still playing the field.'

Like me, Jane came into her grandmotherhood late in life. She had borne a son to a soldier who went off to war and was reported missing in action before he even knew about the baby. They had planned to marry. Jane was a teacher, and an illegitimate child would have ended her career and left her penniless. So the boy was adopted, and Jane lost touch with him, discovering only much later and by accident that she had a grandson. They took to each other from the first, and when Jane finally worked up her courage and told him about the relationship, it only strengthened his love. He was a bright and energetic young man of whom Jane was extremely, and rightly, proud.

'Met her at university, and then did an internship with her. British Museum.'

'So they have lots of interests in common. That's important.'

'Just waiting for steady jobs before they marry. Sensible.'

I wondered if, meanwhile, they were living

together, but I didn't ask. It was none of my business, and attitudes had changed so much since Jane and I were young that it scarcely mattered anyway. How differently things might have turned out if unwed pregnancy had not been such a social disaster back then. Jane might have been able to keep her baby, marry the father when he did after all come home, know her grandson from the first . . . but then she might not have taught all her life, and hundreds of young lives would have been the poorer for not having known her wise influence.

Jane turned toward the church. 'Got to see Margaret about the flower rota. One of the volunteers muddled it, as usual.' She stumped off.

'It would appear that Jane is not a fan of Mr Lovelace. I'd like to see for myself. Do you suppose the dean would mind if I tag along?'

'He suggested it, in fact. He and I are not going together. He thinks we can form better judgements independently. So he and Margaret are visiting the day after tomorrow—'

'On a Saturday? Why not wait until Sunday?'

'At a time like this, he feels he should be here at his own altar on a Sunday. St Barnabas' has a Saturday evening Eucharist. We – you and I – are to go to the Tuesday Evensong. The Archbishops' secretary has made sure that Lovelace will be taking both services.'

'Well, then, I'd better call Lynn and find out if she and Tom can put us up. Unless you're on an expense account and want to go to a hotel?'

'The secretary offered. I said we had friends

in London and could save the Church a little money. And after listening to Jane, I had another idea.'

'Walter!' I said. 'Of course. We can give the kids a meal and listen to his take on Lovelace. All right, dog, I want my tea, too.'

We got Walter's address and phone number from Jane, and Tuesday morning saw us in the train headed for my city of dreams. I'm a country person, really, but London is in a class by itself. Our good friends Tom and Lynn Anderson had professed themselves delighted to put us up for a couple of nights, and we were genuinely delighted to be seeing them again. Tom and Lynn, American expats like me, have a lot of money and a beautiful Georgian house in Belgravia, "Upstairs, Downstairs" territory. They're also great hosts, so the visit promised to be enjoyable.

We had taken the train because driving in London is nightmarish, also expensive, given the Congestion Charge meant to discourage driving in the metropolis. It was a good thing we started early, because there were infuriating delays on the journey. Many of England's railway lines are quite old and in need of repair, and the rail company that serves Sherebury had decided to tear up several miles of track before the highest of high tourist season arrived. So we were shunted aside several times, sat on a siding for a time, and arrived a full hour later than we had planned. Alan was not pleased.

'If they had only notified us ahead of time, the car would have been much quicker,' he grumbled.

41

'The level of public service in this country—'

'Is not what it was in my day,' I finished for him. I tucked my arm through his as we made our way through the rushing throngs in Victoria Station. 'Careful, dear, or you'll begin to qualify as an old fogey. And what does it matter? We told Lynn we'd call when we got to London, so she isn't expecting us at any particular moment. But let's get out of the station first. You can't hear yourself think in here.'

The big railway stations in London were built in Victoria's day, when rail travel was in its heyday and the termini were temples to the train, designed to impress. Many of them have huge vaulted roofs that echo and re-echo the clamour below, making it nearly impossible to hear, among other things, the vital announcements of which train is at which platform. Out on the street, with all the cars and taxis and buses whizzing past, and the tourists wheeling huge suitcases and trying in several languages to figure out where they're going, it's neither convenient nor very safe to stop and use a mobile. So Alan and I ducked into the Grosvenor Hotel, which has an entrance directly from the station and is, by comparison, an oasis of peace and quiet.

After he made the call, we walked out into a gorgeous spring morning. April weather in England can be even more erratic than in the American Midwest, but today it was perfect: crisp, with a light breeze and a brilliantly blue sky – London at its happiest.

'It's crowded,' I said with deep content. 'It's

42

noisy. It reeks of diesel fumes and frying food and beer. It's wonderful!'

Alan chuckled and took my arm to cross the dangerously busy Buckingham Palace Road.

Five

There are lots of little private parks here and there in Belgravia. The one across from the Andersons' house was alive with daffodils, and I breathed a deep sigh of contentment. We rang the bell, and heard Lynn rushing down the stairs to greet us. 'Where's Watson?' were her first loving words.

'Oh, I see. You love us only for our dog. Boo-hoo.'

'You brought him the last time you came to stay with us.' Her tone was still accusatory as she led us up the stairs to the sitting room.

'Yes, but this time we had to leave him and the cats in Jane's care. We've come on a mission, and we could hardly take a dog to church with us.'

'Church? You haven't abandoned the Cathedral, have you? Tell all.'

I hadn't taken the time on the phone to explain our errand, so Alan and I talked while Lynn fetched us some of her superb coffee and lovely homemade pastries.

'But, Alan,' she exclaimed when our tale was finished, 'you never *told* me you were picking

43

out the new bishop! I heard about the murder, of course, but I didn't know *you* had anything to do with it!'

'Well, not with the murder, in fact,' Alan began, a twinkle in his eye.

'Who did it – one of the other hopefuls?'

'We trust not,' said Alan, 'but as far as I know the police haven't got very far with their inquiries.'

'What do you mean, as far as you know? Aren't you in on it?'

'Lynn Anderson, you can be the most exasperating person!' I put down my coffee cup. 'You know perfectly well Alan's retired, and furthermore he's almost a suspect in this case.'

'I also know,' she said, 'that neither of you can keep yourselves out of any juicy murder that remotely concerns you. Is that what you're really doing in London?'

I tried hard to keep a straight face. 'The secretary of the commission sent Alan to get to know Mr Lovelace.'

'I'm sure he did. And if the two of you just happen to stumble across something that incriminates him, you'll be ever so surprised. And I, incidentally, will be ever so pleased.'

'Now, exactly what do you mean by that?'

'Later. After you've seen for yourself.'

Daily Evensong is a fixture in most big London churches, some of them having very fine choirs indeed. Westminster Abbey and St Paul's are usually jammed with tourists for the service, but I didn't know what to expect at St Barnabas', which was in a neighbourhood that could charitably be described as 'mixed'. I was glad for Alan's solid, reassuring presence as we walked from the nearest Tube station, some distance away.

'Maybe we should have taken a taxi,' I said dubiously.

'Not a taxi sort of area, love.'

We walked on. 'Tell me what else you know about Mr Lovelace,' I said to Alan.

'I don't want to prejudice you.'

'That means you don't like him. Tell me anyway. I know how to make up my own mind.'

'Well.' Alan paused to organize his thoughts. 'Our dean doesn't care for him, if I'm reading between the lines properly. He didn't tell me much after his visit, for the same reason I ought not to tell you anything at all.'

I gave him a look.

'Yes, all right. I'm told he preaches compelling sermons and inspires a loyal band of volunteers, who do amazing work amongst the poor in the neighbourhood of the church. The parish is said to be growing rapidly, in a time of declining church attendance nationally. We've also learned that he has some friends in high places.'

I made a face.

'Yes, he's an unabashed politician. But the Church is very politicized these days, and someone who knows how to tread the halls of power without stepping on too many toes can be a real asset to any diocese. Not that he's entirely avoided treading on toes, judging by some of the emails we've received. You know I can't tell you exactly what the writers have against him, but some of the accusations have verged on the hysterical.'

'Oh, dear! He sounds horrible.'

'Then I've given you the wrong impression, love. Kenneth says the man has that quality that used to be called charismatic.'

'I don't care for that sort. I've always distrusted charm.'

'We'll soon see for ourselves, my dear.'

The shops that lined the pavements as we walked from the Tube station were small and rather tacky, selling used electronics, cheap clothing, and the like. A few newsagent/tobacconist shops looked dreary and unprosperous. A payday loan establishment, on the other hand, was plainly doing a roaring business. Several shops were empty, the papers pasted over the windows torn and dirty. Beggars stood at corners hawking copies of *The Big Issue*, the chronicle of the poor and homeless.

'Urban blight,' Alan commented.

'The Archbishop should get on that loan place,' I muttered. 'A scourge.' For the Archbishop of Canterbury had launched a campaign against the loan businesses that prey on the poor, with their ruinous interest rates and crippling fees. He proposed setting up small banks actually in the churches, combining low-interest loans with financial counselling, an interesting idea certain to meet with fierce opposition.

As we neared the church, however, the appearance of the neighbourhood began to improve. Several small restaurants, mostly serving Asian food of one nationality or another, looked clean and inviting. The streets and pavements were free of rubbish. No obvious beggars were present; the pedestrians seemed clean and decently dressed.

'We were told,' said Alan quietly, 'that Lovelace has done a great deal of good in his parish. Now I believe it.'

'Jane said it was his staff who did all the work.'

'Hmm. Well, whoever has done it, it's good work.'

The church itself, as we approached it, was large but not at all attractive. Built of red brick with dirty white granite trim, it was typical Victorian grim in style. Its architect had apparently leaned toward the Old Testament school of religion, the God of wrath, the sort who, as a schoolboy is reputed to have put it, 'watched to see if you were doing anything fun and put a stop to it'. The forecourt, of unadorned paving stones, was surrounded by a high wrought-iron fence topped with spikes, and the gate, though wide open at the moment, had a large and business-like padlock attached to the hasp.

'Brrr,' I said as we turned to enter.

'Indeed.'

'Are we going to introduce ourselves to him?'

'Perhaps after the service.'

The bells began to ring for the service just then, and I was surprised to find them melodious, in tune and well rung. I was surprised, too, to see a steady stream of worshippers turn in at the gates and move toward the door. There weren't hundreds of them, but in an area of working people, it was heartening to find more than a

47

handful of old ladies to attend a church service at three thirty in the afternoon.

Inside, the church was comfortably warm. I looked at Alan in surprise. Virtually all English churches house a chill that even the warmest summer day seems unable to dispel. He nudged me and pointed to the base of the wall. Under each window sat a low electric heater, in the style of American 'baseboard' heating.

Good grief. Central heating in a huge church. Amazing!

For the church was huge, the vaulted roof high overhead, the nave wide. Even the clutter of tombs and memorials that spoils the proportions of any old church couldn't destroy the impression of immensity. It was not beautiful. Actually, the pseudo-Romanesque styling reminded me of a railway station with garish stained-glass windows. But it was undeniably impressive.

A verger was directing people to the front pews – pews, not chairs, I noted – and I exchanged glances with Alan again. Apparently, they expected a large congregation that needed to be properly seated.

And the expectation was fulfilled. The stream of people grew, slowly and then more rapidly, so that by the time the bells ceased their clamorous invitation nearly a third of the church was full. The worshippers were of all ages and descriptions, from the predictable old ladies, most of them white, to young Pakistani mothers with their babies, to Chinese couples, young and old, to young black men. My surprise had by now turned to astonishment. This simply couldn't be

48

happening in an inner-city London church in the twenty-first century. I pinched myself, but the crowd was still there.

The organ struck up a voluntary, and yet again I looked at Alan. I had thought I was beyond surprise, but instead of the reedy sound I'd expected, this was the glorious full-throated sound of a proper pipe organ. I looked around for the pipes.

'Electronic,' Alan whispered in my ear, pointing to a speaker high overhead. 'Not bad, eh?'

Then the choir entered on an opening hymn, and it was more like what I had expected. Obviously not professional, the choir was mixed, with women taking the place of the boys of the usual cathedral choir. But they sang on key, they sang enthusiastically, and the congregation joined them with a will. I watched them file into their pews to one side of the altar, not a formal quire as in a Gothic church, but adequate for their needs. The singers were led by a verger and followed by a clergyman in cassock, snowy surplice, and stole. The rector, presumably.

He turned around to face us, and I was stunned. The man was gorgeous. There is simply no other word for it. His silver hair, thick and wavy, set off a tanned face with eyes that rivalled Paul Newman's: blue, blue, blue. His smile was enough to light up the church, even had the sun not been shining through those ugly windows. He moved with a springy grace that positively radiated energy and belied the evidence of his hair. Surely he was prematurely grey? This had to be a young man, or youngish, anyway.

He spread his arms wide. 'Welcome, brothers and sisters! God is our refuge and strength, an ever-present help in trouble.'

From the moment of that simple and familiar sentence, I was mesmerized. The Reverend Geoffrey Lovelace's voice matched his appearance – deep, warm, compelling. It forced me to really listen to the words of the service rather than just repeat them by rote. His voice was actually more musical than the choir's music. They sang short, simple settings of the Psalms and canticles, and did them competently, but I waited impatiently for them to stop, so I could listen again to the rector.

At last he ascended to the pulpit, and an expectant hush spread through the church. The congregation, too, had eagerly awaited this moment.

He repeated his opening gesture and words. 'Welcome, my brothers and sisters, welcome. Whether friend or stranger, you have come to a place of healing, a place where all may bring their broken and troubled lives and be made whole. Jesus said, "Come to me, all you who are heavy laden, and I will give you rest." He said, "My peace I leave with you." St Paul spoke of the "peace that surpasses all understanding". We live in troubling times, my friends. We all have pain in our lives. We must seek the peace, the rest, that Jesus has promised us, and it is my job to help you find it.'

I hung on every golden syllable. This, I felt, was a man who could change my life, a man who could work miracles. He spoke of new directions for the neighbourhood, new initiatives from St Barnabas' Church. I didn't care what he said. He could have recited lists of laws and rules from Leviticus, and I would still have listened in awe.

At last he pronounced the blessing and there was a final hymn. Choir and clergy filed out in procession while the organ played a postlude, and Alan took my arm. 'Let's get out of here.'

He sounded urgent. I would have stayed to listen to that remarkable organ, but I rose and followed him out.

'I thought you wanted to meet the rector. Alan, slow down!' I was panting to keep up with his long stride.

'Sorry, love, but it's good to breathe some fresh air.'

'But, Alan . . .'

He gave me rather a grim smile and, taking my elbow, steered me up the street to a respectable-looking, if rather plain, pub.

When he had fetched pints for both of us and brought them to the scarred table, I said, 'All right. What's eating you?'

He downed a large quaff of beer and sighed with satisfaction. 'Ahh. That's better. I'd had a bellyful of the Reverend Mr Lovelace.'

I frowned in disappointment. 'I was actually rather impressed. He's such a powerful speaker.'

'Is he? What did he say?'

'Alan, you heard him! He talked about peace, and the needs of this area, and . . . well, I can't quite remember everything offhand, but I know he was good.'

'Anything about Christian love? Redemption?

Loving God and one's neighbour? Anything about Easter, recently past, or Whitsunday, soon to come?'

'I tell you I don't remember the details.' I sipped my beer and tried to remember just what Mr Lovelace had, in fact, said, and my mind began to clear. 'I think I begin to see what you mean,' I said slowly after some reflection. 'He didn't actually say anything very specific, did he?'

'Except for rather a lot about how much he'd done for the parish. Oh, he used the word "we", but it was obviously the royal, singular "we". He also mentioned, fairly subtly, how much more he could do if the parishioners would only shell out a bit more cash. And you lapped it up, didn't you?'

I opened my mouth to utter an indignant reply, but it died on my lips. Yes, I had indeed 'lapped it up'.

Later, back at the Andersons', I was rueful. 'I'm more than a little annoyed with myself.' I shook my head. 'I'm not usually susceptible to a flim-flam artist. I'm feeling very stupid.'

'Don't,' said Lynn. 'I was taken in at first, too. Tom and I had heard so much about him, we went one Sunday, and I thought he was marvellous for about five minutes. I think he employs a form of mass hypnotism, actually.'

'I admit the thought that came to my mind when I first heard his voice was "mesmerized". But I've always thought I was one of those people who can't be hypnotized.'

'You probably can't,' said Alan, 'not when you have any idea what's happening. You have a

52

strong will, so you set yourself against anyone who tries to manipulate your mind. But in this case you had been lulled into a receptive mood by music and the soothing, familiar words of the service. You were open to suggestion. And the fellow has a golden voice and uses it, I have to admit, to maximum advantage.'

'So why didn't you succumb?' I still felt stupid and, illogically, annoyed with Alan.

Alan covered my hand with his. 'Don't shoot the messenger, love. I didn't succumb, as you put it, because, for one, I'm a male. A honey-voiced Greek god has limited appeal for me. Second, I'm a policeman, trained to look behind a façade. What I saw beyond his wasn't very pretty. And third, I remembered what Kenneth had said about the man's "charisma", so I was on my guard.'

Lynn said, 'Tom was livid with the man that one time we went, said he was an Elmer Gantry of the worst sort. He wasn't very happy when the man ended up on your shortlist, Alan, and if we'd known you were on the commission, I imagine you'd have heard from him. We're not C of E, and we don't even go to church all that often, but the man has ambitions, and we'd hate to see him get to be Archbishop. Anyway, enough of that. What will you have to drink?'

After a leisurely cocktail hour and dinner, Tom and Lynn asked about our plans for the next day. 'I trust you're not rushing back on the first train,' said Lynn. 'Because I thought you and I could do some shopping. There are some new spring hats at Harrods you'd adore, Dorothy.'

'You know quite well I can't afford their hats, and I don't need a new one, anyway.'

'When did that ever have anything to do with it?' asked Alan. 'A hat is not an object that one needs, except in the coldest of weather, and very few of yours, my dear, are made so as to keep your ears warm. Here's my credit card. Go and buy yourself a spectacular hat, and we'll call it your birthday present.'

'My birthday is in October.'

'Your unbirthday present, then.'

'Well, we do need to stay in London to spend some time with Walter and his girlfriend. I promised Jane we'd phone him.' I explained to Lynn that we wanted his opinion about Mr Lovelace. 'Though now I'm not sure we need another opinion. But I'd like to see him, anyway, and meet his lady-love.'

'Let's do both,' said Lynn. 'We'll go shopping, just us girls, and then meet Walter and his girl and the guys for lunch. There's a trendy new place in Parliament Square I've been dying to try. That part'll be our unbirthday treat for you, Dorothy.'

Six

When I'm with Lynn, we take taxis. Cost is not an issue with the Andersons. So we pulled up at Harrods' main door in splendour, and found the millinery department after only a brief survey of the Food Halls, which I can never resist.

54

The hats were stunning. Many of them were the 'fascinator' type, entirely unsuited to a woman my age, but the clerk tactfully steered me to the ones designed to flatter grey hair and cover wrinkly foreheads.

The one I chose at last was pale blue, a cloche made of some sort of stiff net, with a bow and spangles. It was utterly impractical, and utterly gorgeous. 'And it goes with that outfit,' said Lynn. 'Leave it on. And we need to hurry a bit if we're to meet Walter and Sue on time.'

We had agreed to pick up the kids at their flat in Bloomsbury before meeting our husbands at the restaurant. There was time for no more than introductions before we all piled back in the taxi and headed down Charing Cross Road.

I hadn't seen Walter for ages, so we had a lot of catching up to do. He was excited about the possibility of a job with the Museum of London.

'I'm really interested in treasure trove and that sort of thing,' he said, 'so this is right up my street. It wouldn't pay a lot at first, but there are lots of possibilities for advancement. And Sue just might be able to get in at the Museum of Childhood.'

'Ooh, that's the one with the dollhouses, isn't it?' I became interested in dollhouses – or dolls' houses, as the Brits call them – some years ago and still enjoyed them, though I no longer had one of my own. So we talked toys, and miniatures, and London history, quite happily until we were jarred by a sudden stop.

'Sorry about that,' said our driver. 'Bleedin' idiots!' He was plainly addressing not his passengers but the drivers ahead. 'Oughtn't to be allowed, if they don't know how to drive in London.'

We were nearing Parliament Square. Traffic on the other side of the street was moving, but nothing on our side. Lynn made a quick decision. 'We'll walk the rest of the way, thanks. Not your fault,' she added to the driver. 'Here you are.'

'Thank you very much indeed, madam,' said the driver with a broad smile that gave me some idea of the size of the tip.

'Is there a parade or something?' I asked. 'I've never seen the traffic this bad.' The pedestrian traffic was thick, too; we were not the only ones to have abandoned wheeled transport.

'Not a parade,' said Lynn. 'The cabbie would have known. It could be a wedding or a funeral at the Abbey, I suppose, but only *really* important people are married or buried there, mostly royalty, and it would have been all over the news . . . Oh, good heavens!'

We had rounded a corner and could see in front of us what looked like a riot scene. People everywhere, placards waving in the air, bull-horns blasting out slogans, on the one hand, and orders from the police to move along, on the other.

'What on earth? Are those cardboard crowns they're wearing?' Sue, who was the shortest of us, craned her neck to see.

'They're mitres,' said Walter. 'A lot of women wearing cardboard mitres!'

The signs were homemade, and were all different, but with the same theme: 'The Church is Sexist!', 'Mitres for Women', 'Equality under God'. I saw one reading 'Diana was Murdered!' which seemed to imply some confusion on the part of the demonstrator, but for the most part the women were united in their demands, and getting quite raucous about it.

As we drew closer, the chants grew better organized. 'What do we want?' shouted one woman with a bullhorn. 'Women bishops!' the crowd chanted back. 'When do we want it?' 'NOW!'

I didn't see exactly what happened next, but one woman either dropped her sign or else deliberately hit a policeman over the head with it. At any rate, she fell, and immediately the women around her were brandishing their signs and shouting at the police. Others began running in that direction.

'Let's get out of here,' said Walter. I hurriedly took off my new hat and crammed it into its box, and then followed as he miraculously shoved his way through the gathering crowd, dragging Sue by the hand.

More than anything in the world right then, I wanted Alan beside me.

'Where are we?' I asked after a few minutes, as we panted in Walter's wake. I thought I knew London pretty well, but there were still plenty of odd backwaters where I could get lost in two minutes without my trusty A to Zed.

'There's a church just along here,' he said. 'I don't know anything about it, but if there's a quiet place anywhere, a church ought to be it.'

'Not if there are any lady bishop wannabes in it,' I thought I heard Lynn mutter.

The church, thank heaven, was quiet. There were a couple of women going purposefully back and forth on some business or other. A young man in a cassock and dog collar glanced our way for a moment, and then stopped to speak to one of the women. A lingering odour of incense hung in the air, and a statue of the Virgin Mary occupied a niche above a small stand of lighted candles.

'Roman Catholic?' I whispered to Walter.

'I don't think so.' He gestured to a Book of Common Prayer in the pew rack. 'Anglo-Catholic, probably.'

'I don't think they'd like me using my mobile, but I must talk to Alan. He and Tom may be waiting for us somewhere in that mob, and they'll be worried.' I stood and approached the young priest. 'Excuse me,' I said in those stifled tones one tends to use in a place of worship, 'but my friends and I came in to get away from an unpleasant demonstration a few streets away. Is there a place where I might use my phone without disturbing anyone?'

'Ah, yes,' he replied in a normal voice. 'The ladies who want to be bishops. Poor things. They've been at it for a few days now, and getting rowdier by the moment. Not exactly the behaviour one would think might tempt the Church to consider their demands. However, yes, certainly you may use your mobile anywhere you like. There is no service scheduled until later this afternoon.'

Once I reached Alan, he had to find a place quiet enough that he could hear me, and then I had to ask Walter where we were, so he could find us. 'Alan, it's really scary out there! I don't know what we would have done if Walter hadn't been able to get us away. Where are you?'

'We did what you did, and took refuge in a church – the Abbey. There's not a lot of peace and quiet, though. Too close to the action. And it may take us a little while to get to you. I'm going to ask a verger if there's a back way out. Stay put and wait for us.'

We finally achieved lunch, not at the lovely restaurant Lynn had planned, but at a Pret a Manger in Victoria Place, the shopping centre in Victoria Station. As fast food goes, theirs is really pretty good, and quite a lot healthier than the fat-laden concoctions one finds in other places. And after fighting our way through the crowds, we were all a bit too hot and dishevelled for any posh place. Besides, this place was crowded and noisy, an ideal spot for a private conversation.

After we'd fetched our food and found a place to sit, the first thing Tom asked was, 'Did you manage to save your hat, D?'

'I did.' I held up the slightly battered hatbox. 'The box suffered a bit, but the hat is fine. I took it off at the first sign of trouble. I'd rather have lost my purse than this!' I took it out for admiration, and all agreed I could wear it to Royal Ascot the next time I was invited, or, of course, to a Buckingham Palace garden party.

'Or even to church on Sunday, which is some-what more likely. Now. What do you two know about that fracas in Parliament Square? Did the Abbey people know anything about it?'

'The vergers were quite knowledgeable, as we were far from the first bystanders to seek sanctuary there. The demonstration started on Monday, while the commission was meeting, apparently in the hope that a woman would be nominated for our position, even in advance of the legislation that would permit her appointment.'

'Some hope,' said Lynn crisply. 'The mills of God may grind slowly, but they're greased lightning compared with Parliament.'

'Indeed. At any rate, when the shortlist was announced late on Tuesday, the demonstrators weren't happy about it, and their numbers grew. Then Brading was killed and the women seemed to believe, using a thought process not entirely clear to me, that his death gave their cause a better chance of success, with the result that you saw today.'

'As if!' Sue was indignant. 'They're fools if they think causing a riot is going to make anyone believe they'd be good bishops. I don't go to church much myself, but even I know that a bishop is supposed to be – well – dignified and that. And acting like louts isn't doing any good to any other women's causes, either.'

'Amen to that,' I said, lifting a glass in salute. 'That's the trouble with organized protest. If it isn't very *carefully* organized and controlled, it can degenerate so quickly into chaos, and worse. I wonder, though, that Mr Lovelace wasn't there, seizing the opportunity to make a speech.'

60

'Oh, yes,' said Walter, with a glint in his eye, 'you were going to ask me about him, weren't you? It does sound as though you've already taken his measure.'

'I've gained an impression, but Alan and I would both like yours.'

'The man's a charlatan and a hypocrite,' said Tom in disgust. 'Taking credit for what other people have done, and lulling everyone with that smooth tongue of his. I despise him.'

'He's worse than that,' said Walter, lowering his voice. 'I did a lot of research a few months ago about London churches, past and present, for a paper I was writing, and I picked up quite a few interesting ideas. Research is a lot like detective work, you know, Mr Nesbitt.'

'I do know,' he said. 'And it's Alan.'

Walter ducked his head. He was still near enough his childhood to be embarrassed at calling an older man by his first name. 'Yes, well, anyway. The thing is, I was especially interested in St Barnabas', because I used to go there pretty regularly, though I was never actually on the parish roll. And you know how somebody once said that truth was not in accounts, but in account books?'

Several of us nodded. I remembered the phrase from Josephine Tey's incomparable *The Daughter of Time*.

'Well, I was able to look into St Barnabas' accounts practically from the dawn of time, because I was with the BM at the time, and that's a pretty respectable credential. And since it's such a big church and I'd never officially become a member, nobody really looked at me twice.'

'You think,' said Alan, 'that if they had known you were a parishioner, or at least an attendee, your access to the records would have been restricted?'

'I'm damn sure they would have been! Sorry, Dorothy. But, you see, I was looking at both historical record books and modern ones. And only someone who'd attended services recently and seen how much money was going into the collection would have been able to compare that with the recorded income. And I tell you, Mr – Alan – there's something rotten in the state of Denmark. Or the parish of St Barnabas'.'

'Fraud,' said Alan.

'I can't prove it,' Walter admitted. 'It's based on personal observation. But it's so terribly easy to steal from a church collection, isn't it? All that cash, with no way to know who gives how much. Probably others besides the rector would have to be involved, and I think some of the parishioners pay by cheque, or even direct debit for the few rich ones, but most of those people are poor, Alan! They give all they can afford, and more, because they trust Lovelace. They love the man, and believe in him, and all the time he's stealing from them. It makes my blood boil!'

'Mine, as well,' said Alan. 'This is a very serious charge, Walter, and one that will have to be looked into. But you do realize that there could be any number of reasons for the apparent discrepancy? You say the congregation is poor, and Dorothy and I observed that for ourselves. Not all of them, but the majority, I'd say.'

He looked at me, and I nodded.

'So it's possible what you saw was a great many coins, but of little value, adding up to a less impressive total than you believe.'

'It wasn't just coins,' said Walter stubbornly. 'Banknotes. Five, ten, even twenty pounds. Euros, too, and they're easy to spot, with those huge numbers. I suppose some people in the parish have family on the Continent who send them money, or come for a visit. I usually sat in the back, so the plate came around to me almost last, and I tell you, if there wasn't at least a thousand pounds in there, I'm a Chinaman. And that was just one of the plates.'

'Plates,' I said. 'Not those bags on long poles? Though, come to think of it, they used plates when we were there, didn't they, Alan?'

'I don't remember, Dorothy. You may be right. We were well to the front, and I didn't notice particularly. But that's a point, actually. It would be far easier to pocket some of the contents of an open collection plate than a locked bag.'

'Well, goodness knows I don't care for the Reverend Mr Lovelace,' I put in, 'but there's another side to be considered. It was obvious that money was being spent in the neighbourhood, and in the church itself. The style didn't appeal to me, but there was the central heating, for one thing. And everything was bright and clean, no signs of neglect or poverty. How do you explain that, if Lovelace is raking some off the top?'

'I don't. Fraud was never my department. But I still know some people in the Met who

63

specialize in that sort of thing. You must understand, though, Walter, that I can't ask them to launch an investigation without more evidence than your observations.'

'That's why I've done nothing about it myself. I'm good at paper research, but my abilities end there. I'd hoped that you and Dorothy might be able to dig a bit deeper into the mess.'

Alan and I looked at each other. I was the one who replied. 'We're here in London for two reasons, Walter. And, Sue, this mustn't go any further.'

'Right.' That was all she said, but I felt she could be trusted. After all, if Walter loved her . . .

'Okay, then. You know Alan is on the Crown Appointments Commission, looking for a new bishop for Sherebury. And you know that Lovelace is one of the nominees for that position, and that another was murdered last week.'

Walter nodded.

'So we came for Alan to get a look at Lovelace, and to meet and talk with him. But we're also acting as unofficial investigators into the murder. No one likes to think that a clergyman could be a murderer, but it's happened before now, so all three of the remaining nominees are potential suspects.'

'I'd back Lovelace any day,' said Tom.

'Me, too,' said Walter. 'At any odds you like. So, what can I do to help you nail him?'

'I've been thinking about that,' said Alan. He looked around. The room was rapidly clearing, as the lunch crowd went on to their other pursuits. 'We can't talk here. Perhaps . . .'

'Come to our place,' said Lynn promptly. 'Lots of room, lots of privacy.'

64

So we walked the few blocks to their house and settled in the sitting room while Lynn went to make us some coffee. I slipped off my shoes and massaged my feet.

'I dressed for elegant shopping this morning, not for tramping the pavements. Ooh, that feels good. Now, Alan, what did you have in mind?'

'Nothing terribly brilliant, I'm afraid. What I propose is this: I will phone St Barnabas' this afternoon and book an appointment with Mr Lovelace, for tomorrow if at all possible. You will, of course, come with me, Dorothy, acting the dutiful wife for all you're worth.'

'What if he doesn't have time to see you? Or pretends he doesn't?'

'A member of the Crown Appointments Commission? He'll make time. And, Walter, I want you to come with us. I'll introduce you as a young friend of ours, living in London, who has heard about his good works and is eager to help. Do you think your acting abilities are up to that?'

Walter gulped. He is an open, candid young man with a face that, like mine (I'm told), reveals his thoughts. I look dubiously at Alan.

'I want you, Walter, to be our undercover agent. Dorothy and I can't spend a lot of time in London just now, but it's important that we learn anything we can about Lovelace. First, if he is what you believe, we certainly don't want him to be our next bishop. In fact, we'd like to see him prosecuted and out of the Church completely. Second, we're looking for a killer, and if Lovelace is engaging in criminal activities, it would give him an excellent motive to silence anyone who knew about them.'

'Alan, don't you see—' I burst out.

He held up his hand, watching Walter.

The boy wasn't stupid. 'So if he figured out what I was doing, he'd have an excellent reason to silence me.'

'Yes.' Alan was still watching his face.

'I hope,' said Walter, sitting up very straight, 'that you don't think that would stop me doing what I think is right.' He had turned a bit pale, and Sue, sitting at his side, put her hand on his.

'If I thought that, I wouldn't have asked. But I do want you to understand that what I'm asking you to do could be dangerous. I think the risk is slight, if you go about this the right way, but it's certainly there.'

Walter took a deep breath. 'Tell me what to do and I'll do it. I would do anything in my power to put that bastard where he belongs.' This time he made no apology for his language, which, in fact, I thought was apt.

Seven

'I don't like it, Alan,' I said. 'You know the police will be looking into Lovelace's record, and they're trained to spot that sort of shenanigans. Why put Walter in harm's way?'

'Because he can get on it right away. The police will be looking at Lovelace, first, in connection with

Brading's murder – trying to determine an alibi, that sort of thing. Despite what you often read in the kind of fiction you prefer, the police aren't stupid.'

'Well, I know that!' I said indignantly. 'Look who I married!'

Alan smiled. 'Point taken. The police are, however, hamstrung by regulations. They would need a warrant to search the books. I've told you how often we knew, in Belleshire, who had committed a crime – knew it beyond all possible doubt – but were unable to prosecute because of some irregularity in the evidence, some mistake in procedure, some obscure point of law. Now, I concede that they're necessary, these laws about evidence and procedure. I even embrace them. They protect the innocent. Unfortunately, they also sometimes protect the guilty. That's why I want you, Walter, to dig up evidence I can present to the Met, evidence that will warrant a full investigation.'

'Evidence of fraud?'

'Or anything else juicy enough to bring the coppers into the act. But the first thing you must do is ingratiate yourself with the good rector.'

'It is Lovelace we're talking about, isn't it?' Walter snickered.

'And for a start, you'll have to rid yourself of that tone of voice. Try to remember what you thought of him early on. Flatter his vanity. Project your concern for the people of his parish, and your admiration of his work. Can you do that convincingly, do you think?'

'I'll see to it.' Sue spoke firmly. 'Alan, you

67

don't need to introduce us. If the Reverend Mr Bloody Wonderful knows you're a retired policeman, he might get suspicious. He can't be stupid, or he wouldn't be where he is. No, I've had an idea. We'll go to him for pre-marital counselling, and then Walter can go into his act.'

They argued about that for a while. My mind drifted away. It was obvious that Walter was going to get involved in this, one way or another. I hated to think what Jane would say when she heard about it. She was our dearest friend, but her tongue could blister paint when she chose, and she was fiercely protective of Walter, her only family.

Was there no other way? Could Alan and I . . . but no, plainly we couldn't. We had no possible excuse for poking around in the finances of a London parish.

'You'd stand a much better chance of getting in with my introduction.' Alan's voice rose rather heatedly. 'He's going to be much too busy to bother with pre-marital counselling. He probably has staff for that.'

'But the connection with you cuts both ways,' Walter insisted. 'We can't risk it.'

'Look.' I held up a hand. 'You're both right. And there's only one way around the problem – that I can see, anyway.'

Five heads turned toward me.

'A bribe,' I said crisply. 'He likes money. Offer him money to do your counselling.'

Five faces wore looks of incredulity.

'Oh, you should see yourselves! I don't mean you to do it that baldly. You go in, Walter. Perhaps with Sue on your arm, perhaps alone. You decide.

You tell his secretary or whoever bars the door that you have two reasons to see Lovelace. First, to discuss with him a major gift to . . . to whatever seems to be his pet project at the time. You can find that out easily enough. Second, to hope that he just might find time to do some counselling, because you and this lovely lady plan to be married . . . well, you'll have to set a date.' I glanced at Sue. She seemed absorbed in my narrative. Maybe they really did plan to marry sooner or later.

'That should get you in,' I went on. 'It's up to you from then on. Lots of enthusiasm for whatever cause you pick. Lots of time to do volunteer work. You stress that you don't need to do anything glamorous; behind-the-scenes secretarial work will be fine if that's what he needs most. And it will be, I can assure you. I've been active enough in various organizations through the years to know that volunteers usually want to do something they think is meaningful, but grow weary of dull routine very quickly. And then you ice the deal with a cheque.'

'And there's the rub,' said Walter. 'The fly in the ointment. The spanner in the works. Choose your cliché, and I'll come up with five more. Sue and I could top the proverbial church mice in the poverty charts. As soon as we land jobs, we'll be fine, but meanwhile we're living on bread and Marmite, and not too much of the latter. Thanks, by the way, for feeding us today. As for large cheques, we could certainly write one, but it would bounce higher than the London Eye as soon as Lovelace took it to the bank.'

'That's where Alan and I come in. You supply the brains and the derring-do. We supply the funds.' I looked at Alan. 'At least, I imagine you wouldn't mind blowing a bit of our savings to feed London's poor, or whatever the money will go to.'

'I mind very much using it to line Lovelace's pockets,' he said warmly. 'But presumably Walter will see that doesn't happen. Or if it does, and it's the means of bringing him to justice, then it's spent in a truly good cause. By all means, my dear, squander such of our substance as you think wise. I'm told the alms-houses in Sherebury are really quite nice.'

Of course, Lynn insisted that Walter and Sue stay for a substantial supper, and sent them home with a large bag of leftovers. 'Nonsense,' she said when Walter protested. 'We have plenty of food, but we were once young church mice ourselves. And now that we've met, you can expect a supper invitation now and then. When you both get jobs, you can take us all to the Savoy for lobster and champagne.'

When they had left, we sat around over drinks and mulled over the day's events. 'I was really horrified by that demonstration in Parliament Square,' I said.

'Why, love? Were you really frightened? I wish I'd been with you.'

'No, not so much that. At least, yes, I was scared. It looked as though things could turn really nasty.'

'In New York or Chicago, they might have,'

said Tom soberly. 'With both the police and a lot of the onlookers carrying guns, it could have turned into a full-scale riot.'

I nodded. 'Of course, it's different here. All the same, emotions were running pretty high, and it could have been ugly. I don't suppose either of you has had a minute to catch up on the news and find out what happened. I hope no one was hurt.'

'A few scrapes and bruises,' said Lynn, 'no worse. I turned on the TV in the kitchen while I was getting supper. The media were out to cover the demonstration, and one of the cameras caught that little business we saw, with the woman and the sign. It looked like a gust of wind caught the sign and it fell on the policeman. It wasn't deliberate. But then the woman fell, and things got messy. It wasn't too bad, though, and nobody was arrested or anything.'

'It was still upsetting.'

Tom frowned. 'D, I thought you were in favour of women bishops. I know you're a raving conservative about the church services, but aren't you pretty liberal about other church business?'

I laughed. 'I'm not sure conservatives rave, Tom. We rather tend to sulk. But you're right, of course. There are women bishops in America, and my friends tell me that some are great and some are awful, just as you'd expect. No, it's not the cause that bothers me, either, though I do think they could have chosen a more dignified way to make their case. It's more about where they chose to demonstrate. I suppose it was the nearest place to the Abbey that they could congregate, but Parliament

Square, of all places! I'm so foolishly sentimental about Parliament. The Houses of Parliament were the first "sight" I ever saw in England that I recognized, and I was so awestruck I couldn't speak.'

'There's a first,' murmured Tom.

'I heard that! But it's not so much the buildings, though I think they're wonderful and I don't care if they're Victorian Gothic. They still stand for representative government, our government as well as yours, Alan, and, with all its flaws, that system is still the best in the world. So yes, I get teary-eyed whenever I look at the buildings, and the idea of a rowdy protest right in front of it seems all wrong!'

I had grown vehement. I had a lot more to say, but I was afraid I couldn't keep the silly tears away. I picked up my glass, which was empty. Lynn smiled and refilled it.

'But don't you see, D?' Tom sounded unusually serious. 'Free speech is what it's all about. It's only in countries like ours that people can gather like that to protest whatever they want, without fear of the army coming in and mowing them down. There are always going to be incidents, of course.'

'Incidents! The 1968 Democratic Convention! Kent State! You call those *incidents*!'

'Calm down, love,' said Alan. 'You're preaching to the choir. And you're confused about which side you're on. Tom's point is that free speech can be messy, and authorities can overreact. Things can go grossly, horribly wrong, as you say, in cases like the Kent State murders and the Chicago riots – but only when authorities lose control. You're waxing emotional about representational government, but forgetting that demonstrations like the one you saw today are an integral part of that democratic system.'

'Which, as somebody said, is the worst form of government, except for all the others,' said Lynn. 'Winston Churchill?'

'Yes, but I think he was quoting somebody else. Okay, okay, you've made your point. I want to eat my cake and have it. A lovely building, symbol of a noble idea of government, but with pristine surroundings that no one is allowed to sully with argument or protest.'

'Furthermore,' said Alan, tenting his hands in his familiar lecturing mode, 'if you think what goes on outside the House is disorderly, you should see what happens inside. Have you never visited the public galleries or watched Question Time on the telly?'

'No. Is it anything like our Congress? I've been in both the House and the Senate a couple of times.'

Both Tom and Lynn were laughing. 'My *dear*, the House and Senate are both models of decorum compared with the Commons! You would not believe the shouting that goes on! Interruptions, vociferous cries of agreement – or disagreement – it's a bear garden! I cannot *imagine* how anything ever gets done, but somehow the government carries on.'

'Which brings us back to where we started, more or less: the demonstrators and their goals. Do you think there's actually a chance the church will approve women bishops any time soon?'

'They're getting closer all the time,' said Alan, 'what with that new woman bishop in Ireland. The Scottish Episcopal Church nearly did it a few years ago, and the Church in Wales has approved women's consecration. England is still holding out. It will happen, sooner rather than later, but almost certainly too late for Shrewsbury.'

'Then what was all the fuss about today? I swear I don't understand!'

'That's because you think logically,' said Tom, and then ruined it by adding, 'for a woman, anyway.'

Lynn and I both glared at him.

He grinned. 'Thought that'd get you. But the thing is, these ladies are thinking that probably the death of Dean Brading will louse up the selection process, and maybe it'll take long enough that the Church will get off its collective duff and agree to women with mitres. They want to push the process along, and I'm sure they have just the candidate for Shrewsbury.'

'Who?' said Alan and I together.

'No idea. Better ask them.' He yawned. 'Sorry. It's been a long day.'

'And it's far too late for you to head for home, so stay with us another day.'

'We'd have to anyway,' I said, standing, and trying not to yawn myself, 'because we never introduced ourselves to Mr Lovelace, which was Alan's ostensible reason for coming to London in the first place. It might even be two days, because it's way too late now to phone for an appointment, and he might not be available tomorrow. I'd better call Jane and tell her we'll see her when we see her.'

'You're lucky to have Jane to look after your menagerie.' Lynn stood and began to collect glasses. 'The two cats are easy, but Watson's a pretty active dog.'

'Rambunctious, some would say, but we love him. And so does Jane. She is indeed a gem, and I should have remembered to buy her a little thank-you gift. Remind me tomorrow.' This time I couldn't stifle the yawn.

'You're asleep on your feet, love. Make that call to Jane, and then come to bed.'

Eight

Next morning, Alan phoned Mr Lovelace, who professed himself delighted to see us at any time that was convenient for us.

Alan was rubbing his fingers together after he clicked the phone off, as if to rub off something sticky. 'That man's personality is so revoltingly saccharine. It oozed down the phone line like treacle, *warm* treacle, flowing all over me. I need a bath.'

Since he had just showered, I proffered the coffee Lynn had brought up, hot, strong, and bitter enough to counteract the treacle. 'I'll go down and ask Lynn to omit anything sweet from the breakfast menu.'

The weather had changed in the night, and we

75

walked out into a depressing drizzle. Alan offered to hail a cab, but I preferred to walk to the Tube. 'We've both got good brollies, and rain is what we both need right now. Something real, to offset the artificial bonhomie Mr Lovelace is no doubt about to offer us.'

It was raining harder than ever when we got to our stop, so we were pretty well drenched by the time we reached the Reverend Mr Lovelace's unattractive church. A functionary took our coats without wincing as they showered all over him. 'One point in favour,' I whispered as we were shown to the office.

The office made a sharp contrast to the church itself. It was small, of necessity since its space had been carved out of the old church. But it was bright, with tasteful modern lamps fighting the drear of the day. It was warm; an 'electric fire' tucked discreetly into a corner glowed cheerily. And it was comfortably furnished. The desk and its chair, the two visitors' chairs, and the few pictures on the wall were designed to suit the room and to welcome and soothe those who entered. They proclaimed good taste and, I thought, no little expense.

'Good morning!' said Mr Lovelace, moving to greet us. 'Mr Nesbitt, Mrs Martin, I'm delighted to meet you!' His handshake was firm but not bone-crushing. One more small point on the plus side. The fact that he knew my name – well, I wasn't sure about that one. Someone might have told him I didn't use my husband's name. Or he might have done some research on his own.

'May I offer you some tea or coffee?' he went

76

on, gesturing us to chairs. 'You must be chilled to the bone.'

'Thank you, sir,' said Alan, 'but we've not got a great deal of time. We're in the city only for a day or two and must return home soon. As you will have gathered, I'm here as a member of the Crown Appointments Commission. As I've never met you in person, I wanted to have an informal chat before the formal interview process.'

'Yes, indeed. The process will continue as scheduled, then? Despite the tragic death of Dean Brading?'

'As to that, we have been given no information. The secretaries are trying to schedule an extraordinary meeting, but, as you will appreciate, everyone concerned is extremely busy, and, of course, one of the first priorities of the Church is to deal with the needs of the people of Chelton Cathedral. Did you know the poor man well?'

Mr Lovelace sighed. 'Hardly at all, actually. The police asked me that when they came to interview me. I seldom have the time to travel far outside my parish, and the dean was also a very busy man. I believe one or two of my parishioners may have known him. A terrible thing, isn't it? I imagine you, as a policeman, are also interested in the matter from a professional point of view?'

'I've been retired for a long time now,' said Alan smoothly, without answering the question. 'My principal interest is to see that we find the right bishop for Sherebury. I very much wish I'd had the chance to meet Dean Brading. I've read his CV, but it isn't quite like seeing him in person, is it?'

'As I say, I didn't really know him, either. Certainly, his conservatism is – was – a counterbalance to some of the more radical movements in the Church. I may say I did not always agree with some of his positions, but I'm sure he will be greatly missed in certain quarters. Now, how can I help you further?'

'I won't ask you any pertinent questions just now, as this is an unofficial visit. I simply wanted to meet you and get a general impression of your parish.'

'Yes. When I learned you were coming, I deputized two of my parishioners to give you a bit of a tour and answer any questions you might have about our activities. That is, if you have time?'

'That's very kind of you,' said Alan, rising. I took my cue, stood and murmured something by way of thanks and farewell, and followed the two men out the door.

A young couple stood waiting for us. They were, I thought, probably Pakistani, and when they introduced themselves, their accent confirmed my idea, as did their names, which I didn't quite catch except as a combination of exotic sounds.

The woman – I couldn't help thinking of her as a girl – smiled brilliantly and spoke with animation. 'We will show you everything! This is a wonderful church and Mr Lovelace is a wonderful man. We knew nothing of Jesus when we came here. He has taught us everything, and he has done so much for our families.'

'Saida, you talk too much.' Her husband

78

– brother? – spoke with a more English accent and more slowly. 'But it is true, we have learned much at this church and have been able, ourselves, to help our families under the guidance of the people here. But let us show you the church. That is what we are here to do.'

He was polite, but his lack of enthusiasm was all the more marked by contrast with Saida's sparkle as she showed us around, pointing out various gifts given to the church by grateful parishioners. 'Look, look at these beautiful paintings of Jesus!' she said, sounding like a little girl opening Christmas presents. I couldn't help but smile, although the paintings were so-so reproductions of works that were a good deal too sentimental for my taste.

Alan waited until she stopped chattering for a moment and then asked both of them, 'Did Mr Lovelace tell you why we are here?'

Saida's face fell. 'Yes, and he said we must be very nice to you and answer all your questions, and this we will do. But, oh, we do not want him to leave! It would be wonderful for *him*, to be a bishop, but we do not know what we would do without him!'

'And you, Mr – I'm sorry, I don't remember your name.'

'It is long and difficult for the English. Call me Akbar.'

'Akbar, then, how do you feel about the possibility that Mr Lovelace might be called to be a bishop?'

He shrugged. 'One holy man is much like another. I do not need a priest to tell me how to

79

speak to God. My wife is devoted to him, so she will be sad if he leaves, and for that I will be sorry.'

'But not for yourself?' I persisted.

He smiled for the first time, his teeth very white in his bronze face. 'My business will perhaps suffer. He has organized many initiatives to make our neighbourhood cleaner and safer, and now more people come to my restaurant. He is a good businessman also, I believe. If conditions become worse again after he leaves, it might not be so well with me. And now, I am sorry, but I believe we have shown you everything, and we must go back to the restaurant. I would be honoured to give you lunch if you would like to eat with us.'

'We'd like that very much,' Alan answered for both of us. 'Tell us how to get there.'

'It is on this same road, not far from here. It is called the Kashmir.'

'Oh, you're Kashmiri, then?'

Again that spectacular smile. 'No, we are Pakistani, but the town where we were born is in a region that is not well known in this country. Kashmir is well known and sounds exotic to English ears. So . . .' He shrugged.

We waved goodbye, retrieved our coats, and went back to the office to pay farewell courtesies to the Rector, but he wasn't there. His secretary, a sturdy, no-nonsense woman with iron-grey hair and sensible shoes, told us he had left for a meeting immediately after we had seen him. 'He's an extremely busy man, you know,' she said in a reproving tone. 'He was late to the meeting as it was.'

80

'Then please apologize to him for us, and thank him for taking the time.' Alan doesn't like being condescended to. For that matter, I don't know anyone who does. But he was more interested in gaining information than in being treated courteously. 'It was good of him to see us at all when he's so busy. He seems the sort of man one would enjoy working for.'

'He is the best employer I've ever had, and the best priest I've ever known, and I've been a communicant of this parish for sixty-three years and its secretary for forty-two. It's a sad congregation he'll leave behind when you take him away to be your bishop, and that's no lie!'

'That's why she was so snippy,' I said as we walked to the Kashmir. 'She's afraid you're going to take away her precious rector. You're not, though, are you?'

'I'm less certain about that than I was a few days ago. He certainly seems beloved of his parishioners.'

'Some of them,' I pointed out. 'Akbar – if I've got his name right – was tepid at best. And don't forget Walter, who fell for him at first but can't stand him now.'

'And believes him guilty of embezzlement. Dorothy, do you really think I'm sending him into danger by asking him to look into the matter? I don't see any other way of finding out anything about it.'

'I think there's some risk, but Walter isn't a child. I think he'll be able to get out of it if he needs to. Alan, did it bother you just a little that he knew my name – that I don't use Nesbitt, I mean – and knew you were a policeman?'

'It surprised me a little that he let us know that he knew. I'd have thought he'd play it a bit closer to his chest. That he took the trouble to learn about us, no, that didn't surprise me. It's just good staff work. He's applying for a job, so to speak. He wants to know as much as he can about us, just as we want to know about him. And here we are. We'd better talk about something else over lunch.'

'Well, of course!' I gave him an indignant look as we walked into a room full of delightful smells.

I was still talking about the meal in the train on our way home. 'The restaurant seems to be doing well, but they're certainly not rich. I feel bad about getting a free meal from them.'

'I imagine,' said Alan, 'he hopes we're going to do him a big favour by taking away the rector.'

'Yes, there's certainly no love lost there. What did you think of him, Alan, or haven't you had time to decide?'

'Are you asking what I thought of him as a potential bishop or as a murder suspect?'

'Either. Both.'

Alan considered that for a long mile or two, while I watched the new lambs gambolling in soft green meadows, and thought about the vast capacity humans had for creating sorrow and trouble in the midst of beauty and joy.

'I think,' said Alan at last, 'that Mr Lovelace will one day be an admirable bishop. He has obvious administrative ability, or his church would not be so well run. You could see that in the little things – the cleanliness, the neat schedule of services posted on the board, the dragon of a secretary. He has the ability to delegate, as many people have told us. They didn't put it quite that way, but "getting everyone else to do the work" amounts to the same thing. And he certainly inspires loyalty.'

'Among the women.'

'And probably many men, as well. Our sample is minute, Dorothy.'

'I still think he'd make a terrible bishop.'

'For Sherebury, I agree. He's not at all a good fit for us, and I'll do my level best to persuade the commission of that. But he'll be a bishop one day. I'm sure you noticed that his concern was not for Dean Brading's family or his flock, but whether the appointment process would continue. He has "ambition" graven on his heart.'

'That's an odd choice for a man of God.'

'And I suppose that's what he thinks he is – a man of God. I have my doubts, but who am I to judge?'

'You're entitled to judge him as a potential murderer, though. That's where you're the expert.'

'Not according to some of the real judges I've met in my time! However, as a matter of speculation, I think the Reverend Mr Lovelace would be quite capable of murder, under the right circumstances. He has a cool head and immense self-esteem, and the kind of mind that can justify almost any action taken for what he deems to be the right motives. Witness his stealing from the collection, if he is, in fact, doing that. *But.* He also has keen sense of self-preservation. Witness his bothering to check us out before he met us. If he wanted to be rid of Brading as a rival to the episcopal throne, he would send someone else to do the job and make quite sure his own hands were clean.'

'And throw his hit man to the wolves.'

'Probably.'

'Well, I think you're right about all that, but I also think the man is too conceited to see anyone as a rival. He didn't want to talk at all about poor Dean Brading, and he acted quite sure about his appointment. Alan, I dislike the man, but I can't spot him as a murderer. Which means this was a wasted trip.'

'Not at all. We formed an opinion of Mr Lovelace, which I can use when the commission reconvenes. We eliminated a murder suspect, at least provisionally. And we had a very good meal!'

'Which is, at this very moment, sitting like lead in my stomach. This subject is not conducive to pleasant digestion. Let's talk about something else.'

'Dear heart, talk about anything you like, but you may be talking to yourself. I intend to nap.'

Nine

We had barely got home, greeted our ecstatic dog and our reproachful cats, and sat down to a cheese-and-biscuits supper, when the phone rang. 'Drat! I'll get it, Alan. You can pour me some wine.'

It was Dean Allenby. 'Dorothy, I'm sorry to bother you the very moment you've come home, but I need to speak with Alan, if that's possible.'

I handed the phone to my husband and sat down to sip some wine. I thought I might need a little soothing before the evening was over.

I could gather little from Alan's end of the conversation, which was brief and consisted mostly of yes and no. From Alan's face, though, I could tell that the news was not especially welcome.

'We're on the road again,' he said when he had clicked off. 'Or I am. You need not go if you don't want to.'

'Of course I want to. Where are we going and when?'

'Birmingham, tomorrow. Kenneth wants me to have a look at Mr Robinson.'

I searched my memory. 'Which one is he?'

'The socialist, according to Jane. Social activist, certainly.'

'Ah, I remember. He didn't sound very attractive. And Birmingham has never been very high on my list of places to visit before I die. In fact, it's not on the list at all.'

'Mr Robinson's church is on the outskirts, though. But, as I say, you needn't come with me if you'd rather not.'

I finished a mouthful of cheese and biscuit. 'Don't be silly. When do you want to leave? And are we going by road or rail?'

As the church we were to visit, St Matthias', was on the outskirts of the city, we drove. I had some hopes that the area would be more attractive than the pictures I'd seen of the inner city. When we got there, however, my hopes were dimmed. Oh, the church wasn't thoroughly ugly, not like the ultra-modern excesses of the Bullring. Built, I was guessing, in the early twentieth century, the church was a red-brick pile of no particular architectural style. It was square and uninteresting, at least from the outside, not a place that welcomed one to worship a God of love and joy.

I turned to Alan, a new and distressing thought entering my mind. 'Alan, is it me? Am I so set in my ways that everything in the least different is automatically bad? This is a perfectly decent building, by its own lights. Why do I hate it so?'

'You have a fixed idea of what a church ought to be,' he responded promptly. 'If something is entirely, wildly different – perhaps a wood-and-glass structure with forest around it – you're able to appreciate it for its own beauty. When you see something like this – a building that suggests the idea "church" without conforming to your concept – you reject it. Stop thinking "church" and think "community building", and see if your perception changes.'

I looked away at surrounding houses and small shops, shut my eyes, and then looked back at St Matthias'. 'Oh. It's really not too bad, is it? Tidy, well-maintained, nice lawn around it.'

Alan grinned. 'See? But it doesn't look like a church to me, either. Let's go and find our B and B.'

It was an attractive house in a pleasant neighbourhood. With my new, unwelcome self-awareness, I was determined to see it as pleasant. The vicinity of St Matthias' was a 'planned community' of houses carefully spaced on winding streets and cul-de-sacs. Nothing was run-down; everything looked new and bright and scrubbed. The shops, when we went out in search of lunch, were also bright and new, built in imitation of Tudor half-timbering. They were charming. I kept telling myself firmly that they were charming.

We had an acceptable lunch in a bright, clean café, and then went back to our B and B to settle in before going to Evensong. Alan chatted for a moment to our hostess, got our key, and led me up the stairs.

Our room was as new and bright and clean as the rest of the package. I plumped down on the bed and looked around, secretly hoping to spot a dust bunny somewhere, or even a tattered magazine, anything that indicated our host and hostess were human, with human failings. Nothing.

And then there was the accent.

'I suppose,' I said tentatively, 'I'm going to sound like a typical arrogant American. But honestly, Alan, I couldn't understand a word that woman said to you. Is this the famous "Brummie accent"?'

'Wait,' he said, 'until you hear them in a pub. You'll wonder if you're still on the same planet.'

'I can't wait to hear our priest *du jour*.'

This church had lovely bells. I gave Alan a thumbs-up as we walked through the agreeable cacophony to the church door.

87

There was a greeter – another positive sign. True, I couldn't understand him, but a smile and a handshake are universal. I gratefully took the service leaflet he handed me. Even if the priest also spoke Brummie, I could follow the service.

The church was bigger on the inside than it had looked on the outside, and it appeared prosperous. It was also warm and welcoming, with flowers in every corner, bright banners everywhere, lots of striking modern chandeliers to banish the gloom of a cloudy April afternoon, and a large, chatty congregation that reminded me a bit of the one at St Barnabas', with its variety of skin colour. These people were mostly young, though.

We had to sit near the back, so we had a good view of the congregants. They seemed to be happy people, chattering in languages I didn't always recognize. Or maybe it was just the accent! I have always gone to churches where silence was kept before the service, the chattering reserved for afterward. I had to admit that these worshippers were 'making a joyful noise', even if I found it a little odd.

Then the musicians entered. My eyes widened. I hadn't noticed, until this minute, a pair of fabric-covered screens to the right of the chancel. These were now removed to reveal a set of drums, music stands, chairs, microphones, and amplifiers. Several young men and one woman carried in their instruments, hooked them up, and began to play a rousing tune.

It wasn't exactly rock. It wasn't exactly reggae.

My musical scope wasn't broad enough to label it, but to my astonishment I rather liked it. The amplifiers weren't cranked all the way up to 'Deafen', and the rhythm was captivating. I found myself softly clapping along and tapping a foot.

At some point, more young people entered and sat in the chancel. They weren't robed, but they carried folders with them, so I guessed they might be the choir. As the band wound up their music, and the congregation shouted a joyful 'Amen!', a tall man strode up to the lectern. He was athletic in build. His short, dark hair showed touches of grey, but his face looked young. He was dressed in grey slacks, a short-sleeved grey shirt with a dog collar, and a brightly coloured African print stole. This, then, was the radical Reverend William Robinson.

He smiled, held out his arms in a gesture of love, and began the service: 'We have come together as the family of God . . .'

It was, I saw from a glance at my leaflet, the standard opening sentence, but he made it sound spontaneous and meaningful. He was really speaking to his flock, and they responded with smiles and nods and the occasional word of agreement.

'It's a Southern Baptist prayer meeting,' I whispered to Alan. 'Call and response. Shades of Martin Luther King.'

The hymn that followed was unfamiliar, but as both words and music were printed in the leaflet, I tried to follow. The words were simple but moving, dealing with grace to meet every need, love to lift every heart. The choir sang, the congregation sang, the band played. It was, I thought, a wonder that the walls didn't come a-tumblin' down.

Much of the service that followed was spoken, rather than sung. The Psalms, though, were sung metrically, to tunes both old and new. The band played praise music at intervals, the congregation clapping along with enthusiasm.

Then Mr Robinson stepped into the centre aisle. No pulpit for him. I sat back, eager to hear what he had to say.

'My dear friends, you have heard the lessons for today. You have heard how the Israelites were freed from their slavery in Egypt. You have heard our brother Paul say that for followers of Jesus there is neither slave nor master. Yet here in our city – yes, in our very parish – there is virtual slavery!' There was a rumble from the congregation. 'Yes, you know what I'm talking about! You know the starvation wages paid by at least one employer in our town. They skirt the law, hiring under-eighteens, giving them short hours, using every nasty trick they can play to keep their profits high.' The rumble grew louder.

'I see many young men and women here who know exactly what I'm talking about. You can't live on what they pay you. "If you don't like it, get another job," you're told. But jobs aren't to be had for the asking. It's work for their pittance or don't work at all. Yes! You are angry, and so am I! I tell you, Paul wasn't just saying that Jesus had abolished slavery. He was saying

90

that we, too, must help abolish it! He wasn't talking about a lovely dream; he was issuing a call to action!'

The church resounded with agreement.

'One of our prayers this afternoon reminded us that serving God is perfect freedom. In his service there is no slavery, no despair, only joy. If there are those who, today, wish to commit yourselves to the service of God and the freeing of his children, meet with me after the service, and we'll make a plan. I have some ideas. You'll have better ones. Together, with the help of almighty God, we can make a difference!'

The congregation erupted, the band moved into a lively hymn tune, and the service ended. Some of the congregation left, but many clustered around the rector, eager to hear about his plans for social reform and contribute their own ideas and energy.

'And how did that strike you, my dear?'

We were having coffee in one of those relentlessly charming little shops in the High Street. I paused to collect my thoughts. 'I think I liked it,' I said slowly. 'I wouldn't have expected to, but I did. And I liked him.' I studied my husband's face, wondering if he was going to accuse me again of falling for a handsome face and a good line.

'So did I. Aha! That surprises you, doesn't it?'

I admitted it.

'He's something of a spellbinder, to be sure. But there his resemblance to Lovelace ends.

91

This man is sincere, which makes all the difference. He really believes in the social gospel, and he'll be right there on the front lines leading his troops into battle.'

'It's a futile battle, though, isn't it? Doomed from the start.'

'Possibly. Possibly not. If it's a local employer he's talking about, he may make some waves, at least. If it's a multinational, he hasn't a prayer.'

'Hmm. I seem to recall one David, who had only a prayer and a good right arm, and brought down the ancient equivalent of a multinational.'

Alan waggled his hand. 'Not entirely comparable. Mr Robinson is a David, yes, but Goliath was a midget compared with a modern corporation. One thing is certain, at least to my mind: the Reverend Mr Robinson would not be a good fit for the Diocese of Sherebury.'

'Amen to that! Can't you just see him marching on the High Street shops, smashing windows with his crozier and demanding higher pay and better working conditions?'

'Actually, I can, and it's not a pretty picture.'

'He'd be a change from our present bishop, anyway. I can't think of a thing that man has actually done since I've lived in Sherebury. Or anything important that he's said, for that matter.'

'You're right. But there's something to be said for peace. More coffee, love?'

It was good coffee. I opted for more, even though we were the only people in the place and I wondered if they were about to close. As the waitress brought it, though, in a large cafetière, a laughing, chattering group entered the café.

One of the crowd was the Reverend Mr Robinson. He smiled and came over to shake our hands.

'I believe I saw you in church earlier, didn't I?'

'You have a keen eye, sir,' said Alan, standing.

'I know most of my parishioners, and if I may say so, ma'am, your hat would make you stand out in any crowd.'

We both laughed. 'And it's one of her less spectacular ones. I'm Alan Nesbitt and this is my wife, Dorothy Martin.'

'Aha! Then I did guess right. You're here from the Appointments Commission, yes?'

'Not exactly. That is, yes, I am a member of the commission, but this visit is entirely unofficial. My wife and I simply wanted to meet you, informally.'

'And see me in action, right?'

'Something like that.' I decided it was time to get into the conversation. 'Won't you sit down, Mr Robinson? If you have time, that is.'

'All the time in the world. My next rabble-rousing isn't scheduled until tomorrow morning at nine a.m. sharp. We're going to the factory to protest unfair wages and labour practices.'

'And what factory would that be?'

'Oh, I forgot you're from the south. For us, there's only one factory. We're what you Americans call a company town. Dudley Chemicals, world-famous maker of cleaning products, pesticides, herbicides, and almost anything that's toxic. Cheers.'

He lifted the cup of coffee Alan had poured for him. I put my cup down. Somehow it didn't taste quite as good as a moment before.

The Rector grinned. He was very boyish, although he must be at least fifty. 'Don't worry. It's made with bottled water. Dudley claim they stopped dumping their waste products in the river years ago, but we take no chances.' He drank some coffee. 'That's heaven. I'm in your debt, sir. I suppose you've come to see if I'd suit Sherebury,' he went on without pause. 'I seriously doubt that I would, you know.'

'You would certainly be a change from our present bishop,' I said.

The Rector grinned again. 'I would at that. I've heard a good deal about your bishop. I'm somewhat more . . .'

'Active? Dramatic? Involved?' I supplied.

'All of those things, perhaps. Of course, I'm much younger, and that makes a difference. But I'll be truthful with you. Oh, I know you said this is unofficial, but I can tell you my views, can't I? And the truth is I'm not at all sure I want the job. I agreed, in the beginning, that I'd think about it. And I have thought. And prayed. Oh, I've prayed a lot. And I honestly think God wants me to stay here. I love this town and these people.'

'And we love you.' Two of the people who had come in with Mr Robinson – a married couple by the look of them – came over to our table. Alan stood again. 'I'm sorry,' the woman went on. 'We didn't mean to eavesdrop, but we couldn't help but hear. And we're all agreed – everyone

94

in the parish, I mean. We don't want to lose our priest!'

A cry of 'Hear, hear!' went around the room, subdued but heartfelt. I looked around at the variety of faces. The shy teen with the bad case of acne. The wrinkled, white-bearded man in his wheelchair. Fair hair, black hair, brown hair, auburn hair, no hair at all. Pale skin, ebony skin, several shades in between. A diverse group, but unanimous in their animated show of love and support.

All except for one man in the corner. I noticed him because he was so quiet. He sat nursing a cup of coffee, his hands wrapped around it as if to warm himself. But the room was warm, almost too warm now that it was crowded.

Mr Robinson noticed the direction of my gaze. 'Poor chap,' he said quietly. 'You mustn't mind him. He's had his troubles. I ought not to have urged him to come to coffee with us, but he looked so lonely, I thought it might do him good. Phone me later; I'd like you and Mr Nesbitt to come to supper, if you can. Now if you'll excuse me . . .' And he went to tend his flock.

'You see what a good priest he is,' said the woman who had come to our table. 'Always ready to help someone. My name's Becca, by the way, Becca Bradley, and this is my husband, Jack.' Her accent was the most understandable I had heard, except for Mr Robinson's. Modified for our benefit, perhaps?

'Do please join us,' said Alan politely. Or maybe it wasn't just politeness. He might

95

simply have wanted to sit back down himself, or he might be interested in getting a little more information from this talkative woman.

'You see that man he's talking to,' Becca went on. She was a small woman, with mousy grey-brown hair and the eyes of an avid gossip, the sort that dart around a room and see everything and everyone. 'I'm surprised he came to church at all. He's fairly regular on Sundays, but not always even then. It's his wife, you see.'

'Becca,' said her husband with a frown.

'Oh, I know,' she said, lowering her voice slightly, 'but what does it matter? Everyone knows, and these people will never see him again anyway. His wife is . . . well, in the old days we'd have said she was mad. Nowadays it's tarted up. Mentally disturbed, emotionally unstable. Pretty words for the same thing: barking.'

'Really, Becca, that's not nice. She has reasons for her illness.'

'I didn't say she didn't, did I?' The voice fell still further. 'Their son died, when he was just a boy at school. Now, no one could say that wasn't a dreadful thing, but it was years ago. She should have pulled up her socks and got on with life. Instead, she's made life miserable for herself and everyone else, ever since. Had to be put in a home, you know. It costs the earth. And how that man puts up with it, I do not know. If you ask me, he's headed for—'

'That's enough, Becca,' said her husband firmly. 'Brian Rawles is a good man, doing the

96

best he can in a difficult situation. I'll not have you saying such things about him.'

'Oh, well.' She smiled, and for a moment her eyes lost their restless, searching look. 'I talk too much, as you've always told me, Jack, but I'm too old to change. Anyway, I'm glad you came to visit, but don't you dare take our rector away!'

Ten

'I hope you won't think too badly of Becca Bradley,' said the rector. We were sitting around his fire with after-dinner drinks. The room was cosy and rather shabby. And our supper had consisted of a good thick soup, to keep out the suddenly chilly spring evening, and homemade bread. I was feeling comfortable and very much at home. 'Becca's a gossip, of course,' he went on, 'but her heart is in the right place, though you wouldn't guess it.'

'Now, Bill, you're too kind about her.' Mrs Robinson sat on a squashy old sofa with her legs tucked up under her, lithe as a thirty-year-old, a mark she'd passed at least twenty years before. 'You always want to think the best of everyone, but there's such a thing as too much Christian charity.'

'There can never be too much charity, Jenny, love. Only misdirected, sometimes. I admit that Becca can be a sore trial, but look at all she does in the parish. There's not a supper she's ever missed, not a volunteer job she hasn't undertaken. She's invaluable.'

Mrs Robinson shook her head with a smile. 'You're too good to live, darling. She'll never miss an opportunity to pick up more gossip. That's why she has her finger in so many pies. Of course, she also worships at your shrine.'

Mr Robinson laughed that one off. 'It's one of the hazards of the priesthood, though it's more often elderly spinsters who fall for their priests, and more often unmarried clergy who are the victims.'

I thought of one of my favourite classic mysteries. 'Have you ever read *Overture to Death*, by Ngaio Marsh?'

'Oh, yes!' Mrs Robinson chuckled. 'The two church hens vying for the attentions of their supremely good-looking rector. You have that in common, Bill, with – what was his name?'

'Copeland,' I said. 'I re-read the book just the other day. He was a different type, but yes, your husband is certainly right up there in the Mr England lists.'

Mr Robinson rapidly changed the subject. 'Mr Nesbitt, I know that you're a retired chief constable, so I assume you still have associates in the police force. Has any progress been made, do you know, towards solving Dean Brading's murder? That was a dreadful thing – a priest murdered in his own church. At least, I suppose it was murder? I've seen very little in the papers or on the telly since it happened.'

'It's possible that it was an accident. I know very little, actually, except what everyone knows. He was found with a frightful wound in his head, which was not inconsistent with it having struck a solid object, such as a bit of carving, in the cathedral. He might have slipped and fallen.'

'But you don't think he did? All right, I understand you can't say a great deal. The police came to talk to us about it, to question me about my whereabouts at the relevant time, I imagine. It's a bit ironic, that. They seem to believe that I'd do murder to get the job, when I don't particularly want it. At any rate, I have an unimpeachable alibi, as there was a conference of the diocesan clergy that day, all day.'

'That is fortunate,' said Alan blandly. But Mr Robinson didn't miss much.

'That sounds as though your alibi isn't quite so good.'

'Bill!' said his wife indignantly.

'It's all right. Yes, I am also under some suspicion, as is everyone on the commission. This is going to be a difficult case to solve, I'm afraid. But we were talking about your parishioners.'

'Yes, well, I do boast that I have an extraordinarily devoted, and devout, congregation, and together we have accomplished a great deal in this little corner of England. Poverty is down, employment is up, and not all of it at slave wages, though there's still much to be done in that area. Best of all, people are helping each other, looking out for one another in a way one usually doesn't find outside a village, and not even always there, nowadays. *And* they're learning to put their trust in God, which, after all, is task number one in my job description.'

'In ours for Sherebury, too,' said Alan. 'Are you quite sure you wouldn't take the job if offered, Mr Robinson?'

'Please call me Bill. Mr Robinson is my father.' He fiddled with the stem of his glass. 'No, I'm not sure. I'd rather stay here. Jenny wants to stay here. The kids live nearby, and our first grandchild is due soon. The question is, does God want me to stay here? I'd have a broader scope as bishop, could help set policy, perhaps change some things that badly need changing. But I'd lose the ability for hands-on pastoral care. Oh, I know, I would be pastor to the clergy in the diocese. But it's not the same.' He put his glass down and let his hands fall to his lap with a little sigh. 'You see, I *know* my people. There's Brian, with all his troubles. There's young Susan, who keeps on having babies she can't support. The old man you saw today in the coffee shop, who needs a hip replacement and stubbornly refuses to have the operation. The Chinese couple struggling to make ends meet. The two young Sikh men who face constant persecution from their neighbours who don't understand they're not Muslim.'

'They're not Christian, either,' I pointed out.

'What does that matter? They're a part of my parish. They need help. If I were a bishop, I might not even know they existed, and if I did, serving them wouldn't be a part of my job, nor would I have time.'

'I understand,' said Alan. 'But I'm sorry. I

100

may say that when I saw you in church this afternoon I admired you, but I was quite sure you were wrong for Sherebury. I've changed my mind. If you change yours, you'll let us know, won't you?'

'I will. And I might. God moves in mysterious ways.'

'A praise band,' I murmured, just before I turned over and went to sleep. 'Never thought I'd live to say I liked a praise band.'

This time we had a few days before our next call to duty. When we were having our coffee and buns after church on Sunday, the dean came up to us. 'I would have phoned you yesterday, except that I didn't get home until quite late, and I do hate to disturb you on a Sunday, but as you're here . . .' He paused, and Alan gestured for him to sit down and continue. 'I won't stay, but I needed to tell you that I got a letter yesterday from the Secretary.' The capital S was apparent in his speech. 'The extraordinary meeting of the commission is scheduled for Monday week. Did you receive the letter?'

'Not yet. Our postman is new and sometimes makes mistakes.'

'I'll make a copy of mine, in case your postman never gets it straight. You can be there?'

'Certainly.'

'I have one more assignment for you before then. You and I have both visited two of the candidates, and we've discussed them. Now I'd like you to visit the third, as soon as possible.

I wish you could be there on a Sunday, as they have a very fine choir, but that's cutting it rather fine, what with the meeting on Monday.'

'Perhaps we can get to a Choral Evensong. We'll manage, Kenneth. Don't worry.'

So we phoned Rotherford Cathedral to check the service schedule and make an appointment with the dean, booked a B and B, and, on Tuesday morning, drove to Sherebury station to catch the first of two trains to take us to Rotherford, not too far from Oxford. I was looking forward to this one. I had looked it up on the internet while searching for B and Bs and found it delightful, its charm reflecting its history and landscape. It seemed to be a real place, not a pseudo-Disneyland of a town.

This time we were taking Watson with us. He was getting very tired of being left out of things, even though Jane took excellent care of him. The cats, of course, scarcely noticed when we were gone, though they scolded us roundly when we returned. The purpose of humans is to serve cats, and we were falling down on the job, they informed us. Watson simply missed us.

'He won't be any trouble,' Alan had said persuasively. 'Our B and B allows well-behaved visiting dogs, and our little chap behaves himself. Don't you, mutt?'

It's amazing how much my large, solid husband can sound like a doting mother.

We had chosen to travel by rail, since both the cathedral and our B and B were in the centre of town, and since most of our way by car would have lain on the motorways, which I detest. Our journey did involve changing trains, and that in London is never fun, especially with luggage and a dog. But we got from Victoria to Paddington without great delay, and from there it was a quick run to Rotherford.

From the first, the town took my breath away. We were near enough to the Cotswolds that much of the building stone was of that lovely honey colour that makes Cotswold villages so warm and inviting. The building style was much the same, too, or so at least it appeared to my untutored eye. Shops and houses were small and unpretentious, but with fine proportions. Flowers were everywhere – not the lush draperies of wisteria and climbing roses that would appear in summer over walls and porches, but bright swathes of daffodils in the sun and carpets of bluebells wherever there was a wood.

'It's almost blinding,' I said in awe. 'I don't quite believe they're real. Nothing could be so perfect.'

We found our room for the night, left our luggage, and took Watson for a long leisurely walk down the High Street, which meandered, following the River Roth that gave the town its name. There were ducks. Watson was disappointed that he was not allowed to chase them. There were cats sunning themselves on doorsteps and walls. Watson stayed a discreet distance away from them, having had an unfortunate experience with an extremely intimidating cat a few months before. There were children who wanted to pet him, which he enjoyed thoroughly.

As for us, we simply looked and listened. The shops were interesting, particularly since they weren't aimed obviously at the tourist trade. I was, as usual, stopped by a display of hats in a window. 'I don't have one that colour,' I said innocently, pointing to a bright chartreuse creation.

'And a jolly good thing, too,' said Alan. 'That is *not* your colour, my dear.'

'Nor anyone else's, I wouldn't think. That navy straw, on the other hand . . .'

We went in the store, of course, though we had to leave Watson outside. The navy straw turned out to be a peculiar shape, not at all flattering, but a peach-coloured one was obviously designed with me in mind. Alan is not a man easily intimidated by a milliner, and he actually rather enjoys shopping with me, at least for a while. He agreed that the hat had my name on it, so we walked out with it to greet a bereft dog, abandoned by his people and plainly unloved.

'You,' I told him, 'are almost as good a liar as the cats.'

And then I clutched Alan's arm and turned toward him a delighted face. 'Bells!'

They were practicing a peal, from the sound of it, and they had a good set of ringers. The bells sounded out clear and true in joyous order. I know almost nothing about change-ringing save what I gleaned from Dorothy L. Sayers' marvellous novel *The Nine Tailors*, so I had no idea what 'method' they were ringing, but it didn't matter. 'This is a *proper* cathedral town,' I said happily.

We stood and listened for a while, but Watson began to get restless, so we strolled back to our B and B to put my new hat safely away, and then left him in the back garden, with the consent of our hostess, and went to seek lunch. Predictably, we ended up at a pub.

'Just a half for me, and I think a ploughman's, if they do them here. A salad, if not.' I was feeling fat. The mirror at the hat shop had revealed puffier cheeks than I liked to think I had.

Alan fetched our beer and ordered our food, and when he had sat down I said, 'Tell me about the cathedral. I understand it's one of the new ones?'

'New as a cathedral, though quite old as a parish church. Fourteenth century, I believe. Decorated.'

The term referred, I realized, to a particular style of English Gothic, not to the work of a painter or interior design artist. 'And big, I think Christopher said?'

'Huge, for a parish church. As you can plainly tell, there's a very nice bell tower with a high steeple. Shall we go take a look after lunch?'

Well, that was one of the less necessary questions. I was dying to see the church, so I polished off most of my ploughman's lunch in short order, virtuously leaving some of the bread and a minute fragment of cheese, and we headed off in the direction of the bells.

There's no point in describing Rotherford Cathedral. Any guide to fine English cathedrals will have pictures. I will just say that it is glorious. Not as beautiful as Sherebury, of course, but almost no church can live up to my own beloved Cathedral. Rotherford is smaller, but quite big enough, and, unlike Sherebury, it's all of a piece. My Cathedral has one transept from a much earlier period than the rest of the structure, but Rotherford never suffered from a devastating fire like that which destroyed most of Sherebury in its early days, requiring rebuilding of all but the one transept. Rotherford, I saw, was also spared the Cromwellian destruction.

'Look, Alan, the statues all still have their heads. Why is that?'

'Ah. Therein lies a tale. Come in and sit, and I'll tell you about it.'

We found chairs near the back that were isolated by some trick of acoustics from the clamour of the bells, and Alan tented his fingers in what I've come to think of as his lecturing position.

'It started with a turn of fate that seemed a disaster at the time. When Henry dissolved the monasteries – this was one, you know.'

I nodded.

'Well, when that happened, most of the abbeys were either sold to private buyers, or given as gifts to those owed favours by the Crown, or simply destroyed. Some were left to decay, some despoiled by locals looking for building materials. Rotherford, however, didn't appeal to any buyers or gift recipients because it was prone to flooding. The river was very much higher then, apparently, or else it's more effectively contained now. At any rate, there was a major flood at just about the time Henry was wanting to get rid of the abbey, and although the buildings weren't touched, the whole place was isolated by the waters. So the place was simply closed and locked up, and looked like decaying slowly.

'But then the people living in the surrounding town and countryside stepped in. They had greatly loved their abbey, it seems, and were determined to save it from devastation, until such time as, in their eyes, sanity was restored to the country.'

'So how did they protect it?'

'By sheer cunning, aided considerably by good fortune. It was one of the last foundations to be dissolved, and by that time the king's attentions were engaged elsewhere. This was not one of the wealthy abbeys, so the pickings weren't as good as elsewhere, and, as I say, nobody really wanted it. Henry more or less forgot about it, in part because the councillor who should have reminded him was from Rotherford, and had a sneaking affection for the place. So, with the tacit cooperation of the councillor, the locals built a high wall around it and then planted the fastest-growing trees and vines they could find up against both sides of the wall. By the time any of the king's men came looking for spoils, all that could be seen was a dense copse.'

'Good heavens! Sleeping Beauty's castle. But surely the tower was visible.'

'The tower and the bells were added much later – late seventeenth century, I believe. So, yes, the place looked exactly like something out of Sleeping Beauty. The secret was kept for years, and then decades, and then over a century. Local men and women passed along to future generations the secret of the way through the wall, so repairs could be made, but so devoted were they to their abbey that no one ever told. Cromwell's men had no idea it was there.'

'You're not making this up, are you? It sounds like a fairy tale.'

'It does, I agree, but no, I'm not making it up. It's true, one of the famous "hidden" tales of English history.'

'But it's so romantic. Why haven't I ever heard it before?'

'The people here still aren't eager for it to get about. You know the English have long memories. I learned about it from a chap I worked with years ago, when he'd had a few over the eight. We'd been talking about secret passages and he said I'd be surprised where one was, right in little Rotherford, where he had lived as a boy. He became dimly aware then that he'd said too much and shut up, but I was intrigued and did a bit of research, and it took some real digging, I can tell you. The outline of the story is mentioned in a local history or two, but with no details, and apparently no one to this day has ever revealed where the entry is – or was. Of course, the wall is long gone, and the concealing vegetation. I don't know when they decided it was safe to start using the church again, but certainly not until the Protectorate was over and the monarchy restored.'

I sighed with delight. 'What a wonderful story! And what a wonderful church. Can we see the rest of it?'

A verger appeared then, and asked us if we wanted a tour, but when we said we preferred to wander by ourselves, he was amenable and handed us a brochure with a floor plan and some mention of principal points of interest.

Our first stop was the chapel devoted to private prayer. Nearly every English cathedral has one, a place set aside from traffic areas and noise, where one can be alone with God, whoever one conceives him to be. We knelt for a moment, each with our own thoughts. I was giving thanks for the beauty that surrounded us, and also put up a fervent petition that Sherebury might find the right bishop. I suspect Alan's prayers had something to do with the search, too.

When we rose, the first thing I wanted to see was the chapter house. Now, not all cathedrals have one of those, only the ones that have been monasteries at some point in their careers. It was the place where the monks gathered once a day to hear a chapter read from the Rule of their order, and to discuss any business matters that might be before the abbey. They vary in style according to the architecture of the building, of course, but the most popular style was circular or octagonal, the roof supported by a single central pillar, with stone benches ranged along the walls. The most famous one of this type is possibly at Wells, where the lovely steps leading to it have been photographed innumerable times. Sherebury's chapter house is also of this pattern, though the room is now used as the Cathedral library, with rows of bookshelves, which rather spoil the effect.

Perhaps Rotherford hadn't been a cathedral long enough to acquire much of a library. At any rate, the fine old octagonal room was bare and washed with sunlight from the high windows all around. They were glazed with plain leaded glass, not stained, so the natural light saturated the already golden stone. My breath caught in my throat.

Alan smiled, put his arm around my shoulder, and drew me close.

Sometimes the best communication is wordless.

We wandered, then, without aim or purpose, finding here a charming little chantry, there an amusing tomb inscription, amazing stained glass, exquisite carvings.

There comes a moment, though, when one is saturated with beauty and wonder, and unable to take in any more. When I responded with a nod and a murmur to something Alan pointed out, he said, 'Tea time, then?' and we walked out in perfect agreement.

It was a little early for tea, so we inspected the churchyard for a bit. It was neatly mowed, by machine, I realized regretfully. It's only the country churches that still allow sheep and goats in the churchyard to keep the grass trimmed. They do a much better job than mechanical devices, especially around the headstones, and of course they fertilize the grass as well, but I suppose a cathedral feels that animal droppings

110

are a trifle undignified. I don't know why. They're small, and smell no worse to my senses than gasoline fumes.

We picked out a few interesting inscriptions to read to each other, and then decided we were now in need of sustenance, so we found a tea shop, crowded on a Tuesday afternoon, and eventually snagged a seat outside.

Of course, our conversation turned to the search.

'So far,' I said, 'it's Robinson by a length. By a lap. By a mile. I'm sorry, but I simply cannot like Lovelace. Even if he isn't an embezzler. I wish we'd hear something from Walter.'

'These things take time, if one is cautious. And we certainly want him to be cautious.'

'We do. Alan, that man is dangerous.'

'He is. He's political and he's manipulative, and he's so damnably persuasive. I truly fear that he may be chosen, and I dread the prospect.'

'Can't you stop it? Does the vote have to be unanimous?'

'No, unfortunately it does not. A simple majority. In less contentious times I understand the candidates were often chosen by acclamation, but it certainly isn't going to be like that this time.'

'No. The Church has become so politicized. In a way, I suppose it's better than indifference, but it doesn't seem very Christian.'

'I do seem to recall,' said Alan drily, 'that our Lord once said that he had come not to bring peace, but division.'

'And how right he was.' I sighed and took another scone.

Eleven

The next morning we were up early. Watson saw to that. It was a beautiful day, there were all sorts of exciting sights and smells outdoors, and he didn't intend to be shut up in a house any longer. So he made much more of a nuisance of himself than usual, and Alan was up, sketchily dressed, and out taking him for a walk before seven. I snoozed for a little, but it *was* a beautiful day, and the birds in the garden were making such a happy racket I couldn't really sleep. So I was showered and dressed and ready for breakfast when husband and dog returned, both in great spirits.

'We walked down to the river. It's quite nice down there. Masses of water fowl – ducks, coots, swans, all sorts.'

'I suppose Watson wanted to chase them.'

'Of course he did, but the cob taught him his manners. A swan can be quite alarming when he wants to be.'

'They certainly terrify me. I hope he didn't get too muddy.'

'A bit, but I cleaned his paws before we came in. He's quite socially acceptable now. Which is more than you can say for me. If you'll see to his breakfast, I'll be with you as soon as I'm fit company.'

We'd brought his food and dishes along with us, so I took him down to the garden where he could eat without worrying too much about mess. He wolfed his food happily and then was reasonably content to stay in the walled garden while his humans had their meal. I promised him a bit of sausage or bacon later. Alan and I have strict rules about feeding him snacks, rules we break every time something especially tempting is on offer.

We felt a bit like sausages ourselves when we'd tucked into the full English breakfast, so we took another stroll around the town, with Watson. The influence of the cathedral was obvious everywhere. The Boys and Girls Club, which was clean, tidy, and plainly in daily use, had a message board outside listing activities for the coming week, many of them involving cathedral personnel. The row of pretty alms-houses was also in good repair, despite its venerable age. 'Church endowed?' I wondered aloud, and Alan pointed out the brass plaque on the end house. 'Est. 1512 by Thos. Swain, Esq. & St Martha's Abbey. Re-estab. 1715 by St Martha's Church.'

It was the same everywhere we looked. A school sported a poster advertising end-of-term activities, with the dean visiting. A village hall advertised a concert a week hence featuring the cathedral choir, in aid of Oxfam. A shop listed times when free food would be distributed, with addenda thanking contributors. The cathedral and Dean Smith headed the list.

We had decided to see the dean first in his cathedral – on stage, so to speak – so we spent most of that Wednesday just being tourists, with the now-routine nap in the middle of the afternoon.

The bells woke us. It was time for me to fetch my hat and my good shoes, banish Watson to the garden, and make our way to church.

For weeks now my mind had kept harking back to Trollope's Barsetshire novels. Alan had compared our present bishop to the henpecked, ineffectual Bishop Proudie in *Barchester Towers*, and I had to admit there was a good deal of truth in that. Now, seated in the cathedral, I saw that the Very Reverend James Smith was, on the other hand, a near-perfect model of Septimus Harding, the sweet, mild-mannered precentor of Trollope's Barchester Cathedral. Dean Smith was a smallish man with sparse greying hair. His wire-rimmed spectacles gave him an earnest look, as did the wrinkled brow produced, I suspected, by poor eyesight. I recognized the peering expression from my own mirror.

I had expected, from his appearance, that the dean would have a quavery voice, but it was, instead, strong and sweet. The service was spoken, rather than chanted, but the dean did intone a few phrases, not only reverently but in tune.

The choir, made up traditionally of boys and men, was excellent; so was the organist. In fact, the service was so lovely in every way that I waited for the sermon with great apprehension. Was this going to be the weak spot?

'My brothers and sisters in Christ,' he began, 'we have come together, friend and stranger, in

114

this beautiful and holy place to worship Almighty God, he who made us, sustains us, redeems us. We have heard the comforting words from the Gospel of John, words that are often read at a funeral: "Let not your hearts be troubled, trust in God, trust also in me."

'But we come here to this cathedral church from many places, from many different religious traditions. Many of you – perhaps most of you – are members of this cathedral parish, and indeed I see many familiar faces. I also see unfamiliar ones. Some of you may have come this afternoon to hear our wonderful music and bask in the beauties of our church. Some have come out of curiosity. Some may be seeking respite from troubled lives. Some have come because you've been sightseeing and your feet hurt.'

There was a little ripple of laughter at that.

'Not all of you are Christians. Not all of you are believers of any sort. What I want to say to all of you is that God doesn't care why you're here. Let me repeat that. God doesn't care *why* you came to church today! He cares *that* you're here. He cares that you are, for a little time, a captive audience, so to speak. Here he can reach out to you in a special way. Our form of worship is designed to help people feel the presence of God, and, of course, he uses the music and the beauty and the solemnity to touch you.

'So I want to warn you, all of you – Christians and non-Christians and those who aren't quite sure what you believe – I want to warn you all that God is, in fact, reaching out to you, and he is quite relentless about it. He's going to use every means

115

at his disposal to draw you into his love. If you're trying to run away from him, my friend, as most of us do from time to time, I have to tell you that you've come to the wrong place. There is never a time or place when he isn't at your side, urging you to know him better, to commit yourself to his way, but this time and place is especially hazardous to anyone trying to avoid him. So if you want to escape his net, I'd advise you to leave right now. Another few minutes, and it might be too late.'

He paused, and silence filled the great sunlit space. Then a titter or two began to run through the congregation. No one now would dare to get up, even if they desperately needed to use the loo! Clever, I thought, and Alan passed the same thought to me with a little smile.

'Ah. Well, then, you can never say you've not been given fair warning.' He leaned forward in the pulpit and grasped the sides. 'You may think me facetious, my friends, and I will admit the charge, to an extent. Perhaps the way I have phrased my message is not as serious as it might be. But the message itself is perfectly true. Our loving God, our God who loved us to the point of dying on the cross, is never going to give up on us. He keeps on urging us to follow in his way, to love our neighbours and seek to help them. If you are trying to escape that necessity, again you have come to the wrong place. We here in this cathedral are keenly committed to helping our neighbours in every way, to feeding them, clothing them, and showing them God's love, and a portion of our offering today will be dedicated to those efforts.

116

'Our Lord is present to us in a special way in his church, but he is always, everywhere, with us. When we reject him, when we turn away from his love, he keeps on loving us and seeking to bring us closer to him. When at last we find him, it is because he has, all along, been searching for us. The parents in this congregation will know that, if one of your children is lost, you will move heaven and earth to find that child and bring it back home. So much more will our heavenly father try to bring us home to him.

'So, my advice to you this morning – my urgent plea, in fact – is to stop running. I absolutely promise you that when you do, you will find a mansion prepared for you, a haven where you may rest and stop worrying. That's what he promised us, and he keeps his promises.

'And now unto God the Father . . .'

'The Hound of Heaven,' I said to Alan as we were having tea at Rotherford's fanciest hotel, Watson waiting sadly outside. He accepts the fact that he cannot go everywhere with us, but he doesn't understand.

'I was reminded,' said Alan, 'of C. S. Lewis writing about "the steady, unrelenting approach of Him whom I so earnestly desired not to meet". It is indeed, in some ways, a frightening idea, though I've never heard a parson approach it quite that way before.'

'He's a good preacher. Short, sweet, clear. In fact, he's a good man altogether. I do like Mr Robinson, but Dean Smith is the best of the lot.'

'I agree, but there's no guarantee the committee

will.' He grimaced. 'Let's talk about something else. What would you like to do for the rest of the afternoon?'

We took Watson for a long walk. We prudently changed into don't-matter clothes and Wellies, in case he took a notion to jump into the water after the ducks.

There can, for me, be nothing closer to Paradise than an English spring afternoon. Robert Browning had it right. April, when the weather behaves itself, is heavenly. The air is warm in the sun, but not too hot, and fragrant with the indescribable freshness of new growth and damp earth. Birdsong is everywhere, and the very ripples of streams sound like joyous laughter.

We were content to amble, saying nothing, with Watson snuffling happily along in a world of delightful sights and smells. He apparently remembered his encounter with the swan, for he kept well away from the waterfowl, only pausing now and then to sit and look at them with longing.

We saw the pair of swans, with their trail of just-hatched cygnets. If there's anything more graceful than a swan in the water, I don't know what it is. Nor anything sillier than any water bird on land. Their legs and feet weren't made for walking.

We rounded a bend of the river and there, over the trees, rose the spire of Rotherford Cathedral, floating like something in a fairy tale. 'Not Septimus Harding, after all,' I said. 'Just as gentle, just as kind, but with more backbone.'

'I, for one, look forward to meeting him tomorrow morning.'

Dean Smith had arranged for us to meet at the Deanery, which was one of the beautiful old houses near the cathedral. His wife opened the door and greeted us warmly. She was exactly the sort of wife I'd expected him to have – around fifty, with hair greying around the temples and a pair of twinkly blue eyes. She had, I thought, been a raving beauty in her youth, and she was still very attractive, with an enviable figure.

'Do please come in! You'll be Mr Nesbitt and Mrs Martin, and I'm Emily Smith. Will you have some coffee?'

'We never turn down coffee. Thank you.' Then I wondered if I'd been too hasty. English coffee varies pretty widely, from heaven-sent to what my family used to call 'damaged water'.

She led us into the pleasant, chintz-covered front room, where two other couples were already sitting. 'We invited some of our parishioners,' she said. 'As this was to be an informal, get-to-know-one-another sort of session, we thought you wouldn't mind.'

'Not at all,' said Alan. 'Delighted.'

'Well, then, let me introduce Mr and Mrs Stewart. Mr Stewart is, as one might suppose, from Edinburgh, and is one of our churchwardens. You know that St Martha's is also a parish church? Mrs Stewart is one of the leading lights in Rotherford's WI. And this is Mr Cho, our organist and choirmaster, and head of our choir school, and Mrs Loften, who manages our cathedral gift shop. And you all know that these people are Mr Nesbitt and his wife Mrs Martin, who are here to talk to us about the appointment of the new Bishop of Sherebury. James will be along any moment; there was a sudden crisis about arrangements for the mission trip.' She spoke as though sudden crises were a regular feature of cathedral life, as, indeed, I imagined they were.

'Here I am, my dear. I'm so very sorry to have kept you all waiting. Emily, have you introduced everyone?'

'Yes, don't worry. I'm just going to get coffee.' She slipped out of the room, smiling kindly at her husband as she left.

I was wrong. This wasn't *Barchester Towers*. It was *The Nine Tailors*, and I was in the home of Mr and Mrs Venables.

'Now then. We are at your disposal, sir. And lady! What would you like to know?'

'Actually, we simply wanted to get to know you. As I explained, I'm not here officially representing the commission. The formal interviews will come later. I'm afraid I don't know how much later. They would ordinarily have begun some time ago. The commission is meeting next week to decide what to do in the face of the recent tragedy.'

'And just what are the police doing about that, I'd like to know!' said the leading light of the Women's Institute belligerently. 'It's been over two weeks now, and no one's been charged!'

'I know very little about it,' said Alan patiently. 'I've been retired for a good many years now, so not much news comes my way. I believe, though, that the police have not yet determined whether the dean might not have met with an accident.'

'Hmph! I'd have thought they'd be able to tell a simple thing like that straight off!'

'One would think so, certainly. There may be complicating factors I'm unaware of.'

'But you came here to learn about us, not we about you,' said Mrs Smith, entering with a tray of coffee things, which she set down on a low table, proceeding to pour the coffee. 'Alice, do tell us how the gift shop's coming along. I know I saw a big crowd in there the other day.'

Mrs Loften smiled and accepted coffee from our hostess. 'That would have been just before Easter, I should imagine. There's always a run on cards and gifts then. And, of course, we have that new CD of the choir that's attracting a good bit of attention. Do you like music, either of you?'

'We both do,' I answered, 'and we thought the choir was lovely at Evensong yesterday. I didn't know the anthem, but I loved it.'

All eyes turned to Mr Cho, who came as near to a blush as his complexion would allow. 'Thank you,' he said quietly.

'He won't tell you, so I will,' said Mrs Smith. 'He wrote it, especially for us. And it's to be sung at King's this summer!'

'King's College? That is an honour! Congratulations, Mr Cho.' Alan stood and held out his hand to the musician, who took it with a slight bow and retired to the farthest corner, as if to efface himself.

'We think our choir is at least as fine as theirs,' said Mr Stewart, with robustly rolled Rs. 'Their voices fill our church, though it's a wee bit bigger than yon college chapel.'

'Yes,' said Dean Smith, 'we're very proud of our choir. And it's all Mr Cho's work. The choir was in a sorry state when he came here ten years ago. The choir school had been allowed to fall into disuse, but he got it back up and running, and it wasn't long before the school's reputation began to be known.'

'Hmph,' said Mrs Stewart. That appeared to be a favourite word, if one could call a grunt a word. 'It had a reputation before, and not the good sort. That's what killed it – that and a poor excuse for a headmaster. It was Dean Smith got it up and running again, and don't let him tell you anything different! His appeals for scholarship funds, the grants he brought in for putting the building to rights and hiring staff, his scouring the country for the best musician to head the school – *that's* what put it on its feet again!' She favoured the room with a glare that might have scorched the curtains.

'Now, now, Mrs Stewart, you exaggerate.' The dean looked embarrassed. The rest of us couldn't think of anything to say, but Mr Cho rose out of his corner chair and bowed to us all.

'It is true what the lady says,' he said in his precise English. 'I could not have come here without Mr Dean's help. He is a very great lover of church music and a very good man. I am deeply indebted to him.'

He bowed again and sat down, leaving even Mrs Stewart speechless.

Twelve

We had to leave early in the morning, because Rotherford was no longer served by a frequent rail service. When British Rail was privatized, back the 1990s, a lot of small stations were closed or suffered greatly reduced schedules. Rotherford Station probably remained open only because of the cathedral, but, as it was well out of easy London commuting range, trains were infrequent. If we'd missed the earliest one, it would have meant waiting another two hours, and we were all eager to get back home. We made it by the skin of our teeth, and then had to do the journey across London, with luggage and dog, at the height of the rush hour (which I have always thought is ludicrously misnamed).

'I'm absolutely in Dean Smith's corner now,' I said while we were stopped in a traffic tangle near Hyde Park Corner. 'He's the perfect man for the job. So I'm glad Mr Robinson doesn't want it, and I hope to heaven Walter manages to get the goods on Lovelace. That would put him out of the running for sure.'

'I wish Walter would get in touch. I'd like to stop and see him, but it's impossible with the dog and all.'

Watson looked up at that and whined slightly. 'Dog' is one of the words he knows, and he hadn't quite liked Alan's tone of voice when he uttered it. Alan patted him absently, but his mind was in the coffers of St Barnabas' church.

The train to Sherebury was delayed again, so it was early afternoon when we arrived, finally, at Sherebury Station. To our surprise, Jane was waiting for us. We had told her when we expected to be back, but hadn't asked her to meet us.

'We have our car here, Jane,' said Alan. 'I'm sorry you went to the trouble . . . No, it's something else, isn't it?'

'Not the cats?' I said anxiously.

'Cats are fine. It's Walter.'

'What about Walter?' asked Alan sharply.

'Missing.'

We left our car at the station so Jane could drive us home and talk on the way. 'Sue called,' she began. 'Wanted to know if Walter was here. Said no, hadn't seen or heard from him. No phone call, no email. Left in the morning to go to the BM. Still working there, unpaid, till his job comes through. Left there at noon to see Sue. Didn't show up. Didn't phone.'

I tried to ignore the little pulse of unease that was beginning to beat insistently in one temple. 'But, Jane, it's only a few hours. You can hardly call him missing until he doesn't come home at night. And even then . . . well, I suppose he's too reliable to assume he'd go on a bender or something.'

'Not an ordinary day,' said Jane gruffly. She sounded as though she was trying hard not to cry. 'Was to meet Sue for lunch and then go to pick out wedding rings.'

I drew in my breath and turned to my husband. 'Oh, Alan—'

'Yes. That puts an entirely different complexion on it. I'd better phone Sue.'

His jaw was set. He stared straight ahead. I could read his thoughts as clearly as though they were imprinted on his brow. *If only I hadn't set him that task . . .*

I was thinking the same thing, but I kept my mouth shut.

He called the moment we got home, using the landline so I could listen in.

'Sue? Alan Nesbitt here. Jane has just told us about Walter.'

Sue's voice was very wobbly. 'I know it sounds foolish, but do you think something might have happened to him?'

'I think it's possible. You've heard nothing from him?'

'Not a word. Oh, Mr Nesbitt, I'm so worried!'

'Yes. I'd like to come and talk to you, if it's convenient. Or would you rather come here?'

'I . . . I hate to make you come all the way to London, but I don't want to leave here, in case he comes home. Would it really be a terrible imposition for you to come here?'

'No imposition at all. I can't say when we might be there. The train schedule's quite unreliable just now. We'll drive in until we hit frightful traffic, and then take the train or the Tube or whatever offers. I'll ring you before we board the Underground and let you know when we might be at Russell Square. If you could meet us there?'

Jane had recovered her equanimity, possibly because she had something to do. Always practical, she had packed us some lunches to eat on the way – sandwiches, chocolate biscuits, and apples. 'Been stored since autumn, but still edible,' she said. 'Can eat everything while driving.'

Jane took charge of Watson, who was bewildered at being abandoned when he had only just got home. I kissed her as I got in the car. 'We'll tell you the moment we know anything.'

Mid-afternoon is a better time than almost any other to drive into London. We penetrated quite far into the suburbs before Alan decided we'd do better off the road. So we spotted an Underground station, parked the car, and got to Russell Square in good time.

Sue was waiting for us, worried and frightened, but in command of herself. I gave her a hug, and Alan asked, 'Any word?' She bit her lip and shook her head.

'Well, then, the first thing is to get you some tea. I don't suppose you've eaten anything lately?'

'No, but—'

'No buts. The Russell Hotel is just around the corner, and you can talk on the way. I'm sure they'll do us a good tea. Trust me, child. You can't think properly with low blood sugar.'

'I can't think properly at all! This was to be a special day for us, and he's simply disappeared!' She was hard put not to burst into tears. 'He's never thoughtless. He would have phoned.'

We went into the venerable hotel, found a

table, and ordered quickly. 'Sue,' said Alan quietly, 'I can't report this to the police and expect them to take it seriously until at least twenty-four hours have passed. But I take it seriously, knowing Walter, and I want to do anything I can to help you. I want you to tell me exactly what you and he said and did from the time you awoke this morning.'

She folded her hands in her lap – to keep them from shaking, I suspected. The effect, with her short blond curls, was of a child determined to behave well in front of its elders. 'We were both pretty excited, because just yesterday we set a date for the wedding, and we were going to pick out rings today. They couldn't be anything very expensive, but we have a bit of money put by. We talked about that at breakfast. We decided to go to Hatton Garden and just browse, and then if we couldn't find anything we could afford there, we'd ask someone to recommend a reputable dealer that was less expensive. We've never bought any jewellery before, not what you'd call jewellery, so we don't actually know how!'

Her voice quavered a little at that, and she clasped her hands more tightly.

Alan said, in his most down-to-earth, practical voice, 'So, you discussed Hatton Garden over breakfast. Then what? You must have decided when and where to meet.'

'Yes. I was going to the V and A this morning to fill out some paperwork. It looks as though I've landed that job at the Museum of Childhood. I was really excited about that.' Her voice held no excitement now. 'So we went online and found a little caff in Smithfield Market that looked pleasant. I could get there easily from the Bethnal Green station, and Walter said it would be handy for him, too.'

Our tea arrived just then. I poured out, giving Sue quite a lot of sugar. I doubted she'd notice the taste, and it would do her good.

'So he was coming from the British Museum?' I prompted, when she'd taken a valiant sip of tea.

'Oh, no. Didn't I tell you? He said we'd have to make lunch a little late, because he was going to be at the museum till around noon, and then he was going to St Barnabas' for a few minutes.'

At that, all my radar went on red alert. St Barnabas'. His last known destination. St Barnabas', where he was trying to uncover evidence of malfeasance on the part of an extremely intelligent, extremely ambitious, and, I suspected, extremely ruthless man.

'And when were you to meet?' Alan sounded calm, but he had that ability, even in moments of great tension.

'Around one, he said. Of course, he couldn't time it to the minute, because London Transport can be infuriatingly slow.' She swallowed, and had to swallow again before she could go on. 'I waited until two. Then I tried to phone him, and he didn't answer. I've left messages, voice and text. I phoned the museum. They said he left around twelve; no one was sure just when.'

'Did you ring the church?'

'Yes. The secretary said no one had seen him. She wouldn't let me talk to Mr Lovelace.'

'So sometime between, let's say, quarter to twelve to quarter past and one o'clock, he seems to have vanished.'

'Yes.' Sue's mobile rang. She dived for it. The hope in her face died when she saw the display. 'Robocall,' she said. The first tear slid down her cheek. 'I'm sorry. It's just that . . .'

'He's going to be fine,' I said, knowing it might be a big fat lie. 'We'll find him. What could happen to a grown man in the middle of London, in the middle of the day?'

I thought as I spoke of the iffy neighbourhood of the church, of the suspicions we had about Lovelace, of the murder of a dean. I was afraid my thoughts would show on my face, and tried strenuously to stop thinking at all.

But Sue was watching Alan's face, not mine. 'There's nothing you can do, is there?'

'There is one thing,' he said, his voice now grim. 'It would be counterproductive for me to go to the church and inquire. The people there know me, and I'm not terribly popular with some of them. Especially the secretary. She wouldn't tell me anything, even if she were inclined to be helpful about Walter. And, of course, we have reason to suspect that she might not be so inclined. If there is some hanky-panky going on with the books, I'd lay fifty pounds she knows about it.

'So I can't go myself. And I no longer have minions at my command. The Metropolitan Police have any number of men who could take on a search, but I can't go to the Met, not just yet, anyway. But there is one person I can send

– a very capable former policeman who owes me a favour.'

'Jonathan!' I brightened up instantly. 'Why didn't I think of him right away? He's the very person!'

'If he's available,' cautioned Alan. 'He's doing consulting work now, you know. He could be anywhere from China to Peru, but if he's in London, or can get here quickly, I know he'll help.'

Alan and I had saved Jonathan Quinn from a difficult and dangerous situation a while back, and I knew he'd do anything for us. 'He's a terrific person,' I said now to Sue. 'Alan was one of his mentors, and he rose to great heights in the Met until an accident left him unable to pursue active police work. But there's nothing wrong with his head, or his heart, either. Now, look, Sue. I know you're scared silly – I would be, too – but try to think. Did you help Walter at all with what he was doing at the church, poking into the books and so on?'

'Not really. We did do one session of counselling with Lovelace, but I had a hard time keeping a straight face. He's so phony! All grave concern on the one hand, full of platitudes about what makes a happy marriage and that, and all the while he couldn't keep his eyes off my legs. I told Walter I'd for sure wear slacks next time! If there was a next time. But, fortunately, he said he would be too busy for a while to meet. So Walter said he'd just go to the church when he could and put in some secretarial work, and, of course, he intended to try to sneak a peek at the books while he was at it. He thought it would look suspicious if I came, too.'

'And was he able to find out anything?'

'Not yet. That secretary – her name is Steele—'

'Appropriate,' I said. 'She's hard and chilly.'

'She's all of that. Anyway, Walter said she was looking over his shoulder every minute, nearly. He didn't dare touch anything he wasn't supposed to, for fear she'd walk into the room.'

'So he didn't tell you anything that might help us.'

'I've thought and thought about that. Truly! Yes, I'm scared, but trying to remember is better than imagining . . . Anyway, he hadn't learned anything. But he had been able to see where the important ledgers and other records were kept. They were in a locked cabinet, and Mrs Steele keeps the key. But she doesn't take her keys when she just leaves the office to go to the loo or something. So one day Walter pinched them and unlocked the cabinet. It's just one of those cheap locks, where a metal slat goes into slots at the top and bottom of the door when the key turns. You know?'

We nodded. My first husband had owned such a cabinet. He always said the lock was useless, except to keep the honest people honest.

'Walter's very strong, you know, and those slat things are pretty thin. He managed to bend the bottom part up, so it didn't go into the slot at all, and he got the key back in Mrs Steele's desk before she came back. He thought, if he got there on her lunch hour, he could manage to work the slat out of place in the top, too, and

131

get the cabinet open. Then he could photocopy some of the ledger pages, and a few other documents. He didn't say what, and I probably wouldn't have understood anyway – finance isn't my thing. And I think that was what he was going to try to do today.'

'Isn't the office kept locked?'

'Yes, but Walter's made friends with the sexton, who doesn't like Mrs Steele much. He was sure Jed would let him into the office if he said he had some work to finish, or something.'

'Then the first person Jonathan needs to talk to is Jed,' said Alan. He leaned over and took her hand. 'Sue, I'm not going to tell you not to worry. This could be nothing. Walter could be following up some sort of lead, and not able for one reason or another to phone you. The problem could be as simple as a mobile that he left behind, or forgot to charge. But it also could be something serious. I'm going to try to reach Jonathan Quinn—'

'Jonathan Quinn! Is *that* who you're talking about! Why, I know who he is! He's that big hero who saved the little girl, and got the George Cross, and everything!'

And everything sort of summed it up, I thought with a private smile. We'd been successful in keeping the rest of the mess out of the media, so Jonathan's image was left untarnished. 'That's the one,' I said. 'And if Alan can find him, I imagine he'll want to come here and go over the same ground we've just covered. Not easy for you, I do realize.'

'I'll do anything, if it'll help find Walter.'

I persuaded her to nibble a sandwich, while

Alan tried to call Jonathan. He tried twice, with no luck. He left a voicemail. I talked Sue into a piece of cake, and we prepared to leave. 'I'll be in touch, Sue. By this evening, I hope. Chin up.' Alan shook her hand gravely, I gave her a hug, and we made our tortuous way back to our car and thence home.

Thirteen

Alan tried to phone Jonathan from the train, but couldn't get a signal. As soon as we got home he tried again, this time with success. Jonathan had gone to a concert, with his phone turned off, and had just turned it on again. Of course he would come to help Sue. Address and phone number, please?

We went over to see Jane to give her the non-news. She looked dreadful, her full age and more. Her face was nearly as grey as her hair, and the lines in it sagged even more than usual. 'Doing what you can,' she said gruffly. And when Alan tried to apologize for putting Walter in harm's way, she shut him up. 'Rubbish. Old enough to make up his own mind. Not your fault.'

We went home, seeing we could do Jane no good, and sat up late, mulling over the situation, trying to think of any way we could help find Walter. We jumped every time the phone rang, hoping it would be good news. It was never anything important.

When we finally went to bed, it was to a troubled sleep. I had one of my recurring nightmares, in which I was in a building and unable to find a way out. I kept wandering from one area to the next, and doors that seemed to lead to the outside would lead instead only into another corridor, or an enclosed courtyard. Sometimes, with the supreme illogic that governs dreams, I was driving a car through the building. Sometimes the building would disappear, and I was trying to drive out of a canyon, or away from a beach where the tide was rising. In one scenario, I was looking for something. It was terribly important that I find it, or something horrible would happen. I tried to run to escape the horrible fate, but my legs felt weighted down. I tried to scream for help . . . and Alan shook me awake.

'Darling, what is it? You sounded terrified. And you're crying.' He brushed a tear away from my cheek.

'I can't find it!' I wailed.

'It's all right. You'll find it in the morning. I'll get you a glass of water.'

He was only a moment, but it was long enough for me to shake away the clinging veils of my dream.

Reality was even worse.

'Alan, I was looking for something, something desperately important. I didn't know it in my dream, but now I'm awake, I think it was Walter. Alan, where *is* Walter?'

Where's Walter? That thought was never out of our minds the next day. As I fed the cats, made

134

coffee, took Watson out for a walk, the refrain kept repeating: Where's Walter? As Alan sat in his den, preparing for Monday's meeting of the commission, I saw him ignoring the papers in front of him and staring into space, and I knew he was thinking: Where's Walter?

Jonathan called to report in, only to say there was very little to report. 'I talked to Jed. Nice old bloke, one of the real characters of London. A dying breed. Christened Jedediah, and had to tell me all about the name and his dear old parents and grandparents and so on, before we could get down to it.

'He said he let Walter into the office, all right. He likes Walter, doesn't like Mr Lovelace, detests Mrs Steele. He said Walter got there at about twelve ten. He was pretty specific about the time because he leaves for his lunch at half twelve, and was watching the clock. He didn't stay to see what Walter did. Why should he, he said; had his own work to do, didn't he? His work, as far as I could tell, consists of keeping the office floors swept and the desks dusted. A crew of cleaning volunteers does the church itself, polishes the brass and all that. Old Jed isn't overworked, I'd say.'

'Hmm,' said Alan thoughtfully. 'He sounds like the sort of old retainer who's kept on out of sentiment. But I wouldn't have suspected either Lovelace or Mrs Steele of being guilty of sentiment.'

'That thought occurred to me, too. I wouldn't be at all surprised to find out Jed knows more than he's telling. Not about Walter, but about what's going on at that church.'

'So you think something's "going on"?'

'I'm sure of it. Something doesn't smell right, and I mean to track it down. But as to Walter, I'm not much further on. Jed let him in and then went back to the little hole where he hangs about. He left promptly at half twelve, and when he got back, Walter was gone, and he, Jed, got a dressing-down for leaving the office unlocked. He told me about that in great detail, which I won't repeat, especially as Dorothy is undoubtedly listening in.'

'I am indeed, and I'll bet I've heard all the words before.'

'No doubt. He seems to have given as good as he got, and relished the battle.'

'Did he say whether Walter was still there when he, Jed, left for lunch?' asked Alan.

'He's not sure. The office door was open, and the light on, which Jed took to mean Walter was there, but he didn't take time to check.'

'And when he returned?'

'The same. Door open, light on, but this time Mrs Steele was there, with fire in her eye. She's next on my list to question. I don't look forward to it.'

'Jonathan, dear, a man who can face a burning building full of terrorists can face one determined woman. Exercise your well-known charm.'

'Dorothy, you are a dreamer. And what would Jemima say if my charm had some unexpected result? I'd better ring off. It's been twenty-four hours now; we can call in the police. They're short-staffed as usual, and won't be able to do very much, but it's a start. Then I'll head for the lion's den.'

'So Jemima and Jonathan are still an item?' I asked Alan when he had hung up. 'I hadn't heard anything for a while.' Jemima was an old friend of Jonathan's, almost as close as a cousin, and though they'd been estranged for a good many years, a crisis had brought them together. I hoped they'd marry one day. They needed each other.

'I suppose they are,' said Alan. He was obviously still worrying about Walter, so I dropped my attempt to change the subject and went back to fretting.

That was Saturday. Alan and the dean were to go to London together on Monday. We spent Sunday as usual: church, Sunday lunch – and then worry. We heard nothing from Jonathan, nothing from Sue. There was only one thought running round and round in my brain like a squirrel in a cage: Where's Walter? Alan had to move that concern temporarily to the back of his mind while the front was occupied with the bishop search.

'Dorothy, should I tell the commission members my suspicions about Lovelace? They are only suspicions, as yet, and a man is innocent until proven guilty.'

'In a court of law, yes. But we're not talking about a court of law. I think it's your duty to tell them what you think. Of course, you'll have to explain why, and I think that explanation will have to include Walter's disappearance.'

'The whole thing may be a mare's nest.'

'But it may not be. You don't think it is. Nor does Jonathan. And you're both policemen with a keen sense of smell for the unsavoury.'

'I'll ask the dean what he thinks.'

'Do. But I think he'll tell you to follow your conscience.'

'My damn conscience is telling me this whole disaster is my fault!'

He went off in the morning to meet the dean and catch their train, still in that same mood. I sighed and said a prayer for them, and then returned to my obsession: Where's Walter?

When I couldn't stand it anymore, I crossed my back garden and knocked on Jane's door. A wild clamour of barking greeted me. Jane came to the door, holding back the dogs. 'Don't know why they always bark at you. Ought to know you by now.'

'They're just saying they're happy to see me, aren't you, dogs? Down, Archibald. I love you, too, but I don't want to pick you up.'

'Any news?' said Jane, automatically filling the kettle while the dogs circled, hoping for a treat.

'No, and I can't stand the inaction any longer. Jonathan is doing what he can, but he hasn't made any real progress. The police are looking, too, but there's no word yet from them. Jane, you know Walter better than anyone. If he had to run somewhere, had to hide, where would he go?'

'Here,' said Jane.

'But he didn't. So maybe there was a reason why he couldn't. Where else? What other family does he have?'

'None.'

I wished Jane wouldn't be quite so laconic. The monosyllables were beginning to toll like doleful bell. 'Friends, then? Someone who would take him in and ask no questions?'

She shook her head. I couldn't tell if that meant 'no friends' or 'don't know'. I wanted to shake her. I decided to try persuasion instead. 'Jane, you're the most sensible person I know. You can't just let yourself sink into depression like this. Look at the situation logically. There are only two possibilities: Walter has been taken somewhere and is not at liberty to leave, or he's gone somewhere of his own accord, in response, we think, to some danger. If someone's made off with him, there's not a lot we can do. But if he's hiding out, we need to find him.'

'One more possibility.'

'Yes, but there's no point in thinking about that. If that's the case, nothing we can do will make any difference. But if Walter's alive, we have to do what we can. Now, once more, where might he have gone?'

She took her time. She spooned tea into the pot, poured the boiling water over it, set out mugs and sugar and milk and a plate of biscuits. They were store-bought, something I'd never before seen in Jane's kitchen. She was truly disintegrating.

'Spent nearly all his time at the museum, before Sue came along.'

'The BM? But that was an internship, wasn't it? I mean, he wasn't getting paid, was he?'

'No. Liked his job. Loved his job.'

'What I was getting at was he wouldn't have had any keys to the museum, would he?'

That caught Jane's interest. It was about time

139

she snapped out of it, I thought. 'No keys, no. But he has a good friend there.'

'Right.' I put down my mug. 'Finish your tea, woman. We're going to London.'

She held out a cautioning hand. 'Dogs.'

Oh. Yes, with both of us gone at the same time . . . 'Margaret. She won't mind, just for the day.'

I made the necessary arrangements with the dean's wife, and Jane and I made it to the station just in time to catch the train to Victoria. Then it was a quick hop to Tottenham Court Road Tube station and the Museum.

The British Museum has been one of my favourite places ever since my first visit, years and years ago with my first husband. There are exhibits I visit every time I'm in the building, old friends I must pay my respects to. Not today. Even the Rosetta Stone was going to have to do without my homage.

'What department?' I asked Jane.

'PAT.' When I looked mystified, she translated. 'Portable Antiquities and Treasure. What used to be called treasure trove.'

'Oh, but that's exciting! When someone finds a hoard of Roman coins, or whatever, you mean?'

'Exactly. It's this way.'

The museum has done a great job of making the galleries and displays lighter, brighter, and more inviting. The innards of the museum, however, where the work is done, are labyrinthine. Jane led me to an uninviting door, which was clearly marked 'No Admittance'. Ignoring the sign, she turned the knob and stepped inside, with me at her heels.

'Public not admitted, madam,' said the bored man at the desk inside the door.

'Looking for Walter Tubbs,' she said. 'Grandson.'

'Oh! You're Jane!' The man sat up. 'Sorry. I've heard about you. Walter talks of no one else. Well, except for Sue. But he isn't here right now.'

'Know that. Hunting for him. Who's his best friend here?'

'Hunting for him?'

I hesitated for only a moment. 'Walter seems to have gone missing, Mr –' I looked at his name badge – 'Mr Johnson. We're trying to talk to anyone who might have heard from him.'

'Oh. Oh! Oh, dear! I do hope nothing untoward has happened to him. Nice chap. Hard-working. Yes, well. Your best chance is Ahmed. I'm afraid that's all of his name I can manage, but that's what everyone calls him. He and Walter are really good friends. Here, let me give you visitor badges, and then he's through there. I'd take you through, except I'm supposed to stay by the door for the next hour or so.'

'Trusting fellow, isn't he?' I murmured as we made our way back along a narrow corridor. 'We could be anybody. Terrorists, thieves . . .'

Jane stopped and looked me over, from my straw hat with the pink roses down to my sensible shoes.

She didn't need to make any other comment.

We found Ahmed without difficulty, and when we introduced ourselves, the first thing he said was, 'Have you found him? I've been stewing ever since Sue called.'

'No. Hoped you could help.'

Jane's clipped style can make explanations somewhat difficult. I stepped in. 'You see, we hope that perhaps he's hiding out somewhere, keeping away from some sort of danger. We thought his friends might have some idea of where to look. You've known him for a long time?'

'Not long. Two years, but we became very close. Before he met Sue, we spent a lot of time together. After that, of course . . .' He spread his hands and smiled.

'Yes, I see. But tell me, *where* did you spend time together? A favourite pub? The theatre?'

'I am Muslim, Mrs Martin. I do not drink alcohol, so pubs don't appeal to me, and Walter drinks only a little. No, but we are both fond of music, so we went to concerts a good deal. Free ones in the parks, when we could! Neither of us has a great deal of money. He is an intern, and though I am paid, it is only a pittance.'

'Concerts.' I must have sounded as disappointed as I felt. A concert hall – or, for that matter, a park – wasn't a likely place for a hideout. Then I wondered just what I'd expected. *Oh, yes, Mrs Martin, we used to go to an opium den. It's very hard to find. He's probably hiding there.*

'Other friends?' asked Jane.

'Not close friends, but there were some uni students. We sometimes went to one of their flats to watch football on the telly. They've taken their degrees now, and I don't know where they are.' He paused for a moment. 'There is one boy who joined us now and again. A rather silly young man; I didn't much care for him. He has a good deal of money, I think, and spends it foolishly.

142

His parents live in Kent in a manor house – very posh. He took Walter and me there once for a weekend. It was not a success.'

I waited.

'His parents did not like my colour, or my religion. I did not like their snobbery, nor did Walter. But the house is very fine, and very large. It might be possible . . . but it is very far-fetched.'

'Name?' asked Jane brusquely.

Ahmed looked apologetic. 'I cannot remember his surname, if I ever knew it. I am not even sure of his first name. Walter called him Jack, but that could mean James or John or . . .' That hand-spreading gesture again.

'Or it could even be unrelated to his real name,' I said. 'C. S. Lewis was known to his friends and family as Jack, and his given names were Clive Staples.'

'Reason enough for a nickname, one would think,' said Ahmed with a little smile.

'House?' asked Jane.

'I beg your pardon?'

'Name of the house. The manor.'

'Oh, that I do remember! How clever of you to think of that! Yes, it is called Ashhurst, and it is near Tunbridge Wells.'

'And do you think Walter might be there?'

A shrug. 'No, I do not think it is likely. He did not enjoy his stay there, and I think he does not like Jack very much. But it is the only place I can think of where one might be able to hide, if hiding were necessary. I live in a bed-sitter, and so do our other friends. We are not rich, any of us, except for Jack.'

We thanked him profusely, gave him our phone numbers in case he had another idea, and left, surrendering our badges to the bored young man at the door. 'Do you think it's a possibility?' I asked Jane as we made our way back to the main door of the museum.

'No. But worth a try.'

'Right. Now all we have to do is try to find a house called Ashhurst, whose exact location we don't know. Nor do we know the names of the owners. Child's play. And I don't know about you, Jane, but I'm starving, and there's the Museum Tavern right there in front of us, and I intend to have some lunch. And a pint, since I'm not a Muslim.'

Fourteen

There are more difficult jobs than finding a large country house. The hunt might have taken a very long time indeed before the days of the Internet and Google, but after we left the Museum Tavern, Jane and I set out in search of a library, since neither of us has a smart phone or any other Internet gadget. We had actually eaten very little. I'd thought I was hungry, but with food in front of me, my throat had seemed to close up. I kept wondering when Walter had eaten last.

We found a library, did the search, and lo! Ashhurst was about halfway in between Tunbridge Wells and Wadhurst. It was owned by a titled family named Everidge. Built circa 1625. Open to the public Sunday afternoons only, June through August, admission three pounds. No children or dogs.

The accompanying map showed a maze of country lanes. There was no railway station nearby, and Jane's car and mine were back in Sherebury.

'Phone,' said Jane.

'But if he's hiding, the Everidges may not even know he's there. And if they do, they'd hardly tell some unknown woman on the phone. And they don't sound like very friendly people.'

Jane's reply was to pull her phone from her handbag and punch in the number showing on the computer screen. Her face was grim. It grew even more so as she held the phone to her ear and finally punched it off.

'House closed until June. Ring then for opening hours.'

'Drat! That's just the number to book a house tour, then. The family must have a private number. Let's search some more.'

There were a good many Everidge families, it turned out. We searched through pages and pages of websites, but at last had to concede defeat. If the Everidges of Kent had a phone number, it wasn't readily available online.

'I'm sorry, madam, but your time is up. This computer is needed by another patron,' said the librarian. 'And the use of mobile phones is prohibited in the library,' she added, pointing to the sign on the wall.

We retired, defeated, to the reading room.

I wished Alan weren't tied up in that tiresome meeting. I wanted to consult him, ask him what we should do. I wondered if they were accomplishing anything in the meeting, while I sat here needing him. I felt useless and helpless without him, but he was as far out of reach as if he'd been on the moon.

But – 'Jonathan!' Jane and I said at the same moment. We were glared at by the librarian, who had put us on her list of Suspicious Persons and was keeping a close eye on us. I meekly approached her desk. 'Do you have a London telephone directory?' I asked in properly muted tones.

She handed it to me from under the desk, saying firmly, 'You will need to copy down the number. You may not—'

'Use my mobile in the library. Yes, I know.' Then I bit my lip. Snippy would get me nowhere. And it wasn't very nice, no matter how irritated I was. 'I'm sorry if I was rude,' I said with a placatory smile. 'My friend and I are rather upset. Her grandson is missing, and we have reason to think he may be in danger. We're trying to figure out where he might be.'

'Oh, dear! You've gone to the police?'

'Yes, but they've not come up with anything yet. I'm looking up a private enquiry agent I happen to know in London.'

'Dear, dear. Well, now, you just take the directory into the staff room –' she pointed – 'and you can use your mobile as much as you like in there. And I do wish you luck!'

But I had no luck. My call to Jonathan went

146

to voicemail, which probably meant that he had silenced his phone. That, in turn, probably meant he was actively searching for Walter, but it was frustrating, all the same. I left a message saying only that I thought I knew of an avenue worth his exploring, and he should call me.

I told Jane I couldn't reach Jonathan, and watched her shoulders sag. 'I'm afraid I'm out of ideas. We could go back to the BM and get the names of Walter's other friends, I suppose.'

'Ahmed said they'd gone. Go back to Sue.'

I hated to go back to her with no news at all. The longer Walter was missing, the less likely it seemed that we would find him easily. And if Jane was worried and frightened, Sue must be nearly out of her mind by now.

Jane was right. We had to go and talk to Sue.

She had been sitting by the front window, watching, waiting, hoping. I was glad. If we had rung the bell unseen, she would have flown down the stairs in hope, only to have it dashed when she opened the door.

One look at our faces told her all she needed to know. 'Nothing?'

'Nothing. I'm sorry.'

'I'll make us some tea.'

I started to follow her into the tiny kitchen, but Jane caught my arm. 'Better for her. Needs to keep busy.'

I made a wry face. 'Of course you're right. Stupid of me.'

The tea tray shook only slightly as Sue brought it in from the kitchen. Along with the pot and mugs and appurtenances, there was a plate of freshly made scones. I knew she had made them for Walter's return, and I was hard put not to let my tears show as she handed them around.

We sat and drank in silence, crumbling the scones none of us had the appetite to eat. Sue, I could tell, was afraid to speak lest she start to cry, and I would have bet money Jane was feeling the same way. As for me, I was trying to find a way to give Sue the one sliver of information we'd gained, without raising false hopes.

'Sue, have you ever heard of a place, a manor house, called Ashhurst?'

'I don't think so.' She looked up from the pile of crumbs on her plate. 'Sounds Kentish. There's Penshurst, I know. I've been there. Penshurst Place is brilliant.'

'No, this is Ashhurst. It is in Kent, though. I thought Walter might have mentioned it.'

'I don't think so. Why?'

She couldn't dredge up any interest, but she was trying hard to be polite.

'Well, you see, the thing is, Jane and I went to the BM this morning to try to talk to Walter's friends. We found a man named Ahmed something-or-other who was very kind to us, but didn't have much to tell us.'

'Oh, Ahmed is a darling! He's going to be our best . . . that is . . .' Her chin started to tremble, and she looked away.

'Yes, well, the thing is, we were trying to think of any place where Walter might have gone if he had to lie low for a little while. He wouldn't have wanted to come here if there was any danger to you, nor to Jane for the same reason, so we asked

Ahmed if he could think of a place. And he mentioned this house. Apparently one of Walter's . . . er . . . acquaintances invited the two of them to come for the weekend. The house belongs to this man's parents, a wealthy, titled family named Everidge. Ring any bells?'

Sue tried to pull herself together. 'I think I remember Walter and Ahmed talking once about someone named Everidge. It's a posh name, that's why I remembered. They didn't seem to be terribly keen on him. I can't imagine why Ahmed would think Walter might go there.'

'Grasping at straws.' Jane's voice was raspy. She drank some of her tea.

'I'm sorry we—' My phone rang. Alan! I pulled it out of my pocket and looked at the display. Not Alan. A number I didn't know. I excused myself and moved to a corner of the room. 'Hello?'

'Dorothy, Jonathan. You phoned.'

'Oh, yes, thank you for calling back. I'm with Sue right now.'

'Is there something you'd rather not talk about in front of her?'

I didn't want to enlarge on the Ashhurst theory, tenuous as it was. 'Yes, that's right.'

'Then let me tell you something. I'm at the church, and something very strange is going on. I haven't quite put my finger on it yet, but the reverend gentleman isn't here, and hasn't been here since Friday. I need to talk to you and Alan.'

'Alan's in a commission meeting, and I don't know when he'll be done. He doesn't even know

I'm in London. I was told to phone him only in case of emergency.'

'I believe this constitutes an emergency – for the commission, at least. Please phone and ask if he can meet us at the pub nearest the church, as soon as possible.'

'Oh, my! Yes, I'll do that right away.' I fussed with my phone, dropped it, retrieved it, put it back in my pocket, trying to give myself time to think, time to figure out how much to tell Jane and Sue. Especially Sue.

I decided on part of the truth. 'That was Jonathan. He's come across something that may be very important to the Appointments Commission. I don't know what, but he wants Alan and me to meet him right away. So I'm going to head over to Lambeth Palace and see if they'll let me wrest Alan away. You two hold the fort.'

'But what about Walter?' cried Sue, not bothering this time to hide her tears.

I gave her a quick hug. 'We've not forgotten him, my dear. It's all going to tie together, I'm sure of it. And I'll report back as soon as I know anything at all.'

I hailed a cab, wondering as I did so if it would be quicker to take the Tube. But I'd walked quite enough for the day and my feet were hurting me. Anyway, I couldn't use my phone underground.

Answer, Alan. Answer! I pleaded as his phone rang and rang. At the very last moment, when I'd given up hope, he picked up. 'Dorothy,' he hissed. 'What is it?' He sounded both irritated and worried.

I didn't waste time with apologies. 'Jonathan told me to tell you this is an emergency. He wants to meet both of us right away. It has to do with Lovelace, and it isn't good.'

There was such a long pause I wondered if my phone had died, or his had. But finally he said, 'I'll do my best. Where?'

I told him, and knocked on the panel separating me from the cab driver. 'Sorry. Change of destination, please. St Barnabas' Church.' I gave him the street name. He seemed annoyed, as best I could tell from the back of his head.

'Not the best area, madam,' he said. 'Being American, you might not know.'

I despair of ever losing my accent. If it still clings after so many years in England, there's no hope. But I thought I knew what was really bothering him. 'I know it's not a good place to pick up another fare, but I'll pay you double if you get me there as fast as you can.'

'Right, madam.' He sounded much more cheerful, and made a sharp left at the next corner.

There was a small crowd of people, perhaps ten or fifteen of them, gathered around the iron gates in front of the courtyard at St Barnabas'. The gates were shut and, apparently, locked, and the crowd's voices were verging on angry.

'Sure you want to stop here, madam?'

'Actually, no. It doesn't appear I could get in. No, I'll settle for that pub on the corner.' It was The Lion, the one where Alan and I had stopped after our first visit to St Barnabas'.

I gave the driver, as promised, double the fare, which left me with exactly fifty-seven pence. He saw me searching in my purse for more, and handed me back a five-pound note with a chuckle. 'Don't you worry about me, madam! Can't leave a lady penniless, now can I? Hope somebody's meetin' you in there.'

'I hope so, too.'

I hurried inside. I had tarried too long as it was. A cab in that neighbourhood attracted attention, and the people gathered outside the church were already beginning to turn and look.

I looked around, but couldn't spot Jonathan. Oh, dear! It had been years since I'd been in a pub on my own, and then it was in Sherebury where they knew me. A tiny panic was beginning to stir inside, when Jonathan moved out of a shadowy corner and beckoned to me.

'My, I'm glad to see you! I was beginning to think . . . well, anyway, I'm glad you're here.'

'Any word from Alan?'

'He said he'd do his best to get here. It might take a little while, though. Jonathan, what's happening at the church?'

'I wish I knew. What I know for certain,' he said quietly, 'is that no one has seen Mr Lovelace since early yesterday morning. Mrs Steele is being typically obstructive. She says he's away at a church event of some sort and has left orders not to be disturbed, but my friend Jed says he's done a bunk. He missed Evensong yesterday, even though he was supposed to take the service. And Whitsun's coming soon, with preparations to be made. They make a great to-do about Whitsunday in this parish, it seems, and he's done nothing about any of it. *And –*' he lowered his voice still further – 'the parish account books are missing. Jed says he saw Mrs Steele hunting frantically for them for hours. When he asked her what she was looking for, she bit his head off, but the cabinet door was open, and he could see that they weren't where they should have been.'

'How did Jed know where they should have been? A sexton wouldn't have anything to do with them, surely.'

'No. But he's been working at this church even longer than Mrs Steele, and she's been here since the Ark. He knows where everything is. He knows a lot of secrets, too. I think he knows – ah! Here's Alan at last.'

'This had better be good, Jonathan. They're very displeased with me at Lambeth.'

'Lovelace and the account books are missing.'

Fifteen

Alan was very still. Then he shook himself, rather like Watson when he's been out in the rain. 'That is absolutely all I needed to put a cap on this day. Dorothy, my dear, Jonathan, what would you like to drink?'

We all settled for beer. I would have liked a Jack Daniel's, but this didn't seem the sort of pub to stock it, and I know Alan was panting for a good tot of whisky, but, there again, what was available at The Lion was probably not the best single malt.

The beer was quite acceptable, though, darkly

amber, clear, and quite refreshing. We each took a long quaff, and then Alan said, 'All right. Who'll go first?'

'I know Jonathan's story, and I haven't a lot to report. You start.'

'Well.' He took another pull at his beer. 'The commission members are a bit rattled, as one can imagine. Never before in the history of episcopal appointments has a candidate been murdered. Not in recent history, at any rate. God knows what Henry the Eighth and his crowd got up to.'

'I don't think they bothered with commissions and all that. They just named people bishops and then expected them to do their bidding. The king's bidding, I mean. Look at Becket. He wasn't even in holy orders when Henry made him Archbishop of Canterbury.'

'Different Henry, quite a few centuries earlier. All right, all right, don't chuck your crisps about. I bought all they had. At any rate, the meeting was pretty well divided. I can speak only in generalities, you understand, but some of the members said that since there was no chance Brading would have been chosen anyway, there was no point in not continuing with the process. They didn't put it quite that way, and they hedged it round with expressions of horror and regret, but it was apparent that was what they meant.

'The other faction – the Brading supporters – claimed to be appalled by the argument. By the time they finished arguing their case, Brading was equipped with a halo and wings and was well on his way to canonization.'

'I didn't think Anglicans canonized people.'

'They're prepared to make an exception. There was a good deal of not-so-subtle finger-pointing, as well.' He finished his beer.

'Finger-pointing? At whom?'

'At me, of course. "Where are the police? Why has no one been arrested for this heinous murder?" Never mind that I have been retired for a good many years and have nothing, officially, to do with the investigation.'

'Oh, honestly! That's just plain mean! They know perfectly well that you're in no position to investigate.'

'It was all politics, love. Grandstanding. But unpleasant enough. Who wants another?'

'Mine this time.' Jonathan got to his feet with only a bit of stiffness. Time was when he couldn't walk without a cane. I was proud of his hard, painful work toward recovery.

'So, are they going to postpone the process?'

'I don't know. They were getting ready to vote on it when you called me away. I gave Kenneth my proxy and escaped.'

'How did you vote?'

'In favour of postponement. That'll take some sort of special dispensation from Canterbury, to let Bishop Hardie stay on past his seventieth birthday. But I can't see how anyone can seriously evaluate the other candidates until Brading's murder has been solved. And now, Jonathan, you tell me we may be down to two candidates!'

'I'm afraid so. It looks very much as though young Walter was quite right about Lovelace cooking the books. We can't prove it until we find Lovelace, and the accounts, but flight is pretty good evidence of guilt.'

'And meanwhile,' I said, 'what about Walter? Everyone's looking high and low for him, and that sweet child he's going to marry is half out of her wits with worry. Where is he? What's happened to him?'

'The one good thing about Lovelace's apparent disappearing act,' Alan pointed out, 'is that now Jonathan and I have enough to ginger up the Met. The "everyone" looking for him really amounts to a few concerned people and what police could be spared. Put the entire Metropolitan Police Force on the job, and he'll be found. Has either of you come up with any leads?'

'I have not,' said Jonathan. 'I do have a number of leads as to where Lovelace might have headed, and it's not impossible to suppose that Walter is with him. I'm sorry to have to say it, but if Lovelace caught him snooping, it's more than likely that he'd have tried to find a way to shut him up. I'm loath to suppose the worst of the man. I think he's a snake-oil salesman of the very highest degree, but I don't think he's a murderer. So I think he'd have tried first to talk Walter out of his suspicions, and then, when that didn't work, he'd have taken the boy with him.'

Despite my worry, I had to smile at Jonathan's references to 'young Walter' and 'the boy'. The age difference between them couldn't be much more than five or six years. But then Jonathan's had some hard knocks in his life, and that ages a person.

'I do have one thin lead. That's why I called

you earlier, Jonathan.' I told them about the country house. 'It isn't very likely at all, and I do realize that, but I had to pass it along.'

'It's possible, though,' said Alan. 'I agree that if Lovelace caught Walter, he'd have abducted him. But if Walter got out of the church safely, with incontrovertible evidence, he'd hardly have wanted to go home, for fear of endangering Sue.'

'That's what I thought,' I said eagerly. 'And listen, Alan! That "incontrovertible evidence" might even be the account books themselves! Walter might have them!'

Both Alan and Jonathan turned on me looks so grim my mouth dropped open. 'What? What did I say?'

'You just gave Lovelace an excellent reason to abduct Walter, or hunt him down,' said Jonathan. 'And if he finds the boy, with the incriminating evidence, then I might have to change my mind about his willingness to do murder.'

'I think,' said Alan, 'that house in Kent is sounding more likely by the moment. Who else knows about it, besides Walter's friend Ahmed?'

'You'd have to ask him, but the visit happened some years ago, and I don't think the friendship – if you can call it that – persisted. Even Sue was vague about the whole thing, and if she doesn't know, I can't think it's likely anyone else would.'

'Nevertheless, it's possible. It's amazing how much Londoners are interconnected. Jonathan, you know more people in the Met than I do. Can you get them genuinely involved in a search for Walter? I must get back to the commission meeting, if it's still in session, and drop this bombshell.'

'I'll do that, and then shall I go to Ashhurst?'

'If you will. You'd best ring them first. I must go! Dorothy, expect me when you see me.'

He gave me a quick kiss and was gone. I turned to Jonathan. 'They don't have a listed telephone number – not that I can find, anyway. The one on their website is just for tourists.'

'Oh, it's that sort of house, is it?'

'More or less. Not exactly Blenheim, but quite old, very elaborate, extremely expensive to keep up, I'd have thought. Which means the family must be quite wealthy. They allow visitors only on summer Sundays, and that can't bring in a lot of cash.'

'No. But I'll find a phone number for them. Police connections can come in handy. And speaking of police, I need to get to the chief straightaway. Would you care to share a taxi?'

'I doubt you'll find one. They're not very thick on the ground hereabouts. I'll gladly accept your escort to the Tube station, though. It's not in the most salubrious of neighbourhoods.'

It was a fair walk. We used the time on our phones. I called Sue, gave her a brief run-down, and asked her to tell Jane I'd be there in half an hour or so to head for home. Jane called back almost immediately, to say she'd meet me at Victoria Station. 'Platform eighteen, unless they've changed it.'

Jonathan called Scotland Yard. 'My old chief is in,' he said when he'd rung off, 'and will see me as soon as I can get there. That's good. I'd

158

rather explain to him than anyone else. Meanwhile, I need to phone Sue for some basic information about Walter.'

All phone calls ceased, of course, once we were in the train, far under the streets. Our District Line train took us straight to Victoria, where Jonathan bid me a hasty farewell and I headed for old familiar platform eighteen.

'How's Sue?' I asked Jane.

She shrugged. 'What you'd expect. Trying to be brave.'

My next question was going to be 'And how are *you* doing?', but I left it unsaid. The set of her shoulders told me everything.

We didn't talk much on the way home. The carriage was crowded and noisy, and what was there to say? I didn't want to tell her about the missing cleric. Jane was no fool. She would draw the same conclusions we had, and she'd only worry more. Leave well enough alone. I did say, choosing my words in consideration of the people all around us, that Jonathan was following up on the suggestion that Sue had given us. She simply nodded and went on pretending to read the *Evening Standard* she'd been given at the station.

It was a great relief to get out of that strained atmosphere and into my own home, where the cats each opened one eye, stretched, and went back to sleep again. Margaret must have fed them. Watson wasn't around, so she was probably taking him for a walk. Dear Margaret!

I was far too tired to do anything much about dinner. Anyway, I didn't know when Alan would be home. I peered in the fridge. There was that bit of leftover pot roast. It wasn't enough by itself, but I could make it into a curry or a casserole or something. Meanwhile, it had been a frustrating and exhausting day, and I was more than ready for my belated nap.

I was awakened by a wet kiss. A very wet kiss. I opened my eyes to see a black nose near mine, and a pink tongue ready for another swipe. I sat up. 'Watson, your teeth need cleaning. Your breath could fell an elephant.'

Alan lifted him off the bed and gave my face a swipe or two with a damp washcloth before offering me a kiss of his own. 'Any better?'

'Much better. We've got to start feeding that dog some of those biscuits that are supposed to keep his teeth clean. What's the latest news?'

'The police are on the lookout for Walter, Jonathan's headed for Ashhurst, and I'm ready for a bit of relaxation and food. Your bourbon is poured and ready, and dinner is warming in the oven.'

'Bless you! Take-away?'

He nodded. 'Lasagne from Azzurro. We've wanted to try it, so I hopped out at London Bridge and got some. Some "pane all' something-or-other", too, for a starter.'

'It smells wonderful, and you're an angel. Oh, my, Alan, life does look brighter when you're around!'

That earned me a more prolonged kiss, until Watson, jealous, jumped back up on the bed and wriggled between us. 'All right, all right, dog. Get down. I'll give you a treat.'

Over a delicious bread-and-cheese concoction

and a libation, Alan told me about the rest of his day.

'They were still meeting, as you will have gathered, and still arguing about whether to postpone further proceedings. When the chairman asked if there was any further discussion, profoundly hoping, I was sure, that there was none, I stood and made myself most unpopular.'

'And dropped your bomb.'

'I did. I'm ashamed to say that I rather enjoyed it. The looks on the faces of the Lovelace supporters were priceless! They didn't believe me at first, of course, but when I cited chapter and verse, and added that the Metropolitan Police were now searching for both Mr Lovelace and Mr Tubbs, they had to believe there was something in it. Of course, it threw the whole selection matter into confusion. The vote came very quickly after that. They decided that we could hardly proceed with only two candidates, and would have to adjourn until a more propitious time.'

'I suppose that means we're stuck with Bishop Hardie for the duration.'

'For a while, at least. The Archbishop will have to make the exception official, but it was obvious that he would do that as soon as possible. He's also going to notify Hardie of the distressing circumstances.'

'Poor old man! He was so looking forward to retirement.'

'Old man indeed! I'll remind you, woman, that he's just about our age.'

'Oh. Well . . . but he *is* old!'

Alan roared at that. 'Some are born old,' he

said, and I instantly followed up with, 'Some achieve oldness, and some have oldness thrust upon them.'

'Thank you, Will. More or less.'

'Shakespeare has a quote for every occasion, doesn't he? I think you're right about Hardie, though. He was born old. He belongs back in the last century, or the one before that, when bishops just sat around wearing their mitres and looking pontifical. Nowadays, we need them to be active leaders.'

'I would remind you, my dear, that most of the English population don't feel the need for bishops at all, or for the Church, for that matter. Except perhaps for weddings and funerals.'

'And christenings. Hatched, matched, and dispatched. And a lot of them don't bother with christenings, get married by a registrar, if at all, and leave this earth with the blessing of a crematory official. Ah, well, we think they're wrong about that. The Church holds the nation together. Where would we all be without the Abbey for royal occasions like weddings and coronations? Can you imagine Prince Harry and his bride-to-be, whoever she may be, rolling up in their gold coaches to a registry office? Come on, that lasagne's calling me.'

Later, as we had settled ourselves in bed more or less comfortably around Watson, who insists on taking his half out of the middle, Alan said, 'You realize we are now free to concentrate on who killed Brading.'

'And finding Walter,' I reminded him.

My only answer was a snore, from both of them.

Sixteen

I woke early the next morning, not quite sure why I had a sense of contentment. Certainly there were worries enough to weigh on my mind. Then I consciously smelled the coffee and the bacon and understood. My incomparable husband was cooking breakfast, and, for the moment, troubles were in abeyance. Watson bounded into the room, presumably sent to waken me. I put my feet on the floor before he could jump up, ruffled his beautifully feathered ears, and gave him a pat. 'Tell Papa I'm on my way.'

Not bothering to dress, I went down to the kitchen, where Alan thrust a mug of coffee into my hand and forbore to talk until I'd downed half of it.

'Oh, my, that's good,' I said, when my brain was more or less functioning. 'And it's a beautiful day.'

'It is that. I've been making plans.' He set plates of scrambled eggs and bacon on the table, along with hot buttered toast. I've taught him American ways in that respect, at least. Immediately, both cats materialized beside us, lured by that irresistible smell. Watson, of course, had been there all along. There was a certain amount of jostling for position, which I ignored for the time being. 'What kind of plans?'

'I thought we ought to visit Chelton for a day or two. I'd like to get to know some of Brading's parishioners.'

'I thought you told me that cathedral wasn't a parish church.'

'It isn't, officially, but you know what I mean. The people he serves. Served. And if I can find a pleasant B and B, perhaps we can take along the d-o-g.'

That took Watson's attention away from the bacon, momentarily. He knows that word, even spelled out. His bright eyes searched both our faces for a clue to what we were saying about him.

'You are a dreadful nuisance, do you know that?' I told him severely, handing down a piece of bacon. Alan did the same for the cats, which kept all of them busy for at least ten seconds. 'Do you think one of his flock did him in, then?'

'I don't think anything at the moment, except that we – and I include the official police – have so far come up with absolutely no suspects, except possibly Lovelace, if he wanted the bishopric badly enough to kill for it.'

'If he did, he's certainly shot himself in the foot now. He'll be lucky to find a parish in Puddleby-in-the Marsh.'

'If he's found guilty of embezzlement from St Barnabas', his ministry for some time may well be in one of Her Majesty's prisons.'

'They'll have to find him first.'

'They will.'

'And speaking of finding . . .'

'Ah, yes. I wanted to wait until you were fully

164

awake. I had a text from Jonathan this morning, just before you woke up. It was brief, as such things always are, and somewhat cryptic, but if I interpreted it correctly, he's on Walter's trail and hopes to track him down very soon.'

'Oh, that is a relief. Almost. Three cautious cheers, then. But don't let's tell Jane or Sue until we're sure.'

Alan smiled. 'Of course not. More coffee?'

We finished our meal and tidied up the kitchen. 'We're going to have to tell Jane something, if we're leaving again and want her to look after the cats. I swear those animals aren't going to know us when we finally settle back down at home.'

'They'll survive,' said Alan. 'Cats are good at that. But I wasn't planning to go right away. I'd rather stay where we can get to London easily, in case something blows up about Lovelace and/ or Walter.'

'That suits me. There's laundry and housework to be done, and I'm just plain tired of being away so much. The old lady's getting set in her ways and wants her familiar comforts.'

'So does her old man. I thought we'd leave on Saturday, perhaps. Then we could take in a Sunday service at Chelton.'

'Sounds fine.' I yawned. 'Along with the housework, I plan to take regular naps.'

So, for a couple of days, we enjoyed a leisurely life, or we would have, if it hadn't been for concern about Walter. A couple of cryptic messages from Jonathan didn't do a lot to reassure us, but, with the police on the trail as well, there wasn't much we could do, except fret. Jane, bless her heart, understood that and kept the traditional stiff upper lip.

One afternoon, when I was just thinking about a nap, and the cats were quite willing to join me, the doorbell rang. The Cathedral organist, Jeremy Sayers, stood there with his partner, Christopher Lewis, who taught at Sherebury University. Jeremy, after happily playing the field for years, had finally settled down with a man whom Alan and I both liked. They had moved into a Georgian house not far from ours and spent all their free time making it into a showplace, where they loved entertaining. They visited often, but there was something about their manner now that told me this was not a social call.

I settled them both in the parlour, called Alan, offered a choice of drinks, poured sherry, and waited to hear what they had to say.

To their credit, they came straight to the point. 'We've known both of you a long time,' said Jeremy. 'And we debated a long time before deciding to come to you with this.'

'We argued,' said Christopher. 'Let's call a spade a bloody shovel. I said we had no right to take advantage of a friendship. Jeremy was determined to come and at least talk to you. So here we are, but I want it on record that I'm here under protest.'

'This will be about the bishop appointment, I presume,' said Alan, and he sounded weary.

'However did you guess?' said Jeremy, in a rather pathetic attempt at levity. 'Alan, Dorothy,

I actually agree with Chris. I don't like to use a friendship, and if this weren't so desperately important, I wouldn't think of it. But –' he spread his hands – 'this may be the only chance we'll ever have to influence church policy, and we can't let the opportunity pass.'

He put down his sherry glass and leaned forward. 'We've been C of E all our lives, Chris and I. We love the church, and this Cathedral has always treated us decently. But we have friends – we could tell you stories – well, I *will* tell you one. No names. A distant friend, another organist, was caught with some gay porn sites on his computer. His personal computer, nothing to do with the church, and nothing to do with children or anything horrid like that. He was harassed, eventually turfed out of his job. He ended up on the streets, got mixed up with a very rough bunch, got AIDS, and died. Hounded to death by bigots.'

I was appalled. 'Jeremy, that's a dreadful story! I had no idea such a thing could happen in this day and age. I'm so very, very sorry.'

Jeremy shrugged. 'I didn't know the man well. I told the story only to make you understand that the bigotry is still very much alive. And a bishop could do so much to change attitudes. Archbishop Welby has already done a bit, with his appearance of tolerance, though he's still . . . well, time will tell how he turns out. But at least he isn't sweeping the issue under the carpet, and that's a step. A bishop in this diocese who cared about gays could be *so* important to us.'

He sat back, blinked away tears, and picked up

his glass in an unsteady hand. Chris reached over to take his hand.

Alan had to clear his throat before he could speak. 'I'm glad you came, both of you. You know that the issue is moot for the moment, and, of course, I am only one voice on the commission, so I can promise nothing, even when discussions begin again.'

'We understand,' said Christopher, rather grimly. 'But *we* can tell *you* things. I still think coming to you like this is unfair, but you might as well know that most of the gay community hopes Bill Robinson will be appointed.'

I was surprised. 'We quite liked him when we met him, but I had an idea you both really liked Dean Smith.'

'We do,' said Christopher. 'It's just that, on this particular issue, Robinson seems to be the best man. True, he's very Low. You wouldn't care at all for his churchmanship, and nor do I. But I'd put up with Rite Q or whatever, even in the Cathedral, for the sake of the chance to feel that Christopher and I were truly accepted in the life of the church.'

I sighed. 'I won't say I understand, Jeremy, because I can't put myself in your place. I've never been despised just for what I am, so I don't know bigotry from the inside. But I know you two well enough to sympathize.'

'I do, as well,' said Alan. 'But remember what I said. My influence is very, very limited.'

Both the young men nodded, and we turned with relief to other subjects. But after they left, I spent a good part of the evening trying to imagine how I'd feel if I were hated and reviled for being white, or American, or old, or any of my other attributes that I could do nothing about. It was a sobering idea.

Alan had apparently been thinking about it, too. As we sat at breakfast the next morning, he said, out of the blue, 'Americans feel a good deal more strongly than the English about homosexuality, don't they, Dorothy?'

I blinked. 'I suppose they do. I haven't lived there for so long, I don't know what it's like now. Certainly there was a good deal of ill feeling about gays in Indiana, when I lived there, but I think attitudes are changing.'

'And what about you? Any opinions on the matter?'

I put down my coffee mug. 'I don't know that I have any opinion about gays and lesbians in general. I don't like treating people as generalities. If you ask me about Jeremy and Christopher, I like them very much and enjoy being with them. And as an American etiquette columnist once wrote, "I don't need to know what my guests plan to do after they leave the party." The one thing I'm sure about is that there is only one person whose behaviour I'm entitled to judge.' I pointed to myself.

By Saturday we were ready to venture forth again, and by mid-morning we were in the car on our way to Chelton. We had somehow missed this pretty little city when we took a walking tour of the Cotswolds a few years ago, so I was glad we were giving ourselves enough time for a little sightseeing.

169

It was a beautiful Saturday, warm and sunny, with spring just beginning to give way to summer. I had never seen the English countryside look lovelier. It's true, of course, that when the countryside includes hedgerows along the road, one can't see much of it from a car. But every so often the hedges gave way to dry-stone walls, and then the lovely rolling fields of green wheat and yellow rapeseed, the meadows alive with sheep and lambs, the tiny groupings of houses, with ancient steeples giving them anchor – these sights so delighted me that I forgot all about Walter and embezzlement and bishops, and just drank in the beauty.

'England's green and pleasant land,' I said, sitting back with a contented sigh.

'Do you know, Dorothy, one of the things I love most about you is your capacity for enjoyment? You look right now like a child who has just been given a marvellous Christmas present.'

I sighed again and waved my hand in a sweeping gesture. 'Alan, look at it! What's not to like?'

Alan chuckled, and we drove on in companionable silence.

We had to stop for lunch, and a couple of times to accommodate Watson, but then we began to look for Chelton. The road sign, when we spotted it, was one of the modern ones, not the old fingers-on-a-stick kind, which were picturesque but almost impossible to read. It read in large clear letters 'Chelton 2.'

'I hate to disturb your idyll,' said Alan, 'but perhaps we should refresh ourselves a little about Brading before we start talking to people about him.'

'Ultra-conservative and rigid, right?'

'Kenneth Allenby summed him up as a man who tried to pretend the Oxford Movement never happened. He was opposed to virtually every innovation in the church for the past hundred years. He detested High Church practices: candles, vestments, incense, the lot. He wanted Matins and Evensong always to be the principal services, with the Eucharist only on especially solemn occasions, and even then with as little ceremonial as possible. Women in the priesthood were, of course, anathema.'

'And this man was being considered for the See of Sherebury.' I shook my head. 'I still can't believe it, political pull or not. And I admit, with shame, that I'm not as sorry as I should be that he's dead. He sounds like a thoroughly disagreeable person.'

'Well, one reason we're here is to find out who, if anyone, found him disagreeable enough to kill him. And here, in fact, we are.'

Seventeen

Well, in a manner of speaking. We were in Chelton, but it took a little while to find our B and B. English towns are laid out not on a grid, but with streets that wind and change their names every little whipstitch. Alan can apparently navigate by instinct; he got mildly lost only once.

Our hostelry was a dignified house called

Lynncroft (I do love the names the English give their houses) on the edge of town, probably once part of a farm, with green fields stretching off behind it. It was built of the traditional honey-coloured Cotswold stone, set off with touches of a white stone over windows and doorway. It would have looked severe had it not been for the riot of colour in the front garden. Every spring flower imaginable seemed to be trying to outdo the others in luxuriant display. I kept a tight hold on Watson's leash as we stepped out of the car. I didn't want to even think about what he could do to those flowers if he decided their bed was a good place to dig.

Our hostess, however, had the situation in hand. 'You can't see it very well, but there's an electric fence around the flower beds, put there long ago to keep our own dogs out. They're gone now, but we found the fence useful when guests brought their dogs, so we've kept it up. And the back garden is walled, so he can run and play as much as he likes there, with no danger from the road. He's a lovely boy, isn't he?'

This last was addressed to Watson, who responded with increased tail wagging and excited little yips. He's been taught not to jump on people, but he still wants to, when he likes someone. He was rewarded with pats and praise, and trotted off happily with me to the broad walled-in expanse of grass behind the house, where I let him off the leash to explore as he wanted.

Alan and I got ourselves situated in our room and then went down to the tea our hostess had prepared for us. It was simple, but the tea was excellent and the scones fresh and as light as feathers.

'I like to get acquainted with my guests, you see, and tea is a good time to do it. Breakfast is too rushed.'

I nodded. 'Everything has to be done at once, and nothing will stand sitting for very long. A lukewarm fried egg . . .'

Mrs Stevens nodded her head in fervent agreement. 'Fit for nothing but to patch a tyre. And bacon can't be reheated, and mushrooms get watery. No, breakfast must be served at once. But tea is a leisurely meal, at least when I have only a few guests.'

'How many can you accommodate?'

'Twelve at a pinch, but I don't like to have more than six, especially now that my husband's gone. He was such a help. I have a cleaner who comes in daily, and a gardener to do the heavy work, but the rest is on my plate. Last week we were full up, so I'm very glad that you're my only guests at the moment.'

'Goodness, so am I! You need a rest. I can't imagine cooking and all the rest of it for twelve people – and strangers at that.'

'Oh, no one stays a stranger for long! My tongue's hung in the middle, my husband always said, but I do seem to get on with most of my guests. Is this your first visit to the Cotswolds?'

I gave Alan a quick smile behind Mrs Stevens' back. It wasn't going to take her long to find out all there was to know about us. All we wanted to let her know, at any rate.

Alan gave her a truncated biography. No, we'd

visited the Cotswolds once before, doing a walking tour. We lived in Sherebury and were both retired. (He carefully didn't say what he'd done before he left his working days behind.)

'And you're American, aren't you, dear?'

I admitted that I was. 'I moved to England after my first husband died, and was lucky enough to meet Alan.' I anticipated her next question. 'I never had any children, so it took Alan's daughter to make me a grandmother.'

'Oh, how lovely for you! Charles and I had four daughters, and there are twelve grandchildren now and three great-grands! Now, you'll let me make you some more tea – no, no, it's no trouble at all, the kettle's hot – and I'll show you my darlings.'

She carried the teapot to the kitchen, thereby observing the strict rule of 'take the pot to the kettle, not the kettle to the pot', and I grinned at Alan. 'Did you choose her on purpose because she's a talker, or is this just luck?'

'Pure luck,' he said. 'I chose this place because I thought you'd like the house, and the rates are reasonable. But we have fallen on our feet, haven't we?'

Mrs Stevens came back with the fresh pot of tea and a photo album. When we had duly admired the children, Alan turned the conversation to the late Dean Brading. It didn't take much. All he had to do was ask about service times in the morning at the cathedral, and she was off.

'Eight and ten. The Early Service, you know, and then Matins. Would you like an early breakfast?'

174

'I thought we might go to the Early Service and then get some coffee and a bun in the town,' I said apologetically. 'We wouldn't want you to go to a lot of trouble to feed us so early.'

'In any case,' said Alan in a deliberate fib, 'we seldom breakfast before church. We're rather High in our views.'

'Oh, well then, I don't know as you'd care for the cathedral. St Dunstan's might be more to your liking; it's just a few streets away. The cathedral's very Low, you see. Although that might change, now that the dean's dead. You'll have heard about that, I'm sure. Dean Brading, murdered in his own cathedral.'

I had a feeling I might grow very tired of that phrase. 'Really?' I said. 'How awful. I think I may have read something about it.'

'All over the telly and the papers for a week,' she said, giving me a sidelong glance as though to make sure I was really of normal intelligence. 'It's died down a bit now, but we here in Chelton haven't forgotten. They say the police haven't found out a thing about who might have done it. Mind you, there are some here in town who might be able to tell the police a few things, if they wanted to.'

I tried to look desperately intelligent and questioning.

'Are you all right, dear?' asked Mrs Stevens with concern.

So much for my acting ability. 'I'm fine. Just a momentary twinge of arthritis. But do go on. You think there are things people aren't telling the police?'

'Well, I'm not one for gossip.'

In one of her books, Dorothy Sayers commented that people who say this often really believe it of themselves.

'But it's a fact,' Mrs Stevens pursued, 'that there are plenty of people around here who didn't like the dean, not one little bit. Not that I'm saying anyone would have struck him down. That's going a bit far, wouldn't you agree?'

We nodded solemnly. I was glad I had swallowed my last sip of tea.

'But what I do say is that not everyone is sad he's gone, and they're not going to go out of their way to help the police catch his killer. So, you won't change your mind and go to St Dunstan's tomorrow? I'm told they have a very pleasant vicar.'

Alan stood. 'Oh, I think we'll try the cathedral, at least for the Early Service. And, as my wife said, please don't bother about breakfast for us.'

'Well, if you're hungry after, you just come and knock on the kitchen door. I'll be home all morning.'

And she bustled off. Watson, meanwhile, had been standing hopefully at the sitting-room door, which gave on to a terrace. When he caught our eye, he whined softly.

'Yes. Supper time for all of us. I'll feed him on the terrace, Alan, if you'll ask Mrs Stevens about where to eat.'

We took Watson with us when we went to find a meal. He'd been left alone far too much lately, and deserved better. If we couldn't find a pub that would admit him, he'd wait outside quite happily, especially since his keen sense of smell would tell him that a treat might be forthcoming.

We found our meal, and Watson got his treat, and then we went for a walk, sightseeing.

There weren't really a lot of sights to see in Chelton. It was a very pleasant, very typical Cotswold market town, with narrow streets, shops built of golden stone or else half-timbered. A market square was dominated by a small but striking arched market hall. The streets had been busy during the day, but were growing quiet as night drew near. There was no particular tourist attraction beyond that of any pretty little English town. Like Sherebury, it was really too small to be considered a city, and acquired that designation only because of its cathedral. As in Sherebury, too, the cathedral was originally a monastic foundation, which functioned as a parish church after Henry the Eighth closed all the monasteries. Unlike our lovely Cathedral, however, Chelton's was quite small and had suffered badly in the years before it was elevated to cathedral status. The monastic buildings – the cloister, the refectory, the dortoir – were destroyed completely, and the north transept of the church had burned down at some point and was never replaced.

'It looks a trifle lopsided,' I said, when we had wandered through the town to the cathedral gates. 'Especially with that ugly building right up against the north wall. Nowadays, no one would ever get planning permission for something like that.' The building in question was of a

177

particularly virulent shade of yellow brick, its ugliness enhanced rather than diminished by lintels decorated with fat, smirking cherub faces.

'No, but that appalling structure went up long before civic planning was instituted. It looks Victorian. They perpetrated all sorts of horrors on churches, inside and out. I should imagine it's a parish hall, or Sunday school, or something of the sort.'

But when we went around to that side to look, a poster out in front said 'Chelton Youth Centre'. The poster was enclosed in a large glass-fronted display box. The glass was dirty and badly cracked in one corner, so that rain had got in and warped the poster. The lettering was badly faded.

Alan went up and peered into one of the windows. They, too, were dirty and in poor repair. 'No furniture inside, as far as I can make out,' he reported. 'I would hazard a guess that the youth centre no longer functions, or at least not here. Quite a contrast to Rotherford's.'

'Indeed,' I said. 'So far, I find Chelton Cathedral distinctly less than splendid. And I'm feeling more and more jaundiced about Dean Brading. I'm assuming that brick thing belongs to the cathedral, and the dean shouldn't have let it get into such shocking condition. What a contrast, too, to the spotless neighbourhood around St Barnabas'.'

'By the logic of opposites, then, Dean Brading ought to have been the perfect example of all that is pure and holy.'

'I'm too tired to be logical. It's been a long day, there's a good television in our room, and

they're re-running *Pride and Prejudice* tonight.
Shall we?'

Eighteen

Morning seemed to come very early, but Watson
needed to go out, and I needed to shower before
the Early Service, so I was actually awake and
functioning when Alan's mobile rang. He was in
the shower, so I answered it.

'Dorothy? Jonathan.'

'Oh, goodness, I'm glad to hear from you.
What's up?'

'I've good news. The best news.'

'You've found Walter!'

Alan walked out of the bathroom just then,
towelling his head. He dropped the towel; his
head shot up.

'We have. Unharmed, and with the St Barnabas'
account books safely in his possession. We've
nailed Lovelace!'

'Oh, heavens, have you found him, too?'

'Not yet, but we will. It's just a matter of time.
I meant that we have all the evidence we need
to prosecute him. Until we do find him, we're
keeping Walter somewhere safe, just in case,
and I'm not telling even you and Alan, much
less Jane and Sue, where he is.'

'They won't be happy about that, but I see your
point. Look, I'd better let you talk to Alan; he's
standing here perishing of curiosity.' He was also

shivering; the room was chilly, and he was dripping wet. I found him another towel and his bathrobe, and started dressing.

'What did he tell you? Where did he find him? What happened to him?' I asked, the minute he was off the phone.

'All he said was that your advice led him to Walter, that he had indeed gone into hiding, and he'd tell us more when Lovelace was found.'

I could hardly wait to get to church, with such cause for rejoicing. Walter was all right! And the nasty Mr Lovelace was going to be caught!

There was little enough other cause for rejoicing. 'Okay, barely' was our verdict about the Early Service. It was celebrated with as little ceremonial as is reasonably possible, in a small side-chapel almost stark in its austerity. No candles burned on the altar, no corpus adorned the plain silver cross. The celebrant wore cassock, surplice and stole, with no other vestments. No one assisted him, and indeed assistance was hardly necessary, since the communicants numbered five, counting Alan and me. The low numbers might have been a reaction to the death of the dean, but somehow I doubted it, since the chapel could seat only perhaps a dozen people.

The liturgy was read from the old Book of Common Prayer, which, with its lovely language, made up for some of the other disappointments. But it confused us no end, for bits of the service were in a different order than we were accustomed to, and the prayer book in the pew was in such small print as to be almost unreadable.

We refrained from the small rituals we used

180

at home – the sign of the cross, genuflecting, and so on – since they were plainly not observed here, and left quietly as soon as the service was over. No one had spoken to us, except in liturgical forms, the whole time.

'Well.' We left the church and went out into the misty morning. It would clear later, but just now the weather was hardly inspiring. 'I'm not sure I feel like I've been to church.'

'Let's go and get some breakfast.'

We hadn't even taken time to make coffee before leaving our room, so we were more than ready for breakfast. There wasn't time to go back to the B and B, though, before Matins, so we found a small tea shop that served tea and doughnuts, and that had to suffice.

The congregation for Matins promised to be larger than for the Early Service, judging by the number of cars parked as we approached the cathedral and the number of people walking in that direction. However – 'Alan! No bells!'

'Popish,' he said with a wry grin.

'Nonsense! There've been church bells in England for centuries!'

'But Cromwell hated them, you know. Here we are. No time now for a canned history of the Church of England.'

The cathedral interior, lit by large and rather ugly chandeliers, was no more impressive than the outside. Nothing can totally destroy the soaring impact of Gothic architecture, but those who'd had charge of Chelton Cathedral over the centuries had done their best. Much of the medieval glass had been replaced by crude Victorian

181

panels or plain leaded glass. The pillars of the nave had been girded by iron bands, presumably to lend some strength, but the effect was to spoil the proportions and stop the upward movement of the eye. The pews were modern and hideously out of place.

It was plain that the dean, lover of the austere, had followed his own strictures. His cathedral was as unadorned as it could well be. All of the statues low enough to be reached had been deprived of their heads, almost certainly by Oliver Cromwell's men during the Civil Wars, a fate Rotherford Cathedral had been spared. The altar did bear two simple vases of daffodils, but none of the elaborate creations that always graced Sherebury Cathedral. Plain, stark, unembellished – those were the watchwords.

'Do they not have much money?' I whispered to Alan. He shrugged and spread his hands in an I-don't-know gesture. We found seats quite near the front, for although we were almost late, most of the worshippers seemed to prefer the middle of the nave. There weren't, after all, that many of them. I looked around discreetly, then nudged Alan again. 'No parish altar.' Evidently, the Eucharist, on the rare occasions when it was celebrated in the main body of the church, was conducted at the far east altar, quite a long way away from most of the congregation. At least there was no rood screen to cut off everyone's view of the proceedings. However, it scarcely mattered for Matins, a service that doesn't use the altar at all.

The organ – I was relieved to hear there was

an organ – sounded the first few bars of a hymn, we opened our books to the page indicated on the hymn board, and the service began.

It was again read according to the 1662 Book of Common Prayer. The choir wasn't wonderful. Not bad, not good. They got through the many psalms and canticles, versicles and responses that are required by the service. First, though, we all knelt and confessed our sins, and were absolved by a small, balding man in wire-rimmed glasses who looked as though he followed the same liturgical practices as the late dean. His surplice was unadorned and somewhat shabby, though it was quite clean. His stole was the simplest possible, with crosses the only decoration, and even these weren't embroidered, but plain white appliqué. His receding hair was neatly trimmed, but with no attempt at styling. His voice was thin and whiny. Not a comfortable sort of voice, even pronouncing the absolution.

The sermon came near the very end of the service. We had prayed for peace and for grace, for the Queen and her family, and for the Church. Then we all sat, and the presider climbed the many stairs up into the pulpit, which had a traditional sounding board looming above it.

'Who is he?' I whispered to Alan. 'One of the canons?'

'Probably. Shh.'

His text was from the Old Testament lesson for the day – 'Of course,' I whispered to Alan – the story about the golden calf. He read it with great solemnity: 'Thy people, which thou broughtest

out of the land of Egypt, have corrupted themselves: They have turned aside quickly out of
the way which I commanded them.' He set the
bible aside and grasped the sides of the pulpit
with both hands.

'As I look around this cathedral, I see no
golden calves. Graven images there are in plenty,
perhaps too many, but we do not, I hope and
trust, fall down and worship them. Ah, but what
happens when we leave this holy place and step
into the world of the streets outside? What idols
do we worship there? Is it the idol of pleasure,
to be found in public houses? The idol of treas-
ures, to be found in shops that sell goods of
which we have no need? The idol of vainglory,
to be found in the establishments that purport
to render us beautiful?

'Yes, we worship many idols. But that is
scarcely the only way in which we defile
ourselves. We daily break the Commandments.
How many of us fail to honour the Sabbath?
How many of us commit adultery, and worse?
How many of us steal, and covet that which is
our neighbour's, and bear false witness?

'And there is at least one among us who has
broken the sixth Commandment: Thou shalt do
no murder!'

His voice had changed. The thin whine had
given way to a raspy sort of shout, unnerving
in the extreme. His eyes, too, behind their rather
sinister spectacles, seemed to grow darker, and
to transfix everyone in the pews, individually. I
found it difficult to look away, to escape his
glare.

184

Here was mesmerism of a very different sort from that practised by Lovelace. Here was no lulling with honeyed words and spellbinding voice. If Lovelace was a snake-oil salesman, this man was the snake, a cobra, paralyzing his victim with his eyes.

I managed to wrench my attention away from those terrible eyes and ventured a quick glance at the people around me. I wished we weren't sitting so far to the front. I could see only the people to my sides, and not many of them, since I didn't want to turn my head and be rudely obvious about my scrutiny. The few faces I could see were perfectly blank, which was annoying. I wanted some reaction, some look of shock, at least.

You wanted, I told myself severely, *to have someone stand and sob out a confession. Idiot!*

I had missed a few words of the sermon, if that was what you could call the diatribe that continued from the pulpit, but that irritating, oddly compelling voice drew me back.

'. . . the perils that await the sinner! And it is not the murderer alone who will face the torments of Hell. Those of you who know who he is, who know and have told no one, are as guilty as the man who struck the blow, who struck down the dean, here in his own church, adding blasphemy and sacrilege to murder! Examine your own consciences, and if you know anything that might help bring this vile murderer to justice, you *must* speak!'

The church was so quiet that I could hear, from the organist's bench behind a screen, the

185

faint rustle of a page of music being turned. The noise ceased instantly. The congregation seemed to stop breathing. Time itself seemed to stop.

Then from the back came the fretful cry of a hungry baby, and the spell broke. The man in the pulpit looked quite humanly annoyed for a moment, and then said, 'You cannot escape God's justice. Repent before it is too late. In the name of the Father, the Son, and the Holy Ghost. Amen.'

The organist played the opening chords of a final hymn, one I didn't know, and the congregation dutifully sang petitions that God would keep us from 'ill sights' and 'vanities'. Then the canon pronounced a blessing, and the organist began a slow, melancholy postlude. Under cover of the music, I whispered to Alan, 'Whew! What on earth is that man doing in the Church of England? He's a Calvinist through and through. Life is real, life is earnest, and you have to watch your step every minute or God will strike you with lightning.'

'He's apparently following in the late dean's footsteps. Let's hurry a bit, love. If this rigid establishment bends enough to offer coffee after the service, it would be a good chance to talk to people.'

This time our position at the front was to our advantage. We had an excellent view of the congregation as they filed out. There were no black faces, or brown or tan, nothing but white. There were very few young faces. The family with the baby scuttled out, and I wondered if they, too, were visiting and regretting it.

186

No one greeted us as visitors. No one spoke to us at all, in fact, but Alan smiled benignly at a middle-aged woman who looked approachable. 'I hope you don't mind, madam, but might there be a café nearby where my wife and I could get some coffee? We're just visiting in Chelton and don't know our way about.'

'Well, as to coffee, there's a tea shop in the High Street that might serve coffee, though I'm not certain of that. I never drink it, myself.'

'Our church at home serves coffee in the parish hall after the main Sunday service,' I said hesitantly. Nothing ventured, nothing gained.

'We don't do that. Not *coffee*.'

'Tea, perhaps?' I persisted.

'Fruit punch. Mostly water.'

'Oh, that sounds perfect!' I said with enough counterfeit enthusiasm to make her, I was sure, doubt my sanity. 'Where should we go? That is, if visitors are welcome.'

'Yes, of course.' I've heard more enthusiasm from a child thanking its maiden aunt for a pair of hand-knit socks. 'Out that door and round to the right. It's the old youth centre.'

I managed not to raise my eyes to heaven, but it was a near thing. 'Thank you *so* much,' I gushed.

'You won't like it,' she muttered before turning away.

'Chelton hospitality,' I said as we turned toward the disgusting erstwhile youth centre.

'All in the day's work, my dear,' said Alan. 'A detective's lot is not a happy one.'

''Appy one,' I echoed, at the bottom of my range.

A single trestle table had been set up in the cavernous room. Dust was everywhere. Apparently, the cathedral authorities saw no need to keep the place in order for one function every Sunday morning. I could see their point. Possibly ten people were in the room, two of them fussing about the table, which held a few very small plastic cups and a litre bottle of something luridly pink. There were no decorations. There were chairs, but they were all stacked neatly against the wall.

I thought longingly of Sherebury's parish hall, jammed with people of a Sunday morning, crowded, noisy, with bad coffee and stale buns and love overflowing. Alan and I should be there right now. Instead, we were strangers in a strange land.

Conversation had stopped abruptly when we entered the room. A man stepped up to us. 'May I help you?' His hair was an even iron grey, his face set in lines of bad temper. His eyes were as sharp as the crease in his trousers, and his inflection made it clear that his subtext was 'You're in the wrong place. Go away.' He reminded me of someone, but I couldn't quite place him.

'Why, yes,' said Alan. 'We were told we might find a bit of refreshment here. We've just been to Matins.'

'Oh. Well. Well, yes, certainly. Mrs Rudge, these people would like some punch.'

The smile I had pasted on my face was beginning to hurt. I turned it on Mrs Rudge, she of the pink apron presiding behind the punch table.

And wonder of wonders, my smile was returned, with interest. 'How nice of you to come and join us,' she said warmly. 'And this is your husband? We're delighted to have you here to worship with us. Are you just visiting us, or were you thinking of joining us?'

'Mrs Rudge, please!' It was the man with the sharp eyes. 'This is hardly the time.' He came over to the table. 'You may not know that our dean was murdered only a few days ago.'

'Yes, our hostess mentioned it.' Alan's tone was a shade or two south of icy. 'Mrs Stevens, at Lynncroft.'

'And, of course,' I chimed in, 'the sermon today . . .'

'Yes,' said Sharp-Eyes. 'So you will see that we're hardly in a position to entertain visitors just now.'

I almost shivered. Raise the drawbridge, lower the portcullis, and prepare to repel invaders.

'Nonsense,' said Mrs Rudge stoutly. 'Visitors are always welcome, particularly now in our time of trouble. You know quite well—'

'That may be, Mrs Rudge, but this is a time of mourning for Chelton Cathedral. We've not even been able to bury poor Dean Brading. The police are being scandalously slow about releasing his body, much less identifying his killer. So I'm sure you can see, sir, why we are not yet quite on dress parade.'

That did it. I knew who he reminded me of, and it was a type, not an individual. This man was, or had been, an officer in some branch of the military. His upright stance, his habit of

189

command, his spit-and-polish grooming – all told the story.

Was he, like some military men I'd known, not terribly intelligent outside his narrow sphere of expertise? I decided to test him.

'Oh, I do understand, Mr . . . ?'

'Pringle,' he said unwillingly. '*Colonel* Pringle.'

'Dorothy Martin,' I said, extending a hand, which he couldn't very well not shake. 'And my husband, Alan Nesbitt.'

His mouth took a firm set when I pronounced the two different surnames, but he said nothing.

'It's lovely to meet you,' I cooed on, 'and I do think it's so brave of you all to try to keep things running normally in the face of such a disaster. Your congregation has dwindled, and probably your income. I'm sure you all must be terribly worried about what's going to happen to the cathedral.'

He could hardly have looked more taken aback if one of the chairs had begun to carry on a conversation with him. He was still trying to figure out whether I was being insolent or deliberately aggravating, or simply as stupid as he assumed all women were, when Mrs Rudge spoke up. 'There, now! Isn't that what I've been saying? We need to encourage people to come to the cathedral, make them feel welcome, make it a happy place, if it's not to fall down about our ears.'

'You're quite right, Mrs Rudge, and I'm sorry indeed to have to tell you we're just visiting. We live in Belleshire, quite a long ways away. But I do so agree with you. A church must

190

welcome everyone, rich, poor, young, old.' I stopped short of saying, 'Black, white, gay, straight.' I didn't want to give the poor colonel apoplexy. 'Not only, of course, because that is our Christian duty, but because the church requires donations to keep its doors open.'

Well, that opened a bit of conversation, men arguing with other men, women being catty with other women, agreement with one point of view or the other. Alan took advantage of it to listen, and now and then make a point himself. I was torn between concentrating on Mrs Rudge and cornering the colonel, but I decided I could almost certainly talk to Mrs Rudge later. She would respond favourably, I was sure, to an offer of tea that afternoon. If I didn't snaffle the colonel now, on the other hand, my opportunity was gone.

'So, Colonel, where are you serving now?'

'I am retired, madam.'

'Really! I wouldn't have thought – that is, the retirement age here must be much lower than in the States. I'm sure you can tell I'm American by birth.'

He thawed a degree or two at the blatant flattery, but said nothing.

'I wonder.' I lowered my voice a bit. 'This business of the dean. You're probably one of the most observant people in the congregation. Have you any idea at all who might have done such a terrible thing? Surely it couldn't have been one of the parishioners, no matter what was said this morning in the sermon.'

Was that laying it on too thick? The colonel

hesitated for a moment, opened his mouth and shut it again, and finally said, 'I have no idea, madam. No idea at all.'

Nineteen

'He was lying,' I said to Alan when we had escaped and were walking Watson. 'I'm absolutely sure of it. He knows, or he thinks he does.'

'Apparently he isn't terrified of hell-fire, then.'

'Oh, I'm sure he thinks that sort of thing applies to lesser mortals, not to him. He, after all, is a colonel. St Peter will salute Colonel Pringle as he approaches the pearly gates, and personally escort him inside. That's if he ever dies at all, which he may think unlikely.'

'Now, Dorothy. Aren't you being a bit hard on the man? You only met him once.'

'It doesn't take me long to size someone up. You know that. It's one of the advantages of age. I've known a lot of people in my life, and they do have a tendency to run in types. But you're right, of course. I admit it. Mea culpa! I'm too quick to pass judgement, which, in any case, we're not supposed to do at all. Sorry.' My apology was directed to Alan, to Colonel Pringle, and to God, who knew exactly how repentant I actually was. 'What did *you* think of him, then? And the rest of them?'

'Pringle seems to be a leading layman of the cathedral. He's a worried man. As you pointed out, attendance is sparse. That bodes ill for the finances of the place. It costs an immense amount to keep a medieval building from falling down, let alone to serve its community. I did mention to you, I think, that, with all his faults, Dean Brading did manage to balance his budget every year.'

'I can't imagine how, with so few attendees.'

'Perhaps there were many more when he was in charge. Would you have chosen to go to the cathedral this morning, if you had known the canon was presiding?'

'Not if I knew anything about the canon. I take your point. Even so, even if the dean did draw a much bigger crowd, it's hard to see how he made ends meet. Unless there are a few extremely wealthy families who keep the place going.'

'You notice, of course,' said Alan, 'that corners have been cut whenever possible. The church has no expensive furnishings, and I'm not sure that's entirely due to the dean's ascetic outlook on life. Even the Prayer Books and hymnals are falling apart, and surely those could have been replaced without offending anyone's Low Church views.'

'So you think Pringle's worried about money?'

'Money and reputation. He doesn't want a scandal, and if it does turn out that someone in the church community killed the dean, there's a scandal of gigantic proportions.'

'I wonder if it was the actual murder, or the possible scandal, that was really worrying the canon this morning. Alan, that sermon! I was reminded of Jonathan Edwards.'

193

'And who's he when he's at home?'

'He was a prominent preacher in America in, I think, the mid 1700s. One of his famous sermons was "Sinners in the hands of an angry God". He likened them to spiders hanging by a slender thread over the raging flames of Hell. It must have been terrifying to listen to him, and I was terrified this morning listening to the canon.'

'That was rather the idea, wasn't it? Frighten someone into confessing? And it didn't work.'

'Alan, you know a lot about how people's minds work, especially criminal minds. Did it not work because someone refused to be intimidated, or because the murderer was not, in fact, in the church?'

'For what it's worth, which isn't much, I think the murderer was not there. There was great tension, but not, to my mind, the unbearable fear and guilt of a murderer. I could be completely wrong, especially because we may not be dealing with a "criminal mind". We have to be careful about that term. There is a mindset common to habitual criminals, I'll agree, and it's fairly easy to spot: the combination of sly cunning with an utterly self-centred outlook on life. You see it in teenage louts all the way up to career criminals. It is simply not possible for such people to understand that anyone else's interests have any value, so when anything or anyone gets in their way, it's just too bad for the obstacle.

'But I'm not sure we're dealing here with a "criminal" in that sense. I think it likely that the dean was killed by an ordinary person who felt he had some overwhelming reason to want the man dead. And if that person was a member of the cathedral, I think he – or she, of course – would either stop attending church at all or, if he attended, would be forced by his conscience to confess. That's the other reason I believe he was not in the church this morning.'

I came to a stop while I digested that. Watson looked back at me and whined. This was unusual behaviour, and he wanted to know what was going on. A human going for a walk with a dog is expected to keep walking.

'Then we need to know more about Brading. So we'll have some idea who would have wanted him dead.'

'That's why we're here, love.'

We walked on in silence for a bit, while I reviewed what we did know about the man. He was married; it was his wife who had raised the alarm when he didn't come home. Hmm. 'Does anybody know what kind of terms he and his wife were on?'

'That's one of the things I hope you'll try to find out this afternoon at that tea you set up with Mrs Rudge. According to the official police report, they were the most devoted of couples.'

'Yes, well, we know what people tell the police, and what they don't. What about children?'

'No children.'

'And I don't suppose there's any convenient hint of a scandal in his background – drugs, sex, anything like that?'

'The police will have looked into all that very

thoroughly, Dorothy. For that matter, so did the commission before naming him to the shortlist.'

'Drat. Yes, of course. Was that your stomach growling, or is Watson upset about something?'

'I confess, it was I. Let's take our lovely boy back for some water and a nap, and find ourselves a thumping good Sunday lunch. We've had no real food all day.'

'And I've walked too far in Sunday shoes. Onward and upward!'

We were not fated to enjoy that Sunday lunch. When we got back to Lynncroft, Alan checked his phone, which he had turned off while we were in church. He looked up, all traces of animation wiped from his face.

'We'll have to go back, Dorothy. They've found Lovelace.'

Looking at his face, I knew there was more.

'He's dead. Apparently by his own hand.'

We packed rapidly. I asked Mrs Stevens to phone Mrs Rudge and explain, and we were off.

Hunger drove us, a few miles down the road, to a motorway café where we had a quick and rather nasty meal. Watson even turned up his nose at the leftovers. On the road again, I said, 'All right. What happened? Did they tell you? Who phoned, by the way?'

Alan, who is accustomed to my multiple questions, answered them methodically. 'Jonathan. He said the police found Lovelace in a pub in Dover. He had apparently intended to take an

196

early ferry to Calais in the morning; he had a ticket in his wallet. He would never have been allowed to board, incidentally; the word was out and all the ports of departure were being watched. He took a room in the pub and was found there in the morning, lying quite peacefully in his bed, with an empty bottle of sleeping tablets on the bedside table.'

'And it's supposed that he discovered that the police were on his trail and killed himself rather than face arrest.'

It wasn't a question, and Alan made no reply.

'It's a reasonable supposition,' I ventured, after a mile or two.

'Mmm.'

'But you don't believe it.'

'I don't like coincidences, and this is a whopping big one, Dorothy. The second death, out of four clergymen selected for the shortlist to be our next bishop. I don't like it one little bit.' He gripped the steering wheel and set his jaw, and I asked no more questions.

It was well past suppertime when we got home, weary, hungry, and upset. We hadn't phoned Jane to tell her we were coming, but Jonathan had. So she had a cottage pie warming in our oven, with a crusty loaf of homemade bread sitting on the table and, I discovered, salad in the fridge.

I found, absurdly, that I had tears in my eyes.

Alan put the car in the garage, brought in our bags, and then told me he was going over to talk to the dean.

'Let's wait, Alan. We're both tired, and Jane's pie won't improve with age. Let's sit down and eat supper and drink a glass of wine, and then go over to talk to the dean. We're both too old to keep running on empty for hours. Go on. Sit.'

Watson thought I was talking to him and obediently sat, looking up with his 'I'm a good dog and deserve a treat' face. That made us both laugh, so he got his treat. Then the cats wanted their share, and also wanted some lap time, so we were a bit more relaxed by the time we got through our meal. Animals are wonderful stress-relievers, except when they're being maddening pests.

'I'd better go over and say a word to Jane,' I said. 'You go on to Kenneth's. I'll be there in a minute or two.'

I found Jane sitting relaxed among her dogs, reading a book. I was stunned at her appearance. She had shed ten years, twenty, since I'd seen her last.

'You're an angel, Jane,' I said, dropping down in a squashy armchair that was going to be very hard to get out of, but was oh! so comfortable. 'We hadn't really eaten all day, and Alan's terribly upset besides. That meal was a lifesaver.'

Jane doesn't enjoy praise. She made a dismissive gesture. 'Not a patch on finding Walter.'

'We didn't find him. Jonathan did.'

The same gesture. 'Alan's idea. And yours.'

'Well, at any rate, we're very grateful indeed. And now I have to go over and try to calm some of the troubled waters at the Deanery. This is a very dreadful thing, this second death, but I won't have Alan worrying himself to a frazzle over it, or the dean, either.'

I struggled out of the chair, with Jane's help, and made my way through the Close to the Deanery.

May would soon be June, and Whitsunday was almost upon us, so the twilight was lingering late. The Cathedral floated, immense but serene, against the darkening sky. Though Evensong was long past, Jeremy was still at the organ; I could hear music drifting softly through an open door somewhere, and gentle light shone through the stained glass. 'Lighten our darkness, O Lord,' I prayed softly, 'and in your mercy defend us from all perils and dangers of this night.'

At the Deanery I found the serenity less in evidence. Margaret greeted me at the door. 'I'm glad you're here, Dorothy. I've been trying to persuade those two old dears that the end of the world has not come, but I'm not sure they're buying it. Maybe you can talk some sense into them. Kenneth takes everything so dreadfully to heart, you see.'

I walked into the room, where Alan and the dean were seated in front of a small fire, glasses of sherry at their sides. They were speaking in low, funereal tones, and the sherry appeared to be untouched. Oh, dear.

Shock tactics, perhaps?

'Margaret, if you happen to have some bourbon on hand,' I said in a clear, carrying voice, 'I think I'd prefer that. We have occasion to celebrate, after all.'

My husband and the dean looked up. The dean looked slightly shocked. Alan looked exasperated.

I went on. 'I've just been to see Jane, and the difference since they've found Walter is amazing! She looks younger than I do, and she has fifteen years on me, at least. Thank you, Margaret.' I remained standing and raised the glass she had handed me. 'To Jane and the happy issue out of her afflictions!' The two men stood, perforce, and raised their glasses. 'To Jane,' they muttered.

I kept my glass in the air. 'And to the gallant men and women who helped find Walter and keep him safe, and to them and the God who will help all of us resolve our other tribulations!'

Both men raised their glasses a bit higher at that. 'Hear, hear,' said Alan softly, and gave me a rather weary smile.

Both men then sat back down as the dean said, 'You're quite right, Dorothy. I've let temporal concerns make me lose sight of the important things in life. We must give thanks to God, and Jonathan and the police, that Walter is safe, and trust him to see us safely out of our difficulties. But oh, dear heaven, I don't want to read the newspapers tomorrow!'

I sat down, having achieved my object. The two men had come out of their funk and were ready for reasonable thought. 'What's the worst that can happen?' I asked, really wanting to hear their answer.

'Everyone concerned will be pilloried, of course,' said Alan. 'All of us on the commission, for choosing such unchancy candidates. The police, for not taking action sooner against Lovelace, and not solving Brading's murder. But the worst is the beating the Church itself will take at the hands of the tabloids and the broadcast media. Back in the day, the Church was sacrosanct, like royalty. Criticism had to be veiled. No more. The media will leap with fiendish joy on yet another huge blot on the ecclesial copybook.'

'Yes. That's serious. The police can stand the racket; so can the members of the commission. Oh, none of you will like it, but it isn't a matter of life or death for any of you.' I took a rather large sip of my bourbon. 'Sorry, poor choice of words. I meant that all of you will survive the attacks. But attacks on the Church are another matter. The dear old C of E doesn't rank high enough in public opinion these days that it can risk publicity as damaging as this. What are you going to do about it?' I was determined to keep them out of the Slough of Despond if I possibly could. Not that they weren't right. This was a pit deep enough to drown anyone's spirits. But positive action was needed, if we could think of any.

The dean sipped his sherry, and then put his glass down and stood. 'I'll tell you what I am *not* going to do about it. I am not going to hide, or cover up, or prevaricate. I am going to call a press conference for an hour from now, and I am going to make sure all of the commission members who can attend are there. The ones from this diocese ought to be able to make it, at least. The Archbishops are, of course, not mine to command, but I will request.'

'Isn't that stepping a bit outside the bounds of your authority, Kenneth?' asked Alan diffidently.

'Yes. But this is my Cathedral, and it's my bishop we're trying to appoint, and the buck, as your president once said, Dorothy, stops here. Now, if you'll excuse me, ladies, I'd best get to the phone. Alan, can you help make the calls? I'll put my secretary on it, too, but they need to go out as quickly as we can manage, and I'll want the Chapter here, as well – as many of them as we can reach.' He turned to leave the room. 'Oh, and Dorothy –' he looked me in the eye – 'thank you for reminding me from whence cometh our help. Sometimes the world is too much with me, and I forget.'

'Never for long, Kenneth. You've certainly reminded me often enough.'

We watched them go, then Margaret sat back in her chair with a long sigh. 'He's a man of great faith, but he takes things so seriously, and sometimes forgets that all the responsibility isn't on his shoulders.'

'The wonder, in this age of cynicism, is that he ever remembers. What was it like, Margaret, back when he was just a parish priest, without all this burden of administration?'

'We had a lovely parish,' she said, smiling reminiscently. 'Not very big, and not so many of them went to church, but they were delightful people.'

'Come, now. All of them?'

'All of them. Truly. Oh, there was the usual run of grumblers, the old women with the bad legs, the old men who didn't bathe often enough, and one or two young toughs who thought they could terrorize the village, but we all got on comfortably enough. And when anyone was in trouble, the rest rallied round. Our children were young when we first went there, and that made a difference. That huge, draughty old rectory would have been much different without the girls giggling and the boys racing up and down the stairs.'

'And did Kenneth worry as much about his parishioners then as he does now?'

She laughed a little. 'More, perhaps. There were fewer of them, and much less to do on the business side of things, so he knew more about their troubles, and took them all upon himself. I speak of a parish, but we actually had three to look after, so Sundays got a bit hectic, especially in bad weather. But it was a wonderful time in our lives.'

'And then he was made dean.'

'And then he was made dean. He didn't want the job at first, you know. We were so happy where we were, and the responsibilities here were so much greater. He prayed about it for a long time. Well, we both did, really. I didn't want to go, either. I had so many friends in the villages. But the children had grown and gone, as children will, and we didn't need that big house anymore, so it seemed quite selfish to stay there. And really, we could see that the Cathedral needed us. You weren't here then, so

203

you never knew how badly it had been allowed to deteriorate. Lack of funds, of course, but also lack of attention. Kenneth finally decided that this was where God wanted him, so this is where we are. And I have to say housekeeping is much easier in a place this size, even if it is several hundred years older than the old rectory. And this is a parish church as well, of course, so he still has the pastoral work he loves. But this appointment process . . .' She sighed and shook her head. 'Kenneth isn't as young as he once was, and this was never going to be easy, with feelings running so high about so many issues.'

'And the deaths have made it much, much worse. I've been worried about Alan, too. The crime aspects he can deal with. That's what he's done all his life, after all – deal with crime and criminals. But he isn't and never has been a politician or a diplomat, so the negotiations within the diocese and then on the commission have taken a lot out of him. You know, Margaret, if there's a bright spot anywhere in this mess, it's that the appointment process has been put on hold until the smoke clears. That gives us all a little time to concentrate on the crime, or crimes, if the Lovelace death turns out not to be suicide.'

'Suicide is a crime,' said Margaret. 'As well as a sin.'

'So it is, but, Margaret, I don't mind telling you that I'm hoping it *was* suicide. The idea of a serial killer of clergymen makes my blood run cold.'

'You do realize that's exactly what the gutter press is going to make of it.'

'Oh, Lord, I suppose you're right.' I levered myself to my feet. 'I'm dead. I'm going home before I fall asleep right here in your sitting room. Thanks for the drink and the company.'

I walked home through the soft spring night. Darkness had fully fallen, and the Cathedral organ was silent. I could see no light streaming from the stained-glass windows, though the Cathedral itself glowed, reflecting the light from the discreet spotlights trained on it from the Close. I shivered suddenly. It seemed suddenly an aloof, almost menacing presence, looming over the tiny humans who served it.

I was glad to get home, and very glad when both cats wanted to cuddle in my lap. I needed the warmth and comfort.

Twenty

I took Watson and a book to bed with me, intending to stay awake until Alan came home. I was sure I couldn't sleep anyway, but I must have dropped off from sheer emotional exhaustion. I didn't know a thing until Alan woke me with coffee.

'Mmph. What time is it?'

'Almost nine.'

'In the morning?'

'As ever was. I found you last night with the light on and an open book on your chest, and Watson sprawled over half the bed. Drink up, and let me know when you want some breakfast.'

I don't know what I ever did to deserve such a jewel of a husband.

A shower completed my return to consciousness, and I went downstairs feeling almost ready to face the day.

Alan has learned how to make French toast, for which he has developed a quite un-British liking, although he claims the stuff would make any Frenchman cringe. So we had that for breakfast, along with some lovely sausages. Watson got his share of the sausage, of course, and when I finally pushed my plate away, I was sure I'd never want to eat again. 'Salad for lunch,' I proclaimed, and Alan just nodded. He knows quite well that I often feel hungrier by lunchtime than I think possible after a big breakfast.

'Alan, I've been thinking,' I said after a second cup of coffee had fully restored my faculties. 'What we need is a council of war – you and me and Jonathan.'

'War?'

'Figure of speech. We need to get together, pool our ideas, work out how we're going to track down Brading's murderer.'

I expected an argument. *Leave it to the police, not our job, et cetera, et cetera.* He surprised me. 'That's very much the decision reached at the dean's meeting after the press conference last night.'

'Oh! I forgot all about that. I intended to find out about it when you got home; I really was dead to the world. Too much has been happening. Tell me about it.'

'Dorothy, Kenneth was simply splendid. I've handled a fair number of press conferences in my time, but he outperformed anything I ever managed.'

'What did he say?'

'First of all, he stole their best line. He said that he knew what they must be thinking: some mad killer on the loose, targeting clergymen. And then he said, "If some of you ladies and gentlemen are broadcasting this conference live, and the killer is watching or listening, I hope he or she realizes that there'll never be a better opportunity to bag a dozen or so of us at one fell swoop!" Of course, everyone roared, including the canons and the other clergy who were there. And then he changed tone and spoke of the vast sorrow of the Church as a whole, that a priest should feel so much despair as to take his own life, and he was sure that extenuating circumstances would be found that would make those actions perhaps easier to understand and forgive. And then – can you believe it? – he read a few of the more moving bits of the Burial Service and asked for a moment of silence and prayer for the Reverend Mr Lovelace. That shut off the questions they were panting to ask. Even the media aren't quite so rude as to break into silent prayer offered by a dean in his own great cathedral!'

'Brilliant!'

'Then, before they could gather their wits again, Kenneth said that he was grateful to the press and the broadcast media for giving him this opportunity to "enlist the aid of the nation" – that was his exact phrase – in discovering the person who killed Dean Brading. He added that he and the Chapter would be in continual prayer for that person, who must, he said, be suffering great anguish of conscience. And then, to their vast astonishment, he pronounced a blessing and the dismissal. They were so caught up in the liturgical atmosphere he'd created that a lot of them responded with "Thanks be to God" before they could help themselves, and then found Kenneth had vanished. Now, what do you think of that?'

'I think I owe him an apology. I've been feeling sorry for him, thinking he was entirely out of his depth and wondering how he could possibly cope. But the performance you've just described was nothing short of miraculous. The man's turning out to be a genius.'

'He credits it all to God, you know. When we met with him afterwards, Chapter and commission members, he said he hadn't the slightest idea what he was going to say when he got up there in front of them all. He'd had no real time to prepare, so he had to wing it. "I was given the right words," he insisted.'

'And I believe him. So, what did you all talk about in the meeting?'

'He expanded on his remarks about finding Brading's murderer. He stressed that most of us had no experience in such matters, of course, so the main job would be simply to keep our eyes and ears open, and report any unusual behaviour to the proper authorities. He asked me, then, to give some pointers about what might constitute "unusual behaviour". I obliged, listing some of the less obvious things such as lights being on or off at times that didn't seem to fit the usual pattern, comings and goings, any changes in someone's usual routine, as well as the moods and actions that usually constitute what one thinks of as behaviour. I also hammered home his point that they were to report anything they found odd, and on no account to try to take any action. And I do hope, my dear, that you are taking heed. Over the years, you've escaped any truly catastrophic consequences of some of your reckless acts of derring-do, but the law of averages is bound to catch up with you one of these days.'

I put my hand on his. 'You know I don't *try* to get into trouble. Somehow it just seems to follow me.'

'*You* follow *it*.'

'But not deliberately. The thing is, when I'm about to discover something important, I don't actually abandon common sense. I consciously decide how far I can go without disaster. It's just that sometimes my judgement is off by a hair's breadth or two.'

'Which is the main reason my hair is grey.'

'That, and the number of birthdays you've had. Now, when are we going to convene our council?'

Alan sighed and pulled out his phone. 'I'll see what Jonathan's schedule is for the next few days. And I think perhaps we'd best include Jane and Walter. Walter for his knowledge of Lovelace and the goings-on at St Barnabas', and

Jane for her knowledge of nearly everything and everyone.'

'Good idea. Do you think we could possibly meet here? I'm so very tired of travelling, and the cats are acting much more clingy than usual. I think they're feeling neglected.'

'If Jonathan can bring Walter here, I think that's an excellent suggestion.'

I tidied up the kitchen while Alan made his phone calls, and then I was about to head across my back garden to talk to Jane, when a hard little head butted my ankle, and a Siamese wail sounded. A quiet one, for a Siamese, but peremptory.

'Sam, you rascal, you need attention, don't you? Where's Emmy?'

Samantha indicated, in her feline fashion, that she didn't give a damn where Emmy was. She, Sam, was right here and wanted a lap. And I, come to think of it, wanted a break. So I picked up the willing cat and settled down on the sofa with her. Her purrs brought Esmeralda from wherever she'd been hanging out, so in no time at all I had two furry heads to stroke, two pairs of eyes gazing up at me (one pair green and one bright blue), and two sets of front paws ecstatically kneading my legs. It was only those paws, their needle-sharp claws occasionally coming through to skin, that kept me from falling asleep right there.

'Cat therapy?' asked Alan, walking into the room.

'Mmm. Very soothing. The massage is a trifle painful, though.' I tried to shove both of them away, but cats can gain weight at will and become immovable. If I persisted, the claws would come into play.

Alan grinned and walked into the kitchen, where he opened a cupboard door. That brought both the cats to full alert. Purrs stopped, ears pricked, whiskers stiffened. Then they heard Alan pop the lid off a can.

That did the trick, of course. It might be a can of soup or something equally boring, but it might be cat food or even, joy of joys, tuna! They shot off my lap, racing each other to the kitchen. I followed.

'They don't need any more food,' I said. 'They're both getting fat. And so are you, dog.' Because Watson had appeared, too, of course, and was jostling for position.

'I know that, and you know it, but they would all disagree. They're healthy. They deserve an occasional treat.'

Oh, well, what are pets for, if not to spoil?

'Did you manage to reach Jonathan and Walter?'

'Yes, and they're both coming this afternoon. Tea time is the earliest they could make it. Jane's free, too, and she said you were not to bother to bake anything. She'll bring something.'

'Whew! That's a relief. I don't know what we have in the house, and she's a better baker than I am, anyway. But my word, Alan, the house! We've been home so little it looks like Miss Havisham's parlour.'

He looked around with exaggerated horror. 'No decaying wedding cake that I can see.'

211

'Enough cat and dog hair to stuff a mattress, though. Would you rather vacuum or dust?'

Our house is very old – early seventeenth-century (although by English standards that's only sort of middle-aged) – and has a good many nooks and crannies where dirt can accumulate. But it's not very big, so with two of us working at top speed we got it back in good time to its usual state of slightly shabby, but orderly, comfort. I did make us salads for lunch, since we were going to have a more substantial tea than usual, and the animals were so tired, what with all their narrow escapes from the vacuum, that they didn't even come to the kitchen to complain about the dearth of hand-outs.

After lunch I sat down in my tiny office and tried to put my thoughts in as good order as the house. There seemed to be so many threads to pursue, so many unconnected events, so many people to try to catalogue, that my head felt filled with mashed potatoes when the bell rang and Alan admitted our guests. Jane arrived a moment later with trays and baskets full of goodies, and we all sat down to a sumptuous tea: all my favourite sandwiches, and scones and jam tarts, and a plum cake that I would have eaten first of all if I hadn't been taught manners.

We didn't say much at first. The food was too good, and it was too pleasant to sit with good friends, rested, and with anxiety, if not banished, at least at bay. But when we were sated with food and had gone through three large pots of tea, I sat back. 'Now, before we get to anything else, Walter, I have to know what happened to you. I'm perishing of curiosity.'

'Gosh, I don't know where to start.'

'You went to St Barnabas' to try to find evidence that Lovelace was embezzling,' I prompted.

'Yes. Dear old Jed let me in, and I went right to work in the office. I knew I had to work fast, because someone might come back any time, and then I was to meet Sue—'

'Yes, we know about that. Go on.'

'Well, I found the ledgers with no trouble. Mrs Steele had locked them up, of course, but she hadn't locked her desk, and the keys were in the top drawer. It didn't take me long to spot trouble. I'm no accountant, but they hadn't even bothered to cover their tracks! I suppose Lovelace thought no one could ever possibly suspect him, great man that he was. I'm sorry – he's dead, and I shouldn't—'

'Scoundrel!' said Jane vehemently. 'Deserves no sympathy!'

'Well, anyway, I got interested in what I found. You wouldn't believe what he managed to get away with! He'd received huge contributions from some businesses. He knew how to twist arms; I'll give him that. That money was what was running the church and reviving the neighbourhood and all that, while he stole most of the offering from the plates. And I was making notes like mad, when I heard people talking, and realized it was Lovelace and Steele!

'You can imagine how scared I was. If they caught me in there . . . well, I made tracks.

There's a little sort of storage room off the office, not used much, but it has a good big window. I ducked in there, pulled the door shut, and headed out the window. That was a bad moment, because I almost got stuck, and I had to more or less fall out of the window. I don't know how I managed not to break something, but I was okay. And then I ran, across the car park at the back and in between buildings and I don't know where. And when I finally fetched up on some street a long way away, I realized I had the ledgers under my arm. I hadn't even remembered I had them.'

'But that meant you really did have to get away.'

'With bells on! I had some money, luckily, and I was close to a Tube station. So I just got on a train, I didn't care where it was headed, and eventually found myself at Victoria Station. And I remembered, I don't know why, about that ghastly Jack Everidge and his revolting family, and I thought I knew which station was nearest that country house, Ashhurst. I had just about enough for a cheap ticket, and I was pretty sure no one would think of looking for me there, so I climbed on the first train. Is there any water, Dorothy?'

'Of course. Or there's beer.'

'Water will be lovely, thank you.'

When he had his water, he continued. 'The station was really quite a long way from the house, and I was pretty cold and tired and hungry by the time I got there, but I was out of money. I didn't think Jack's parents would let me in, and I didn't like them, anyway, so I dossed down in one of the barns. It was full of hay, and really quite cosy. And in the morning there was an apple tree, and a pump in the stable yard, so I was all right for food and water. I was worried about Sue, but I didn't want to call her. I thought it was safer for her if she didn't know where I was. The only thing was, I didn't know quite what to do. I couldn't exactly stay there for ever, and someone needed to know about the ledgers, but I didn't dare call Gran, either, in case I endangered *her*. And I didn't think the police would believe a word of what I had to say, not to mention the fact that I had in my possession stolen ledgers. I didn't have your phone numbers.' He nodded to Alan and me. 'And then Jonathan came along, and Gran had told me about him, so I thought I could trust him, and . . . here I am.'

'Thanks be.' I sighed. 'Well, that was an amazing story, but now we need to get busy. You know what we're here to do, or try to do. All five of us have some special skills or knowledge that might help the police in their search for the killer of Dean Brading. I propose for the time being that we accept the death of Mr Lovelace as the suicide it apparently was, so we can concentrate on the other. I've made some lists.'

Alan chuckled.

'Yes, well, I know I'm forever making lists, but sometimes they do help. I've made copies of them so you can each have one. I thought that maybe if we worked our way through these, some kind of pattern might emerge that we could follow up. But I realize it's all pretty haphazard,

215

and if any of you have a better idea of how to proceed, do please tell us. I don't mind admitting I'm pretty much at sea.'

I passed out the lists, thinking as I did so that they made a pretty poor showing for several hours of solid thought.

The first page was headed 'Suspects', and included the subheadings 'Other Candidates', 'Commission Members', 'Brading's Congregation', 'Family', and 'Other'. I'd listed a few names under the 'Commission' and 'Congregation' headings, and, of course, the two remaining names under 'Candidates'.

The second list was headed 'Facts about the Murder', and though there were subheadings, there was almost nothing under them. We didn't know 'Time of Murder', or at least I didn't. We didn't know 'Weapon'. Under 'Place' I'd put the obvious – Chelton Cathedral – but I didn't know exactly where in that vast, unfriendly church he had been found.

The third was also almost blank, but it was the one I hoped we could best fill in, and the one in which I'd put my trust. It was headed 'Facts about Brading', and had listed only 'Dean, Chelton Cathedral' and the dates, and a couple of notes about his religious views.

'I've got lots of blank paper here as well, so one of us can write down whatever brilliant ideas we come up with. Now. Who has anything to contribute?'

'I have a few facts about the murder,' said Alan, pulling out a notebook, 'though I don't know if they'll be very useful. I wasn't entirely idle while you were whipping this together this afternoon, Dorothy. I talked to Derek, asked him a few things. He isn't in charge of the investigation, of course. That's Gloucester's headache, and, incidentally – and between ourselves – they're still not making much progress. They're having to do too much tiptoeing about. However, they do have a cause of death and an approximate time. Brading died of a subdural haematoma, caused by that terrific blow to the head. They have not yet found the weapon, and, because of the nature of the injury, they can only guess about the time, or even the place, when the blow was struck.'

'"A gentleman was thrown out of a chaise,"' I intoned dreamily.

Three of my audience looked at me with alarm. Alan smiled. 'Dorothy is quoting from one of Dorothy Sayers' novels. The gentleman in question, who was, by the way, a real person in a genuine medical report Sayers dug up somewhere, fell on his head and was badly injured, but got up, got back in his chaise (whatever that might have been), went home, and didn't die until some little time later. The poor fellow died sometime in the middle of the 1800s, if I remember correctly, but the science of it is still perfectly sound. That hapless gentleman helped solve the fictional death in the Sayers novel, but it only serves to confuse our problem. The point is that a subdural haematoma – that is, bleeding between the brain and the skull, to put it roughly – can take its time to kill. There is a blow to the head. The victim staggers a bit, falls, gets

217

up, probably says a few things he wouldn't want his mother to hear, and then goes on about his business. He probably has a terrible headache, and he may feel a bit dizzy and sick. But he may have no idea that his brain is being attacked by more and more pressure as the haemorrhage becomes bigger and bigger. Eventually, if the haematoma gets big enough, and the victim is not treated, he dies.'

'But the kicker,' I chimed in, 'is that word "eventually". Because there's no really good way to tell how much time passed between the injury and the death – right, Alan?'

'Right. Now the ME down in Gloucestershire puts the time of death at about nine in the evening, based on body temperature and other indications. It couldn't well have been much later than that, because the body was found at around midnight and rigor was just beginning. However, given the fact that the cathedral was quite cold, which delays the onset of rigor, death could have been quite a bit earlier. The official report says "17.00 to 22.00". But!' He held up a cautioning finger. 'Remember that's just the time of death. The actual blow, the attack, could have been much earlier, depending on how long it took the poor man to die.'

'So, in practical terms,' said Jonathan, 'we haven't the slightest idea when Brading might have been attacked.'

'Well, sometime the day he died, but, aside from that, it comes down to when he was last seen alive on that day.'

'His wife said he'd been to a meeting in

218

London,' I said. 'Didn't the *Telegraph* say that, or am I making it up?'

'That,' said Alan, 'is what Mrs Brading told the *Telegraph*, but it was apparently not true, or at any rate the police have not been able to trace any meeting that he might have attended. Nor did anyone see him getting on or off a London train at any time that day. Now, that doesn't say he wasn't in London. London is a big place, and there are other ways to get there than by train. But it can't, at this point, be proven.'

'Which means,' said Jonathan, 'that his wife was the last person known to have seen him alive.'

Twenty-One

There was a long pause. I drew a breath. 'That leads me back to the question I wanted to ask Mrs Rudge, or one of the questions, anyway. What sort of terms was the dean on with his wife? I'm sure the police asked that, but people don't always tell the police everything.'

We all looked at Jane. This was her area of expertise.

She shrugged. 'Never heard any scandal. Never heard they were Darby and Joan, either. No children.'

She let that remark and its implications hang in the air. I thought of my own first marriage, childless, but certainly not for want of trying. I held my peace.

'Right,' said Alan briskly, and I thought he knew what I was thinking. 'Talk to Mrs Rudge. She's certain to know about the dean's family life. Now, what other facts about the dean can we dredge up?'

'What does it say in his CV?' I asked. 'I don't suppose you have a copy here.'

'It's meant to be confidential, you know, and in any case it's not terribly exciting. Place and date of birth, date of marriage, date of ordination, posts he held before his move to Chelton.'

'Did he move around a lot?' Walter asked.

'Not a great deal, if I remember correctly. He followed the usual path of the successful clergyman: curate, schoolmaster, rector, finally dean, all in the Midlands. What's your idea, Walter?'

'Probably a stupid one, but I thought that people who knew him in his earlier days might give us some ideas about, you know, what he was like . . .' Walter trailed off into uncertainty.

'I agree,' said Jonathan instantly. 'I'm sure Church officials did a background check on him, but they were looking only for anything that might be dicey. We need to know all we can about the man. It would take quite a lot of time, though, to talk to everyone who might have known him.'

'There are five of us,' I pointed out. 'Walter, can you take, say, a week off from the BM?'

'I can take a month if I have to. The job I'm working on isn't urgent, and since I'm volunteering my time, they can't fire me.'

'It won't jeopardize your real job, though, will

it?' I asked anxiously. 'The one with the Museum of London?'

'That's not a dead cert yet, and if they hire me, I wouldn't start till the end of the summer, so I should be good.'

'And I can devote all my time to this for the next few days,' said Jonathan. 'And before you come over all mother hen again, Dorothy, no, I won't starve with no income for a few days. You never remember that I have a bit of a nest-egg to see me through.'

I did frequently forget that Jonathan had inherited enough money from his parents that he didn't actually have to work at all. He lived simply in a tiny bed-sitter in London because he wanted to, and hadn't employed any help, even back when he could barely walk. 'Oh, yes, I keep forgetting you're Mr Gotrocks. Well, that's you two, then. And, of course, there's Alan and me. Jane?'

I had some uncertainty about Jane. I didn't know her age, but she was for sure quite a lot older than Alan and me, and we're no spring chickens.

'Count me in,' she growled. 'Not too old or feeble to use the phone, am I?'

'Of course not!' I said too heartily, and got a very sharp look from Jane. 'Then that leaves Alan and me, and I think we'd better split up. We'll cover more ground that way. Now, dear, don't look at me that way. You've made great strides in conquering your overprotectiveness, so don't ruin it. I'm only going to be talking to some old acquaintances of Dean Brading's,

221

back when he was a humble parish priest or whatever. It's not as if I were walking into a lion's den.'

'Your middle name should be Daniel,' he muttered, but he said no more. Not then. I knew there would be a discussion later, when Jane had gone home and our guests had retired for the night.

'All right, then. We'll divvy up the assignments later. For now, let's go back to the lists. Any more to put down under "Facts about Brading" for the moment?'

'His religious and philosophical views are important, I think,' said Jonathan. 'A good many people could have either hated or adored him for them, I should imagine.'

'Very well.' I started to write. 'Ultra-conservative about role of women in the Church.'

'And in life,' said Jane. '*Kinder, Küche, Kirche.*'

'But there were no *Kinder* in his household. I wonder what was left for his wife to do?' asked Walter.

'Look after him,' said Jane, and again there was that hint of a growl in her voice.

'She must have had a lot of time on her hands,' said Walter thoughtfully.

'If you're thinking what I think you're thinking,' said Jonathan, 'don't forget the woman is nearing sixty.'

Alan, Jane, and I burst into laughter. 'Go on thinking it, Walter! I can testify that there's life well beyond fifty.' And Alan winked at me.

'So we need,' I said, when order was restored, 'to find out if there's any hint of Mrs Brading having an affair. Given her husband's exalted position, it would have had to be handled very discreetly.'

'Somebody would know,' said Jane. 'No stopping talk in a cathedral town.'

'Do tell!' I grinned at Jane.

'It would make for a great motive.' Walter frowned. 'But then the murder should have been the other way around, shouldn't it? Husband kills lover, or wife, or both?'

'Usually,' said Alan, the expert on crime. 'But if the lover is a robust man and the husband is not, it could end by the attacker becoming the attackee, if I may coin a word.'

'All right, then, whoever gets landed with the Chelton assignments makes that gossip a priority.'

'And maybe we shouldn't forget,' said Walter, 'that it could have been the dean having the affair. Maybe with his attacker.'

'A woman bashing someone on the head?'

'Or not,' said Walter.

Oh. That possibility hadn't occurred to me, though I don't know why not. At least one English dean is openly gay and living with a partner. Why not another? 'That would have had to be even more discreet,' I mused, thinking aloud, 'considering Brading's ultra-conservatism. So you're positing a lovers' quarrel?'

'Just thinking it might have been.'

Jane cuffed him gently. 'Too timid, boy. Good ideas. Stick to your guns.'

He gave her a million-watt smile, and I could have cried. I wasn't sure why. Maybe for all the years these two had lost, when neither knew the

223

other existed. Maybe for all I'd lost, never having grandchildren of my own. Maybe just because I'm a sentimental idiot.

Alan said, 'If I may, I can perhaps speed this along a bit. I take it we'd like to work out the main points before bedtime. Dorothy, I believe we were listing Brading's views?'

'Yes, and I admit we haven't got very far. All right. Conservative social views. Conservative religious views, extremely Low Church in all respects. I don't know if we know his political views, or if they matter.'

'Probably Tory all the way. Don't know if it matters.'

'But we'll try to find out anyway.' Alan made a note on his list. 'Let's move on now,' he said, glancing at his watch, 'to "Suspects". Perhaps I should leave the room.'

It was years before I learned to interpret that deadpan English style of humour, and I still make mistakes. 'Right,' I said. 'You're the obvious top suspect. You know a lot about murder, and how murderers evade capture. And you haven't a shadow of an alibi.'

'Motive?' he asked.

'You couldn't bear the idea of him as our bishop.'

Alan held out his hands, wrists together, as if for handcuffs.

'Thought you wanted to speed things up,' said Jane, with a mighty frown that deceived nobody.

Alan shrugged comically, and proceeded. 'Very well. I surrender. I'll leave my name off the list. Also Dean Allenby. The day he murders

224

someone will be the day the world comes to an end. And I presume we can rule out the two Archbishops and their secretary, and the Prime Minister's secretary, all for want of motive. Actually, Dorothy, I think we can leave all the other members of the commission off the list for now. The police will certainly have been checking their stories.'

'I'll concede, for now. I still think we, as amateurs, might be able to find out a lot the police couldn't, but we have enough on our plates without them. We'll save them for later, if we don't come up with anyone more likely in the meantime.'

'And your "Other" heading can presumably be filled with our extensive catch in the net we're spreading around his background.'

'I'm not sure the metaphor works,' said Jonathan, 'but I agree that's the most likely side of the boat to fish from.' He moved restlessly in his chair. 'Sorry. Getting a bit stiff.'

'And so am I, and my only excuse is age. Or maybe two artificial knees count. I say it's time to take a break, go for a walk, have some supper, and then resume. All in favour?'

We deliberately spoke of other things over supper, which was informal in the extreme. I set out odds and ends of cheese that had accumulated in the fridge, heated soup out of the freezer, and made a salad. Jane the baker contributed a couple of fresh loaves of bread and another plum cake, and we all ate sitting in the parlour with plates in our laps. The two young members of the party sat on the floor. The weather wasn't really cold enough for a fire, but Alan lit one anyway, just for the cosiness of it.

'Walter, I don't suppose you've had time to get that ring for Sue yet, have you?' I said, my mouth not quite full of bread and cheese.

'No, you've kept me pretty busy with other things,' he said with a chuckle. 'And now I suppose you're going to send me off chasing possible murderers.'

'I wouldn't have put it quite that way,' I began.

Alan finished my sentence. 'She never does think of it that way, you know, my boy. She calls it innocent curiosity, or perfectly safe little expeditions, or harmless questions anybody might ask – and half the time ends up very nearly in the soup.'

'But never quite. I do feel guilty about keeping you away from Sue so long, though. She hardly knows me and already she has reason to find me obnoxious.'

'She thinks you're terrific. She wants you to come to the wedding.'

'You couldn't keep us away,' said Alan. 'Have you set a date?'

'We're hoping for August sometime. We haven't talked yet to Dean Allenby, but we'd like to be married here, in the Cathedral. Sherebury is – well, the closest thing I've ever had to a home.' He didn't look at Jane, and she didn't look at him, lest they break that ironclad English rule about showing emotion. I'm American, and didn't care how many people saw me blink away a tear or two.

So the talk drifted to weddings, with the women interested in the clothes and the food, and the men trading rather mild ribaldry. I ventured at one point to ask Jonathan how Jemima was doing.

'Well, I think,' he said, looking down at his plate. 'I . . . we . . . I see her now and again, and she's coping quite well. She's been assigned to work with the Royal Collection, you know.'

'No, I didn't! How wonderful! It's what she's always wanted, isn't it?'

'Certainly since she started working at the Palace.' He stopped there, and I was sorry I'd brought it up. The memories of Jemima's job at Buckingham Palace were painful.

'I hope she'll be happy,' was all I said. I could have added hopes about the two of them, but that was their business.

After we'd cleared away and washed the dishes, we settled down again to our task. 'How should we organize the search for Brading's friends and/or enemies, Alan? You're much better at deploying troops than I am.'

'By location, I should think. That's the most efficient. One person can talk to quite a few people in a short time, if they're all in the same neighbourhood, so to speak.'

'You're going to have to tell us, then, what the locations are. I know you said the CV was confidential, but the man's dead and we're trying to find his murderer. Surely that makes a difference.'

'Not according to the letter of the law, but if one considers the spirit, I agree. Let me fetch the paperwork.'

He was back in a moment with a thick folder in his hand. 'This has everything about the appointment process,' he explained. 'I thought there might be other information we'd need. But here's Brading's CV. Where do you want to start?'

'I say with his first assignment. You said he was a curate?'

'Yes, but only for a little over a year. That was St Margaret's, Godwick, in Bucks. The rector at the time was the Reverend Mr Coates. Now deceased, the file says.'

'Drat!' I said. 'But there will be other people there who remember him. It couldn't have been that long ago.'

'Early eighties. Yes, there will still be a few. And Godwick is a village. Much easier to gather information in a place like that. His next step up the ladder wasn't actually up, more lateral. He was asked to take over a small prep school in a nearby village, Stony Estcott. It was apparently a struggling concern at the time, and Brading was felt to have the kind of qualities needed to revive it.'

'I can imagine,' said Walter. 'Rigid discipline and very little attention to the boys' actual needs. Did it succeed?'

'Seems to have done. At least, he was there for ten years. Surely they would have booted him out if he hadn't brought the school around.'

'Ten years.' I was doing arithmetic in my head. 'So he left there in the nineties sometime. Is the school still flourishing?'

'Don't know,' said Alan. 'I'll find out. Should

be an easy search on the Internet.' He made a note and then continued. 'He left the school upon receiving a call to be rector at St John's, in Upper Longwood. That's a fair-sized church in Oxfordshire, so this time it was definitely a step up. His stipend was just about doubled, and he had a good congregation. In time he hired a curate of his own, so things plainly went well for him there.'

'Wife must have been pleased,' commented Jane.

'We have no information about that,' said Alan with a grin, 'but I imagine you'll find out. At any rate, that post was beginning to look like the church where he would live out his days, until the call came from Chelton Cathedral. His wife was, in fact, pleased about that, Jane, or it seems that way. There's an article here from the *Church Times* about the appointment, with a picture of the new dean and his wife, and Mrs Brading is beaming.'

'And that was how long ago?' I asked.

'Just on three years.'

'And we know there are plenty of people there willing to talk about him, both pro and con.'

'Indeed. Now, who would like to take on his early ministry at Godwick?'

'I will, if no one else wants it,' said Jonathan. 'I do have some training in detection, and it's far enough back that I may have to really dig.'

'And I'll do the school,' Walter offered. 'I'm near enough to my own school days to make me fairly comfortable there. Though I certainly never went to a prep school; I'm a child of state schools.'

229

'Okay, then, let's switch,' said Jonathan. 'I did go to a public school, from the age of twelve. Hated it, but there you are. Not exactly a prep school – wrong ages – but close enough.'

'That sounds good. Not that I have any training in detection,' Walter said with a grin, 'but I am trained in research, and this sounds like a job for a good researcher.'

'That's done, then. Now, there are two assignments left, and three people to cover them.'

'Odd man out,' said Jane. 'Call me when you hit a snag, or need a follow-up. Put my network in play.'

'That's brilliant, Jane!' I exclaimed. 'Our central research station. As for me, I'd just as soon go back to Chelton, if you're happy with Upper Longwood, Alan.'

'Hmm.' That irritating noise he makes that can mean anything. This time I was pretty sure it was another 'We'll hash this out later'. The poor man does try to fall in with my fierce independence, but he's an Englishman, trained to chivalry, and at moments like these it comes out in spots, like a measles rash.

All he actually said was, 'Right. Now there's the question of expense. I'm afraid the diocese doesn't have the funds to send us all chasing what may well be a wild goose, but I—'

Jonathan raised a hand. 'Stop. I know what you're going to say. I can afford to finance my travels, and Walter's, and Jane's phone bill if necessary. You two are on your own.'

There was the usual bickering over that, but in the end Jonathan won out.

230

That seemed to wrap up the evening. It was still early, but we were all tired, and we wanted to get an early start in the morning. So Jane gathered up the leftovers of the food she had brought, and Jonathan and Walter were about to go up to bed, when I had a sudden thought. 'Wait!'

They all turned to look at me. 'We've forgotten three important people: the other candidates.'

'Two,' said Alan gently. 'Don't forget Lovelace is dead.'

'And why does that make him innocent of Brading's murder?'

Twenty-Two

Alan smacked his head. 'Idiot! You'd better put me out to pasture, Dorothy. I'm getting senile. How could I have overlooked Lovelace?'

'We all did. And besides, we've been exploring the possibility that Lovelace was murdered himself. Look, why don't you get drinks for anyone who wants them, and we can hash it out. The night is yet young.'

'But, like me, getting older by the moment.' Alan shook his head and sighed. 'Orders, everyone?'

I didn't have to tell him I wanted bourbon. The two young men opted for beer, and Jane allowed as how she wouldn't mind a tot of whisky.

231

When everyone was content, Alan sat down and opened his notebook again. 'First, does anyone have a case to make against either Dean Smith or Mr Robinson?'

Silence.

'You and I have met them both, Alan. And I have to say I absolutely can't see either of them as a murderer. They're devoted priests, and beloved of their congregations.'

'You will remember, my love, that apparently delightful people have murdered in the past, and will again.'

'I know that. But if personal attributes mean anything at all, those two aren't murderers. Anyway, the police will have checked them out pretty thoroughly, as to alibis and so on. I don't think there's much for us to do there. Lovelace, on the other hand . . .'

'The police will have interviewed him, also. If you remember, he told us they had done, when we talked to him.'

'Vaguely. But that was before he died. The police are calling that a suicide, and are, I suppose, putting it down to his guilt over his thefts. But don't you see? If it was suicide, he could just as easily be suffering the guilt of murder.'

'If it *was* suicide.'

'Yes. Alan, can you get hold of the police report on Lovelace? Both of them, I mean – before and after his death.'

Alan shook his head dubiously. 'That's the Met, Dorothy. I'm not at all sure . . .'

'I might be able to get the Met report on his

232

death,' said Jonathan. 'No promises, but I still have a good many friends at the Yard.'

'And do you think, Alan,' I pursued, 'that Derek could get you the earlier one? We are, after all, talking about a crime, or series of crimes, that directly affects Sherebury and the Cathedral.'

'I can ask. No promises.'

'What's your idea, Dorothy?' asked Walter.

I paused a moment to formulate it clearly. 'It begins with Lovelace's ambition, and his vanity. He was so sure he was the right man for this job, and that it would be the stepping stone to Canterbury. Suppose he decided that his most formidable competitor was Dean Brading.'

'Why?'

'I don't know, Jane. That's the kind of thing you're good at, working out how people's minds work. Maybe Lovelace was worried because Brading was so much of a steam-roller. He might have rolled right over the commission, just by the sheer force of his convictions. Oh!'

Everyone looked at me.

'Wait a minute, wait a minute. It's coming – yes! What if Brading really did have a meeting in London that day? A meeting with Lovelace! And Lovelace became more and more afraid that Brading would get the appointment, and so he followed him home and killed him!'

Objections came from all over the room, and they all apologized and let someone else go first. Alan won the round. 'Dorothy, you forget that the police checked all the candidates' movements that day. I haven't seen the reports, but I understand that they all had sound alibis.'

'Of course they did. But who gave Lovelace his alibi?'

'I don't know. I may be able to find out.'

'Because, if it was that secretary of his—'

'Mrs Steele,' said Walter. 'And she would lie her head off for him. Would have, I mean. She thought he walked on water. If he said he was at the church all that day, she would have agreed.'

'Did he have a family? Wife, children?' asked Jonathan.

'That I can tell you.' He pulled out the dossiers and glanced through Lovelace's. 'No. He lived alone in a flat in Chelsea.'

'Long way from his parish,' said Jane with a sniff.

'Also a long stretch above the income level of the average parish priest,' said Jonathan. 'So we can guess where part of his embezzled funds went.'

'This is all the purest speculation,' said Alan with some impatience. 'It's an interesting theory, but there's not a scrap of evidence to back it up.'

'Then why don't we try to find some!' I was getting impatient, too.

Again protests. This time Jonathan's came to the fore. 'Dorothy, if our murderer does turn out to be Lovelace, there's really no hurry about finding evidence. He can't be prosecuted, at least not by any court we could summon. He's not going anywhere. If he didn't do the deed, though, someone else did, and that person is presumably still alive and free. It seems to me that it would be best to follow up on Brading's background, as we've planned, and see if that leads us in any interesting direction.'

'Good sense.' Jane's concurrence was echoed by everyone else, and I retired, defeated.

'Okay, okay. I thought it was such a brilliant idea, but you're right. Other investigations come first.' But I was still enamoured of my idea, and resolved privately to do anything I could to follow it up.

Not now, though. A mighty yawn broke through, despite my efforts to suppress it. 'Sorry,' I said. 'I guess I'm too sleepy to think straight.'

'We all are, love. Time for bed.'

At the magic word, Watson stood, shook himself vigorously, and headed up the stairs ahead of us.

Alan waited until morning to deliver himself of what he'd been pining to say to me for hours. I had barely returned from the shower before he started in. 'Dorothy, I don't like it.'

'You don't like it that I'm going back to Chelton, where a murderer may be running loose, maybe even a double-murderer – I mean, someone who's killed twice. You'd much rather I stayed home and helped Jane with her phone calls, or, alternatively, let you go to Chelton where the greatest danger may be, while I go to Upper Longwood. You see, I know how you think.'

I started to dress. He sat down on the bed. 'Do you really mind so much that I want you to be safe?'

I sat down next to him. 'I love it that you want me to be safe. I love being cared for and cherished. And I love you. It's just that I want – I *need* – to make my own decisions. I'm old enough to know a thing or two, and smart enough to assess dangers.'

'I grant you all that. You are intelligent and you do have good judgement. Most of the time. But you sometimes get swept away by impulse, and then your judgement may fail you badly. It is that fear that I carry with me, every time you go off on your own tangent.'

He took my hand. 'Dorothy, I don't want to lose you. And you're so fearless, so sure of your own ability to get yourself out of a dicey situation . . . I don't want to limit your freedom, but I do so want to keep you safe.'

'I know. And I understand. But . . .'

We sat there for a moment or two, at an impasse. Finally I spoke. 'Alan, it must surely have been like this when your daughter was growing up. Frank and I never had children, so I don't know for myself, but there must have come a time when Elizabeth's need to cut the apron strings conflicted with your and Helen's need to protect her. How did you resolve that?'

He thought for what seemed a long time. 'It wasn't a question of one time, a clean dividing line between childhood and adulthood. The decision came every time she wanted to do something new. An overnight at a friend's house. A journey out of town with a friend's family, and later, alone. Dating. University. Marriage. Every time it was as if my heart was being torn in two. I knew we had to let her grow up, and I rejoiced in her growing self-confidence, but I knew how dangerous the world could be, and part of me – part of us – wanted to keep her in cotton wool for ever.'

'And how did you resolve the impasse?'

'We talked it out, the three of us. We explained our doubts and fears, and she explained the reasons she wanted to do whatever it was, and we came to an agreement, negotiated limitations. Where she had to be, when she had to be home, that sort of thing. Everything was a compromise, and I remember many a sleepless night wondering if we'd done the right thing, if she were all right.'

'But obviously it worked. She stayed safe, she grew up to be a responsible, sensible adult, and, from what I've seen, she's raising her own children along similar lines. So, Alan, let's do the same. Let's talk this over like two rational adults and work out what compromises we can both accept.'

It was, I knew, a vital moment in our marriage. We'd had this discussion before, often, but we'd never resolved the issue. Now we'd reached a point when it had to be resolved.

'Well.' He ran a hand down the back of his head. 'For a start, I'd like to know where you are, all the time.'

'I'm not sure that's practical. I'll be going to various places: people's homes, the church, who knows where. It wouldn't always be convenient, or courteous, to pull out my phone in each place. Suppose I call you, say, twice a day, and tell you where I plan to go and approximately when.'

'And if I feel that's a place where you will face great danger, and I ask you not to go?'

'Then we'll talk it out, and if in the end you're really disturbed by what I plan to do, I won't do it.'

'Or I might ask you to take someone with you, someone we both trust.'

'I don't know how many people we know and trust in Chelton and environs, but if we can come up with someone, I can't imagine that would be a problem. And how about this? We could set a time for the calls. Then if I don't call at the prescribed time, you could push the panic button and start trying to find me.'

'I devoutly hope that doesn't happen.'

'Me, too. But it would be a sort of alarm system. Only, it works both ways. If I call and you don't answer, then I start trying to move heaven and earth to find you.'

'Dorothy, really! I can take care of myself!'

'Gotcha!'

He stared at me.

'I wanted you to know how it felt, this protectiveness. Irritating, isn't it?'

He simply sat there for a moment, and then he began to laugh. His laugh is irresistible. I joined in. He clasped me in a bear hug, I kissed him, and . . . we were a bit late for breakfast.

There was a flurry of travel arrangements to be made after we'd eaten a hasty meal. I booked the same B and B where we'd stayed before; the others decided to take their chances. Alan was going to take our car to Upper Longwood, since I'm still not entirely at ease driving in England, and the train service to Chelton was fairly good. Jonathan and Walter were both headed back to London to pack what they would need for perhaps a week, then Jonathan would drive to the school at Stony Estcott. Jonathan supplied funds to Walter so he could rent a car to Godwick, a village with no train service at all. He was reluctant to take the money.

'I do have some money, you know. And there's no reason you should pay for this, when it's something the police should be doing.'

'But they don't seem to be getting very far,' I put in. 'Remember, we agreed we could do it better anyway, just because we're not the police, and people will be more willing to talk to us. And you must save your money. You're going to be married soon, and you'll need it.' I gave him a friendly pat.

'We're both going to have good jobs.'

'Ah, but wait until you have a family,' said Alan. 'Then Sue may well want to stay home with the baby, and trust me, my boy, children eat up money faster than they grow. You need to save every penny you can just now.'

'You can pay me later if you insist,' said Jonathan. 'And I want an accounting, mind!'

As soon as they were both gone, I packed rapidly for both of us and said goodbye to Sam and Emmy and Watson. They had all known what was happening as soon as they saw the suitcases come out, and Watson was terribly disappointed when we told him he couldn't come this time.

'You'll be spoiled by Jane,' I told him. He whined mournfully.

Then we both hopped in the car, Alan drove me to the station, and I kissed him goodbye. 'Alan, don't worry about me. I'll be fine. I'm going to an English cathedral city, for Pete's sake.'

'Where a man was killed. Of course I'll worry, but I'll try to keep it in reasonable bounds. And you'll call me . . . when?'

'Better make it three. I should be there and settled by then, and have some idea of my plan of action. But I'll call you, even if the trains are dreadful and I'm still in Upper Podunk.'

We kissed again, and then he was gone and I climbed aboard my train.

I seldom travel alone, and I'd forgotten how much I depended on Alan to make the process go smoothly. He it is who always buys the tickets, manages the luggage, finds the taxi stand, knows which station the next train leaves from – all the bothersome details. Fortunately, the guard on my train to London was very helpful about train schedules, and told me I needed to go from Victoria Station to Paddington. He told me where to find a taxi, too, and though I know Victoria well enough to remember that part, I thanked him for his kindness. While I was dithering over whether to give him a tip, he was gone. That, too, is the kind of thing Alan manages when we travel. Without him, I began to feel very much like an ignorant American.

I coped, however, and it wasn't until the stop just before Chelton that I began to wonder how

I was going to get to the B and B. It was at the very edge of town, much too far to walk, especially with luggage. Alan and I had both forgotten that detail when we made our hasty plans.

I sighed, gathered up my luggage, and stepped down on to the platform at Chelton.

One of the delightful things about England that I had forgotten since I married Alan was the extent to which strangers can be helpful. I must have looked as I felt – a bit stranded – because a young man who had got off the train with me asked if he could help.

'I've done a stupid thing,' I told him. 'Booked a B and B on the edge of town, with no car to get there. Would there be a taxi, do you think?'

'Where is it you're going?'

'The house is called Lynncroft.'

'Oh, Mrs Stevens. If you'd like, I can drive you there. But how are you going to get about, once you're there?'

'Well, I hadn't thought about that, either, to tell the truth. I'm afraid I'm sadly disorganized.'

'You're American, aren't you?'

I admitted it.

'Do you drive over here?'

'Actually, I've lived in England for several years, and yes, I can drive on the left. I don't enjoy it on the motorways, though, and roundabouts terrify me.'

My new friend laughed. 'My wife doesn't like motorways, either. Look, would you like to hire a car? I can take you to a hire garage.'

I sighed. 'Thank you. I really do hate to impose . . .'

'No imposition. I'm just through here, in the car park.'

He cheerfully picked up my bags, stowed them in the boot of his very small car, and held the door for me while I shoehorned myself into the front seat.

'My name's Simon, by the way, Simon Grey.' He shot out of the car park with an insouciance that took my breath away. When I'd regained it, I said, 'Dorothy Martin. I live in Sherebury.'

'Long way from home, aren't you? What brings you to Chelton?'

I didn't have my cover story worked out yet, and I panicked for a moment. I could hardly tell him I was looking for a murderer. Maybe part of the truth?

I coughed. 'Sorry. Frog in my throat. It has to do with the cathedral. We . . . I wanted to learn a bit more about the late dean. Sherebury is a cathedral city, too, of course, but our Cathedral is also a parish church, and we want to have a piece about Dean Brading in the parish magazine. No one in Sherebury seems to know much about him, and I used to do a little writing, so I've come to talk to people about him.' My fingers were crossed, but it wasn't actually a lie. There would certainly be something about his death in the next parish magazine, and I've written lists all my life, and lesson plans back when I was teaching.

Simon frowned. 'I don't know that anyone knew him very well here, either. I'm not a church-goer, but he seemed a chilly sort of chap, the few times I saw him. Speeches, dedications, that kind

242

of thing. I don't mean to be rude about clergy, but, honestly, he was a sanctimonious bloke. Wasn't he . . . do I remember reading that he was going to be the next bishop in – yes! In Sherebury! How did you come to pick him?'

'He wasn't the final choice. That is, he was one of the four on the shortlist, but the Appointments Commission was due to meet after various interviews and so on, to narrow the list down to two. It's a complicated process, appointing a new bishop.'

'Well, *de mortuis* and all that, but I think you've had a lucky escape.'

'I'm beginning to think so, too.'

Twenty-Three

I had mapped out a plan of action, and as soon as I was settled at Lynncroft, and had called Alan to reassure him that I was alive and well, I got back in the car and headed for the cathedral. I looked first for a café where I could get myself some lunch, and found one not far from a car park. I was hungry enough to eat the limp prawn salad (three prawns of a size that in America would have been called 'shrimp') and even the apple tart tasting mostly of cardboard, which apparently comprised the crust. I wondered fleetingly if any establishment in this town served edible food, but forgot about it as I walked back to the cathedral.

My goal was the office. It was in a building adjacent to the church itself, and was staffed by a business-like middle-aged woman and a young assistant.

I had my story straight now. I introduced myself to the woman in charge and said, 'I asked a guest to tea the last time my husband and I were in Chelton, but we had to leave for an emergency that came up suddenly. Unfortunately, I've lost her phone number, but she's one of your parishioners, and I'd really like to get in touch with her, since I'm in town for a few days. Would you have a number for Mrs Rudge? I'm sorry, I don't know her first name.'

I had summoned up the most American accent I could manage. I've found that the accent often causes people to decide I'm none too bright, and therefore not a threat. Mrs Strictly Business said, 'Well, we don't usually supply phone numbers unless we know the person requesting them, but in this case . . .' She went to her computer, punched a few keys, wrote something on a piece of paper, and handed it to me. 'Here you are. Is there anything else I can help you with?'

There are friendly ways of saying that, and then there is the tone of voice that makes it less a question than a clear message: 'Please leave.'

I thanked her profusely and obeyed.

On impulse, instead of going back to my car, I walked over to the church. Most English cathedrals, and other big churches, are open every day. Without a dean, though, I wasn't sure if this one would be.

I was in luck. I slipped in through the south

porch and walked around a bit. The cathedral was full of nooks and crannies. I explored every inch of it, hearing my own footsteps echo off the stone floor. Nave. Aisles. Chancel. Choir stalls. Organ and surroundings. Vestry. Side chapels.

There was not another living soul in the church, unless one counted a spider that scuttled away when I approached a window. (And a good thing it did, for both our sakes.)

As soon as I got back to Lynncroft, I hunted up Mrs Stevens. She was in the kitchen.

'Mrs Stevens, I need some advice. I want to take a new friend to tea, someone I met when I was here before, but I don't know where to go. I've been in a couple of cafés in town, and they were both pretty dire.'

'Have her come here, of course! Unless you'd rather go to a tea room, but I don't know one I could recommend for a really slap-up tea, except the Chelton Arms, and it's quite pricey.'

'Oh, I was hoping you'd say that! If it's a bother, though—'

'Nonsense. I love cooking for people, and, as it happens, I've a cake I made just because I wanted to, so if that and sandwiches will do – oh, and scones, of course – I've still some strawberry jam left from last year—'

I held up a hand and laughed. 'That sounds like the best tea I could possibly imagine. I'll phone Mrs Rudge and ask—'

'Oh, Martha Rudge, is it? Well, then, I'll make some éclairs as well. Very fond of my éclairs, is Martha. What time did you want it, dear?'

245

'I'll ask her what might be convenient. Would four thirty suit you if it's all right with her?'

We agreed, and Mrs Rudge, when I reached her, was delighted, so I went back to the kitchen. 'Four thirty will be fine, Mrs Stevens, and I do hope you'll join us, especially since you seem to know Mrs Rudge well.'

'That'll be lovely, dear. Now, I'd best get to work on those éclairs.'

I left her to get on with it, and went up to my room to ponder several ideas. I lay down to do it, so nature took its course, and when I woke it was a quarter past four. I jumped up, tidied my hair, and got downstairs as fast as two titanium knees would allow. Mrs Rudge was ringing the bell.

'Answer it, would you, dear?' Mrs Stevens called from the kitchen. 'I'm just wetting the tea.'

Mrs Rudge, I was embarrassed to see, was dressed rather more nicely than I, in dressy pants, a light blue pullover that looked like cashmere, and pearls. 'I apologize,' I said as I let her in and gestured to my jeans and sweatshirt. New jeans and an attractive sweatshirt, but still. 'I'm afraid I dozed off this afternoon and didn't have time to change out of my travel clothes.'

'Not to worry,' said Mrs Rudge comfortably, and softly. 'I dressed up a bit because Ruth always takes notice of my clothes. You wait and see what she says.'

Sure enough, when Mrs Stevens came in with the tea tray, the first thing she said was, 'New

246

jumper, I see, Martha. That's a nice colour for you. A bit young, though, perhaps, don't you think?'

'I've always liked pastels,' said Mrs Rudge calmly. 'And you've made éclairs for me. How kind of you!'

'I remembered you liked them. The sandwiches are cheese, cucumber, and ham.'

And then for a while the only conversation was about the food. I was truly hungry after my miserable lunch and ate far more than I should have.

I was polishing off a second éclair when Mrs Rudge said, 'I suppose you're looking into Dean Brading's death.'

My full mouth gave me a good excuse for not replying immediately.

She went on. 'I know who you are, you see. Or at least I know who your husband is, and I've heard about you.'

'That sounds ominous,' I said tentatively.

'My cousin lives in Belleshire, or did. She's moved to Bournemouth, which I wouldn't touch with a bargepole, but she's happy there. Likes the climate, I suppose. But Mr Nesbitt was the chief constable when she was there, and she says he was held in very high regard.'

'Mr Nesbitt is a policeman?' asked Mrs Stevens, her voice almost squeaking.

'Not anymore. He's been retired for several years now.' I had finally recovered my wits. 'And yes, he and I are trying to make sense of Dean Brading's death, but not from the police point of view. Alan is a member of the Crown

247

Appointments Commission, searching for a new Bishop of Sherebury. He is deeply distressed by the death of one of the candidates, as are we all.'

'And my cousin has heard about you, too,' Mrs Rudge went on. 'You've been mixed up in murders.'

Mrs Stevens' eyes grew even wider.

'I have indeed. Only as an investigator, I hasten to say. It turns out I'm good at talking to people and putting two and two together, and that's why I'm here, to help Alan understand why Dean Brading died. Now, Mrs Stevens, if you'd rather I found another place to stay, I'll quite understand. I love your house and I'd be sorry to leave, but if you think I'm . . . I don't know . . . a dangerous guest, or apt to steal the towels, or something, I'll go.'

It hung in the balance for a moment, then my hostess sighed. 'No. I took to you and your husband when I first saw you, and I fancy myself a good judge of people. Goodness knows I've seen enough of them in and out of my house these past few years. And though I was no friend of the dean, if a parson can be murdered in his own church, nobody's safe. Whoever did it needs to be caught. Stay as long as you like, Mrs Martin.'

'That's very good of you, Mrs Stevens. But I do wish you'd call me Dorothy.'

'And we're Ruth and Martha,' said Mrs Rudge. 'We may be old, but we're not old trouts. And I'll have another piece of cake, Ruth, if you wouldn't mind.'

That cleared the air, and my conscience as well. I don't like lying, even though I can do it fluently when necessary. And I had begun to think of these women as friends. When Ruth had poured me another cup of tea, and I had reluctantly turned down another piece of cake, I got down to business. 'We have decided,' I said, 'those of us who are trying to figure out this business of Dean Brading, we've decided that we need to know as much as possible about his background. My husband and a few friends are looking into other places where he lived and worked, and I chose to come here. I wish you two would tell me anything you can remember about him. Not just things that might bear on his death, I don't mean, but any little tidbits you can think of.'

I hesitated for a moment and then plunged ahead. 'You see, I've read a lot of mystery fiction in a long life, starting years ago with Agatha Christie and Dorothy Sayers, and right on into P. D. James and the other contemporary writers. And though their books are fiction, they have a lot of wise insights into human psychology and behaviour. One thing that Hercule Poirot used to say strikes me as profoundly true, and that is that the secret of a murder lies in the character and personality of the victim. Not a street crime, not the drug addict who kills anyone he can find for money. That sort of thing is brutal and horrible, but there's nothing mysterious about it, and the police usually track down the villain in a matter of hours.

'A crime like this, though, directed against a

particular person, for reasons unknown – in this kind of crime, the more you know about the victim, the more likely you are to understand the murderer. And that makes it easier to find him, or her. So tell me what you can, and, as Lord Peter Wimsey said on one occasion, forget all about Christian charity for the moment.'

That brought a laugh from both of them. 'Well,' said Ruth, 'I hope I won't offend you, Martha. I know he was your vicar and all, but I personally couldn't abide the man. This isn't all that big a place, you know, and I keep my ear to the ground, and I could tell you a thing or two about Andrew Brading.'

'I wish you would,' I said. 'Gossip, rumour – you never know what may help.'

Martha looked a little shocked, but sat back to listen critically.

'You know he had a wife.'

It wasn't a question, but I nodded. 'And no children, I believe?'

'He didn't like children. I've heard there were almost no young people going to the cathedral anymore, because the feeling was that children were definitely not welcome at services.'

'I'm afraid that's true,' said Martha reluctantly. 'I've been attending the cathedral nearly all my life, and there were quite a number of young people years ago, before Dean Brading came. There were children's sermons now and again, and outings for them, and even a youth choir of children from the community. But Dean Brading has – *had* – a very different style. He wanted the services to be quiet and reverent, with everything just so. It upset him when children made noise, and do what you will, babies *will* cry, and toddlers *will* get restless. Of course, he didn't take all the services, and some of the canons were more tolerant, but one was never quite sure when the dean would be officiating, so the young couples stopped attending. I thought it a great pity, though there were those who agreed with the dean about the disruptions.'

I nodded. 'When we were here before, I said some things I probably shouldn't have about attendance dropping off. It sounds as though I might have been right about that, though.'

'It's true enough, but I don't know that you can lay that at the feet of the dean. There aren't nearly as many people going to church these days as when I was a girl.'

'It was the war,' said Ruth. 'When bombs were falling everywhere and everyone thought they might meet their Maker any minute, they took care to be on good terms with Him. Not that I remember the war, mind you, but my mum told me about the air raids and all, and the younger kids from London being billeted with country families. And even afterwards, there was so little food. One can understand why most people went to church then. They had to find hope somewhere. Nowadays we have it too easy. We don't need religion anymore.'

I disagreed with that, but I kept my peace. We had established a rather fragile pact of understanding, and I didn't want to shatter it.

Martha spoke up, though. 'Oh, you know I

251

can't agree, Ruth. It isn't just the hope and peace you can find at church, the rituals and the sermons and that – it's the community. The church used to be the centre of community life. Now the centre, if we have one, is – I don't know – the shopping mall, I suppose. And I think we've lost something.'

We were getting off the track. 'It seemed to me, when I visited, that the cathedral community was rather fragile, with some large cracks in it. Was I wrong?'

Ruth cackled. 'You've been talking to Archie Pringle!'

I nearly choked on a sip of tea. 'Archie?' I asked when I could speak again.

'Oh, he never uses it,' said Ruth, filling my cup with hot tea. 'I'll stake a fiver his wife calls him Colonel. I call him Archie whenever we run into each other, just to watch that ramrod back get even stiffer.'

Martha smiled tolerantly. 'He does look like a caricature, doesn't he? And acts like one, too, at times. But there's good in Archie. He truly loves the cathedral and its traditions, and tries to preserve them against a rising tide of change.'

'I take it he was a strong supporter of Dean Brading,' I said, trying to steer the conversation back toward my goals.

'The strongest, at least at first. He's quite well off, and he's donated a good bit to the cathedral.'

'Pots of it,' said Ruth. 'Archie's problem is that he's stuck in the nineteenth century, if not the one before that. And Martha won't tell you, because she's so good-natured she'd see the good in the devil himself, but Archie Pringle is the main reason the cathedral is dying. He can't – or won't – see that his way is not everybody's way. He agreed with Dean Brading in every detail, and that's just not the way a church can function in this day and age.'

'Now, Ruth.' Martha's voice was verging on annoyed. 'You haven't been to church in years, dear. Archie has changed. He truly loves the cathedral. In any case, I'm not sure you know what should and shouldn't be done there.'

'What you really mean is that I've no right to set myself up as judge. And you're right, but you've forgotten that I know quite a few people, and I've heard quite a lot of talk from people who've left the cathedral because they couldn't abide the dean.'

'Why not?' I got in before Martha could protest.

'In a word, he was stuffy. Oh, there are quite a few more words. Self-righteous, domineering, stern, unforgiving – but stuffy sums it up.'

'Was there any attempt to have him – gosh, I don't know the word. Impeached? Deposed?'

'He was neither an American president nor a monarch,' said Ruth tartly. 'I suppose the dean of a cathedral can be removed, but I have no idea how.'

'I read about that the other day,' said Martha. 'With all the problems the Church has been having lately, there's been discussion of it in the news, and someone wrote that the only way to remove a cathedral dean is to find him legally

253

guilty of immorality. And say what you will about Dean Brading, no one could ever have imagined him immoral.'

That disappointed me, of course. 'His relationship with his wife was good, then? You said they had no children.'

'There was never any talk about them,' said Ruth, almost reluctantly, I thought.

'She came to church every Sunday,' said Martha. 'Sat in a front pew, so I never saw her face, at least not during the service.'

'Did you gain any impression of her? As a regular attendee at the cathedral, you must have chatted with her from time to time.'

'She isn't the chatty sort, and even before the dean's death, the gatherings after church were sparse. I don't think I've ever exchanged more than a few words with her. She is . . . very correct.'

Sounds as cold and forbidding as her husband, I thought. Didn't spoil two couples, my mother would have said. I changed tack. 'Do you have any idea of how the dean felt about being considered for our diocese?'

'I never spoke to him after he was shortlisted, but he knew he was being considered, of course, and I got the impression, from some things he said in sermons, that he liked the idea. He thought he could bring Sherebury back to its traditions, its foundations, and do away with what he considered popish practices.' She made a little face, and her hands seemed to disavow the dean's sentiments.

'That, of course, would have been one way to

get him out of Chelton,' said Ruth. 'Kick him upstairs.'

'There was another way,' I said. The remark lay amongst the tea things like a stone.

Twenty-Four

I accompanied Martha Rudge to the door as she was leaving. Ruth was dealing with the tea tray, and Martha said in a low voice, 'There are some things I didn't want to talk about in front of Ruth. It doesn't do to air dirty church linen in front of a non-believer. Are you staying long in Chelton?'

'A few days.'

'Then could you come to lunch tomorrow? I live quite near the cathedral.'

'I'd love to,' I said, and meant it. I hadn't yet gathered nearly enough information. We agreed that she'd ring me near noon.

I made a brief foray to a nearby Sainsbury's, one of the small ones, and laid in a supply of cheese and biscuits and fruit, and, after a quick call to Alan, spent the rest of the afternoon and evening in my room, making lists.

Alan may laugh at me, but lists can be a big help, even without counting the feeling of accomplishment derived from simply having made one. They do force me to organize my thoughts, and that leads to organizing my actions.

I had brought my notes from our discussion back at home, and started from there.

'Suspects.' Well, I had learned that Brading's wife was apparently on good terms with her husband. I left her on the list anyway. Appearances can be deceiving, and I intended to pump Martha a little more on the subject of possible infidelity on the part of one party or the other. Other relatives, if any, also needed to be discussed, and certainly I wanted to know a lot more about the congregation. I wasn't ready to cross the Colonel off the list yet, either. If he truly loved the cathedral, and Brading was damaging the cathedral, might he have thought Brading should go? And there might be, among the former congregants, some who hated Brading enough to kill him.

So that list read: Mrs Brading, Other Family, Former Congregants, and Archie Pringle. I thought of Archie Bunker, and snickered. Actually, with his extreme conservatism and outmoded ideas, the Colonel was not unlike his namesake. How he would hate the comparison!

The next list, 'Facts about the Murder', had been filled in fairly well at our discussion. I didn't yet know exactly where the body had been found, though, and surely Martha could tell me. Could show me, perhaps, if the cathedral was still open. That was another thing I needed to know, come to think of it. Had it been open all day, every day, when the dean was alive? If so, the murderer might have been lying in wait for his or her victim. If not, then it was quite possible that the dean let him or her in, which implied that he knew his killer or, at the least, found the person non-threatening.

Now. 'Facts about Brading'. I thought I might

be able to scrap the idea of an affair. If neither Ruth nor Martha had heard even a hint of such a thing, and if they were as good at gossip as dear Jane, then there had been no affair. Drat. Sexual jealousy is such a powerful motive. But there are other sorts of jealousy. Any time anyone covets something possessed by someone else, there's jealousy and a motive to violence. God got it right, I thought irrelevantly (and probably irreverently), when he gave Moses only the ten forbidden actions. Those ten led to all the others.

So, what are some of the other motives created by jealousy? A lust for power was certainly one. That led directly to the other candidates for our mitre. There was no doubt that Lovelace had lusted for power. I wanted to explore that much further. There might, of course, be someone at Chelton Cathedral – one of the canons – who wanted Brading's job. If he was afraid Brading wouldn't be named as Sherebury's bishop, then might he have taken the other way to make sure the dean needed to be replaced? I made a note: who wanted to be dean of Chelton? Or, as a corollary, who dearly loved someone who wanted to be the dean? Love has prompted murder before now, and not always from the sex angle.

I mentally went through the other deadly sins. Greed seemed an unlikely motive. The clergy aren't at all well paid. Although some of the bishops do get to live in gorgeous historic palaces, and the deans in ancient deaneries, I couldn't imagine that anyone would kill to occupy such inconvenient homes. Gorgeous they may be, but the plumbing is frantically unreliable.

The Archbishop of Canterbury, on the other hand, is paid reasonably well. And, of course, that was what Lovelace was aiming for. His motives were becoming stronger and stronger.

Pride. Well, that was at the root of all evil, wasn't it? I couldn't see how it applied specifically to this case, though, except in relation to ambition.

Sloth was a terrible burden, but a lazy person doesn't often hit someone on the head. Too much trouble. Anger, though . . . there was a real killer. I groaned over my mental pun. Who was so angry with Brading, who hated him so much as to incite murder? Had he done something frightful to one of the cathedral staff or congregation, or someone in his family, something perceived as unforgiveable?

I made copious notes, and then looked at what I'd written. There was plenty of food for thought there, but my instinct told me that anger and/or hatred was the most likely motive. It fit the crime. A cold-blooded murderer plans a crime. An intelligent one plans it so well that he may never get caught. It's the man or woman in the grip of sudden uncontrollable rage who hits someone over the head in a place where the victim is bound to be found, where traces of the murderer's presence will lead to certain conviction.

But only, I reminded myself with a sigh, if the person matching those traces can be identified.

I made myself a last cup of tea and went to
bed.

I went down to breakfast with no very clear idea
of what I would do with my morning. There
were so many possible avenues to explore that
I hardly knew where to begin, and I kept
reminding myself that my time was not
unlimited.

Ruth brought in my breakfast, enough choles-
terol to keep my arteries clogged for the rest of
my (shortened) life. It was delicious. I ate every
bite and was just wondering if there was more
coffee when Ruth came in with a fresh cafetière.
'You'll want to let it steep for a minute or two,
dear. I just put in the water. And would you
mind if I shared a cup with you?'

'I'd love it,' I said, and mused about the odd
situation a B and B hostess finds herself in. An
employee of sorts in her own house, asking
permission of her guests to sit down in her own
dining room.

'There! I knew you weren't the haughty sort.'
She pulled out a chair. 'The fact is, I wanted to
talk to you for a bit. I didn't like to say so in
front of Martha, but that Dean Brading was Not
Liked in Chelton.'

I could hear the capital letters, and inwardly
I rejoiced. This was *just* what I needed. Aloud,
I said, 'Really? Why not?'

'He put people's backs up. He was always
right, you see. Anyone who disagreed with him
was simply wrong, and he never minded telling
them so. Oh, he battled with everyone. He had

a run-in with the mayor over a car park. The mayor wanted to tear down that frightful youth centre, which hasn't been used in donkey's years except for a handful of people on Sunday morning. He was going to build a car park for churchgoers to use on Sundays, and shoppers on weekdays. He was prepared to find the money for it, and he thought the dean would be delighted. I think that coffee's ready now, dear. Would you like me to pour it out?'

I shoved my cup over. 'I'd have thought that was a wonderful idea. The parking around the cathedral is pretty sparse, as far as I could see, and you're right: the youth centre is a sinfully ugly building. The dean didn't like the mayor's proposal?'

'Tore a strip off the mayor. The building was church property and could not be touched. Car parks were a work of the devil. People should walk to church. I think his father and grandfather came into it, walking at the head of a long file, coming piously to worship, heeding the bells calling them to God.'

'I thought he didn't approve of bells.'

'Only those in days of yore. The demonic practice of change-ringing had turned the simple call to prayer into an entertainment, you see.'

'Whew! Then there was no love lost between him and the mayor.'

Ruth grinned. 'Actually, he viewed the mayor as an enemy from then on, but it did the mayor a lot of good politically. The youth centre is a blight on the city centre, and the extra parking on weekdays would have been a boon to merchants. So the dean turned much of the city against him from that moment.'

'Ruth, you're not a churchgoer. How did you hear all this?'

'From a woman you know. Or at least you've met her, when you and your husband went to church on your last visit here. Her name's Caroline White, and she says you asked her about coffee after the service.'

'Oh, yes, I do remember her.' I chuckled. 'She told us we wouldn't enjoy the gathering at the youth centre. She was quite right, as it turned out, although meeting Martha was a delight. I got the impression that Mrs . . . um –'

'White.'

'White, yes – that she wasn't a great fan of Dean Brading. Or of the present cathedral clergy, for that matter. Does she go to church as a matter of habit, or for fire insurance, or what?'

'Fire insurance?'

'What some of my irreverent American friends call it. Just in case that story about hell is true.'

Ruth laughed. 'I see. I'll have to remember that. No, I think she goes because she thinks it's the right thing to do. Not socially. She doesn't really care what people think. But she has a strong sense of right and wrong, and she thinks some form of worship is necessary. She's argued it with me many a time.'

'Do you know, I think I'd like a chance to meet her.'

'So she can tell you who really hated the dean?'

'Partly that, and partly . . . well, she just sounds like a person I'd like to know.'

'Nothing easier. I'll just clear away, and then I'll ring her up.'

'I'll help. This morning would be good for me, if it works for her,' I added, stacking my breakfast dishes.

'No, no, that's my job.'

'Look, Ruth. I'm still an American at heart. This distinction between hostess and guest – landlady and lodger if you will – just doesn't work with me. You've become a friend. Granted, a friend who happens to be sharing your home with me, and I'm paying you for the privilege because I'm not a sponger, but if you don't mind, I'll still act like a friend. Here, if you'll hand me the tray, the cafetière will fit, too.'

Ruth rolled her eyes but handed me the tray. 'You are the oddest guest I've ever had stay here.'

I grinned. 'And probably the most troublesome. Can you get the door?'

She flatly refused to let me help load the dishwasher. 'I despise the thing, but when the house is full it's a help, I suppose. It's the inspectors who say I must have one. I must say, I never poisoned any of my family when I was doing the washing-up in the sink, but . . .' She shrugged elaborately and continued loading the few plates and cups and cutlery. 'Now, you go and do whatever you need to do, and I'll come up as soon as I've talked to Caroline.'

I had barely washed my face and brushed my teeth when Ruth was knocking on my door with news that Mrs White would meet me at the cathedral at ten thirty. 'If that's not too soon.'

'That's perfect. Thank you, thank you. I'll be off, then.' I gave Ruth a hug as I headed down the stairs, calling Alan as I went to give him my morning's itinerary, such as it was.

I was early at the cathedral, but Mrs White was ahead of me. She came out of the shadows, looking at my hat, this time a modest pull-on affair. 'Knew I'd know you,' she said without preamble.

'I know. Nobody except the royals still wears hats. I like them.'

'Good for you. Do what you want. I always have. Do you want some coffee?' She gave me a sly smile.

'Not right now. I've had what a southern friend of mine used to call "a gracious plenty" this morning. But I'd be happy to buy you some if you know a place where it's drinkable.'

'Don't drink the stuff. Ruth Stevens tells me you want to know who killed the dean.'

I searched my mind frantically for some misleading response and decided it wasn't worth the effort, not with this forthright woman. 'Yes,' I said. 'Do you know?'

'No. But I have some ideas. This isn't the place to talk about it.'

'No. Too many echoes, and it seems wrong, anyway. But can you show me where he died?'

'Show you where they found him. Might not be the same, you know.'

'I do know. My husband is a retired chief constable.'

263

She made no reply, but led me up the north aisle, past tombs and memorials, some very elaborate, some very ugly. I spared a moment of pity for Dean Brading, who had not been able to strip his church of these offenses to his austere sensibilities.

A turn into the north transept took us to a very small chapel, screened off with a curtain and the usual sign saying it was reserved for private prayer. It was empty, so Mrs White and I were free to talk. She pointed to the altar rail, a simple marble affair of two railings, each set into the wall at the far end and supported by a short marble post in the middle, next to the opening that led to the altar. The posts were square in cross-section, like fence posts, and were topped by two squares of marble, a larger one resting on the post and a smaller one atop that. They had very sharp corners.

'Was that . . . ?' I whispered.

'They don't know. He was found lying on the kneeler, his head close to one of the posts. No blood on the post or the newels, but there wasn't much blood anywhere. A bit on the kneeler.'

There was no kneeling pad on the chilly marble now. Presumably they had taken it away for cleaning, or perhaps for replacement.

The atmosphere was oppressive, despite the chill of the place. I turned my head away, and Mrs White followed me out of the chapel. 'I think I could use that coffee after all,' I said.

The café was several grades above any Alan or I had found. Bright yellow curtains and tablecloths lent cheer, and the coffee was excellent. Mrs White had tea and a cream bun that looked both delicious and calorie-laden. The room was nearly full, and the gentle buzz of conversation gave us privacy at our corner table.

Nevertheless, I chose my words with care. 'You said you had some ideas,' I prompted.

'He was not a popular man,' said Mrs White. 'Lots of enemies. Don't know if any of them would have gone so far, but some might've. I made a list.'

She rummaged in her handbag and pulled out an old envelope, torn at the top. In tiny, cramped handwriting on the back were three paragraphs. Each seemed to be headed with a name, followed by a few words I couldn't decipher at all.

Mrs White watched me squinting and moving the envelope closer to my eyes. She snorted. 'I forgot Americans can never read English handwriting.'

By now I thought I had the measure of this woman. 'It's my belief no one on this earth could read this writing.' I said it with a smile, and, to my relief, she smiled back.

'A trifle small, perhaps. I thought of it just before I left home, and the only paper I could lay hands on right then was that envelope.'

'Can't you just tell me?'

Her eyes scanned the room. 'More discreet this way. Get Ruth Stevens to read it to you.'

'I will, and then I'll copy it. But could you at least give me a brief rundown? I'm not going to be in Chelton very long, and I want to check out these people.'

'Here. Give it back to me.' She took the envelope back, took a pen from her purse, and on the front of the envelope wrote three names in block capitals. 'The rest of what I wrote is just explanation,' she said as she handed it back to me.

The name that headed the list was Archibald Pringle.

Why didn't that surprise me?

She told me a little about the other two on the list, speaking quietly. 'This one, Sarah Cunningham, leads the sacristans.' To my puzzled look she said, impatiently, 'You Americans call them the Altar Guild, I've heard. Silly name. They're not a guild. Anyway, at this point she is virtually the only sacristan. She's a bossy woman and very High Church. Hated him with a passion because he had most of the plate locked away. Built like a lorry, and works out regularly.'

'So she could, physically, have done it.'

'Easy as breathing. The only problem is, I don't think she'd have done it in the church. She's very devout.'

'A difference of opinion about churchmanship hardly seems a motive for murder.'

'You don't know Sarah.'

I let it go. 'And the other?' I looked down at the last name she'd copied for me. David Worthman.

She picked up her teaspoon. Stirred tea that must by now be stone cold. Replaced the spoon on the saucer. Picked up the cup, sipped, made a face, and put it down. 'The fact is,' she said

at last, 'I didn't want to give you his name at
all. I had a struggle with my conscience.'

I looked hard at her. 'You think he's the one,
don't you?'

'He has the best motive, but I'm one of the
few who know about it. Oh, hell.' She paused,
got her voice back under control, and started
again. 'I've gone this far, I'll have to tell you.
That bloody priest killed his wife and child.'

Twenty-Five

I bit back the startled response that came to my
lips. 'Let's get out of here,' I said unceremoni-
ously, pushing my chair back and putting some
money on the table.

'My car,' I said urgently. 'Where we can be
completely private.' It wasn't far away. When
we had got in and closed the doors, I said,
'Now. My first question is this. If what you say
is true, why didn't it show up in Brading's
background check? The commission is very
thorough.'

It was a warm day, and the car was hot and
stuffy. I asked Mrs White if she'd like some air
conditioning. She shook her head and began her
story.

'It wasn't like that. He wasn't criminally
responsible, only morally. *Only!*' Again she had
to pause. 'They were a young couple, expecting
their first baby. Both of them had been attending

267

the cathedral for years; they were married there. By the old dean. She was having a hard time with her pregnancy so the doctor put her on bed rest. She was about six months along. The dean came to call.'

Mrs White rolled her window down a bit and wiped her face. She pointed to the envelope I still clutched in my hand. 'He asked the dean to anoint Lisa. That was her name – Lisa. She wasn't exactly ill, but she was very tired and discouraged and depressed. The dean refused. He said that was a papist practice, and all that was needed was good strong prayer. David pleaded with him, said he believed in the power of the Holy Spirit through ritual. I don't know all that was said, but it ended in a flaming row, the two men shouting at each other, and Lisa crying and sobbing. The dean stalked out, and Lisa got out of bed to call after him and try to get him to come back. David thinks she wanted to try to patch things up, but she tripped on her nightie and fell down the stairs.'

'Oh, dear God.'

'They got her to hospital right away, but she lost the baby and bled to death in the process. And the dean never once apologized, never once came to visit David, never mentioned anything about it.'

There was nothing to say.

'And if,' said Mrs White, 'if what I've told you leads to David's arrest for murder, I'll move heaven and earth for a verdict of justifiable homicide. I'm off.'

After a while, I turned on the ignition and sat

while chilled air washed over me, trying not to think about anything in particular.

My cell phone rang. It was Martha Rudge, giving me directions to her house for lunch. I wrote them down with some trepidation. I can still get lost in Sherebury, let alone a strange town, and I was feeling too wrung out to think clearly. But I set out and made only two wrong turns. In the end, it would have been quicker to walk, but I was so shaky from the awful story Mrs White had told me that walking might have been iffy, too.

Martha greeted me at the door of a neat, modern terrace house. It was tiny and in the sort of perfect order that I despair of ever achieving. Martha saw the admiration in my eyes and beamed. 'It's only a council house, but I like to keep it spick and span. Easier when a place is new, isn't it?'

I thought of my own house, four hundred odd years old, and said, 'Indeed.'

There was a pocket garden at the back of the house, just big enough for a tiny bed of cottage-garden flowers about to burst into bloom, a small cherry tree, and a patch of grass with a wicker table and two chairs. The table was laid with colourful mats.

'It's such a lovely day, I thought we'd eat out here,' said Martha, 'if that suits you.'

I helped carry out the plates and so on, and we settled down to our salads. It was a lovely meal, prawns and salmon and snow peas on a bed of greens that looked fresh from the garden.

I picked up a forkful of salad and found I couldn't bear the sight of it.

Martha looked at me anxiously. 'If you don't care for salmon, I can easily get you something else. There's cold chicken—'

'I love salmon. It's just . . . I guess I'm not very hungry.'

'There's something wrong, isn't there, dear?'

I took a deep breath. 'I just heard the most horrible story, and I let it upset me more than I should have. I'm sorry.'

'A story about the cathedral?'

'About the dean, and some of the congregation.' I shuddered involuntarily, and felt a tear trying to force its way out of one eye.

'Is this something Ruth Stevens told you?'

'No, I talked to another woman this morning. Mrs White. I forget her first name.'

'Oh, dear. And she told you about the Worthman family.'

'Yes.' I couldn't seem to stop the tears. I picked up my pretty paper napkin and dabbed at my eyes.

'You sit still. I'll be right back.'

I sniffed, blew my nose, and tried to pull myself together. Martha was back in less than a minute with a juice glass containing a puddle of amber liquid. 'Brandy. Drink it down.'

I obeyed. It was pretty terrible stuff, raw and biting, but it did the trick. I made myself finish what was in the glass and took a deep, shuddery breath. 'Thank you. I did actually need that.'

'You're thinking it was frightful brandy, and you're right. It's what I keep for the Christmas pudding, all I had in the house. Are you feeling better?'

'Much.'

'Here's a tissue. Have a good blow, then eat what you can of your lunch, or you'll find yourself staggering out of here too drunk to drive, what with strong drink on an empty stomach!'

I ate a forkful and found I was hungry. So we ate and talked only in snatches, about inconsequential matters, until we had finished our salad. Then Martha brought out coffee. 'We can have our sweet later. I'd like to know what Caroline White told you.'

'She gave me names of three people she thought capable of . . . of killing Dean Brading.'

'And those names were Captain Pringle, David Worthman, and perhaps Sarah Cunningham.'

'Exactly. She'd written it all out on the back of an envelope, but the writing was too tiny to read, so she told me the important parts.'

'May I see?'

She studied it in silence and then handed it back to me. 'I told you I wanted to air some dirty church linen. The Worthman story is the worst, but there are so many more nasty little stories. I hate to have to say it of a priest, but the fact is that Dean Brading was a fanatic, and, like all fanatics, he saw only one side of any issue. I don't want you to misunderstand me. He was a devout Christian who practiced exactly what he preached. The trouble is, his preaching was very narrow. If someone didn't believe *exactly* what he did, didn't worship *exactly* as he prescribed, then they were cast into the outer darkness. That

271

was what happened to Lisa Worthman. She asked the dean for something he saw as anathema, positively Satanic. In his eyes, her death was justice. She had turned away from the truth. If David had asked that the dean conduct her funeral, he would have refused. David didn't ask, of course. He turned away from the church completely and had her cremated, with no service at all.'

'What's happened to him?'

'I've tried to reach him, tried to help, but he's drinking a lot these days. Almost all the time, if truth were told. He's trying to kill the pain, but . . .' She spread her hands.

'Is he . . . I'm sorry, but I have to ask. Is he capable of murder?'

'If he were ever sober, yes, I think he would be. But he's never sober. He makes sure of that. Most days he can't even walk properly, and he won't consider a substance-abuse program.'

I shook my head. 'Sad. Worse than sad. Tragic. But you were going to tell me about some other . . . scandals, I guess is the word.'

'No. Not scandals, or not the way people usually use the word. There was never the slightest hint of sexual immorality about the dean.'

'I hope you don't mind my saying so, but he sounds as though he wasn't human enough for that. No wonder he never had any children.'

'Mrs Brading is rather . . . withdrawn, as well. I think perhaps they suited each other quite well. What I really wanted to tell you, Dorothy, is that whilst there may have been any number of people who would have had the dean sacked if

272

they could have found a way, and a good few who were ready to slap him in the face, or worse, should the occasion arise, I can think of only the one who hated him enough to murder him. And David Worthman scarcely exists anymore.'

'You mentioned Colonel Pringle.'

'I don't care a great deal about the Colonel, as you may have gathered, but he thinks far too much of his own image ever to do anything so undignified as bashing someone on the head, or pushing him into something that would have the same effect. Words are his weapons. As I said before, he's not a wicked man, only pompous and narrow-minded. He's a staunch supporter of the cathedral, emotionally and financially. That was why, finally, he quarrelled with the dean. He agreed with his churchmanship and his morality and theology, but he saw that the cathedral was dying from the dean's attitudes.'

'He would not have killed to keep the cathedral alive?'

'No. He was a soldier, Dorothy. He has killed, and has issued orders to kill, but only in war. He doesn't hold with murder, as my old granny would have said.'

I sighed. 'Someone killed Dean Brading. So far, all I've done here is apparently rule out everyone who wanted to.'

'You don't have to take my word for it. In fact, I know you and your husband won't. But check alibis as you will, I'll lay any odds you like you won't find a murderer at Chelton Cathedral.'

'Is there no one who hated the idea of him

273

maybe becoming bishop, hated it badly enough to stop it?'

'Hated the idea! My dear, haven't you been listening to me? There wasn't a man or woman in the congregation who wasn't praying daily for him to be bishop!'

'But . . . oh.' I rummaged in my mind for a memory. 'I think I understand,' I said slowly. 'Years ago, back when I lived in America, my town had a mayor I very much disliked. He ran for governor of the state. I voted for him. I would have voted twice, three times, if I could have. And he did win, and it got him out of Hillsburg, for a while anyway.'

'Exactly!'

Back at Lynncroft, I stretched out on the bed and called Alan. He answered on the first ring. 'I'm fine, love. No axe murderers have assaulted me, I've had no notes inviting me to midnight trysts in dungeons, nobody's even laced my tea with arsenic.'

'I'm delighted to hear it. And somewhat surprised. You've plainly been frittering away your time.'

'Actually, I've managed very usefully to prove, at least to my own satisfaction, that nobody in Chelton murdered the dean. Martha Rudge convinced me that everyone desperately wanted him to win the bishopric, to get him out of Chelton. He had a few loyal followers, apparently, but most of the congregation hated him heartily.'

'But not enough to murder him.'

274

'Not when a much simpler way of getting rid of him loomed. It seems there was only one man who probably would have murdered Brading if he could. I won't tell you the story now; it's very sad and I only want to tell it once, to everyone. But the man has become a hopeless drunk, trying his best, I suspect, to drink himself to death. Martha says, and Ruth Stevens confirms, that the poor guy can hardly stand up straight, let alone assault someone.'

'That should be checked.'

'Of course, and I'll give you the name when I get home. You can set the cops on it. But I trust Martha and Ruth to know. How about you? Have you come up with anything interesting at St Whoever's-it-is?'

'Much the same sort of thing. I haven't your gift of gossiping over teacups, and it's apparent I still come across as a policeman, no matter how hard I try to look harmless.'

'You're about as harmless as an irritated adder when you need to act. Most of the time you're a pussycat, of course, but it's true you look like a policeman. Of the very nicest kind, that is.'

'Adder, eh? I shall have to remember that. Anyway, I did manage to talk to quite a few people connected with St John's. They were a bit cautious, but one thing I can do well is read between the lines, and I got the distinct impression that the parishioners were mightily relieved when their vicar was elevated to dean of Chelton.'

'Any active hatred?'

'Not that I could detect. Nor did I learn of any particular scandal about him, to my regret.

I begin to think we're barking up the wrong tree, looking into his past.'

'I'm sure we're not. We just haven't hit the right branch yet. Have you heard from the others?'

'Not a word. When are you coming home?'

'Tomorrow. It's a bit late today, with the train schedules the way they are, but I've come to a dead end here, to mix the metaphor, and it's easier to think logically at home. And don't you dare laugh! I'm a very logical person, even if my connections sometimes mystify you.'

'You always mystify me. That's part of the charm, you know.' And our talk drifted into matters that had nothing whatever to do with the murder of Dean Brading. I went to sleep smiling.

Twenty-Six

I had told Alan I think best at home, and it's true. Sitting on my own sofa, with a cat or two in my lap and a sleeping dog at my feet, I can let my thoughts drift until they focus on whatever problem I'm trying to work out, and then I get into gear and start making my lists and getting organized. But I can think pretty well on trains, too, as long as no one's screaming into a mobile phone. (Why do people think they have to shout into those things?)

I was lucky this time. I didn't catch the first train out of Chelton, which would have carried the commuters, but the second, which was nearly

276

empty. I had the carriage to myself for a while, in fact. I found my little notebook in my purse and started to write some random thoughts.

Why murder? I wrote. Was there really no other way to keep the man from becoming a bishop, if that was what the murderer had in mind? I could think of any number of ways. Manufacturing a scandal about the man would be the easiest. Start a rumour on Facebook or one of the other social media. I don't understand them well, myself, but I do know that really hot news can spread across the globe far faster than a raging wildfire, and once it's out there, it becomes almost impossible to deny. Doesn't matter that poor so-and-so never did any of what's being said about him. Try proving a negative.

Or you could just start a whispering campaign. Slower, but equally effective. In some ways, even more so, because the story would get changed from one source to another. I remembered the old game of Telephone. The message at the end was hardly recognizable. And the whispering campaign had the advantage that it was almost impossible to track the rumour to its source.

Or call an anonymous tip to a newspaper, or TV station. That isn't so easy now, in these days of universal caller ID and almost no public telephones. But it could be done.

Oh, there were any number of nasty ways to bring a man down, especially a clergyman. The clergy are human beings like the rest of us, but they are held to a higher standard, and there are few things the human race enjoys more than discovering someone's feet of clay.

So, why murder?

I had once held forth to Alan that the root of almost all motives to murder was fear. Fear that the victim would harm the killer in some way – steal his job, or his wife, or reveal something the killer wanted hidden. Or, conversely, that the victim would keep from the killer something that he passionately wanted – the better job, the woman, the riches.

I saw now that I had left out one of the most powerful motives of all: sheer hatred. I had no doubt, from what Caroline and Martha had told me, that David Worthman would have killed Dean Brading had he been capable of it. And, God help me, I wasn't so sure it wouldn't have been justified. But if what they had said was true, he had crawled so far into the bottle that he was incapable of any action.

We had been concentrating, at least all of us acting as 'private detectives', on church politics. What liberal might have hated and feared the idea of Dean Brading becoming a bishop, hated it so much that hatred turned to murder? What conservative might have seen that Brading's rigid approach to the life of the Church would harm their cause, instead of enhancing it? What proponent of women's consecration? What gay activist? Which one, from any of the many contentious groups, might have felt forced to act in this terrible way?

But maybe it had nothing to do with church politics. Maybe the vitriol of hatred was poured out on Andrew Brading the man, rather than Dean Brading the potential bishop.

I mulled that over the whole way home.

Alan had planned to come home today, too, but he wasn't there when I got to the station, so I took a cab home. Jane would have been happy to pick me up, but she isn't getting any younger, and I didn't want to give her the trouble.

Watson greeted me effusively, and the cats condescended to twine themselves around my ankles a bit. Cats are not, as some people think, indifferent to their humans. They love us, but in a less needy way than dogs. I do think a dog's world is shattered when his people are away. And how, after all, can he know we're coming back? We always have before, true, but I'm not sure a dog's mind can remember that and draw the obvious conclusion. At any rate, for Watson it was Christmas and his birthday and all the happy times together, just because I was home. It was a heart-warming reception.

I went over to Jane's to thank her for looking after my babies, and, of course, she invited me to share her lunch. As we partook of homemade bread and chicken salad, we also shared what information we'd been able to amass. I related some of what I'd learned and then waited for her gleanings.

Jane had been busy on the phone. She was a teacher for years, and as her students grew up and moved on, a lot of them kept in touch, so her network spread all over the country and as far as Australia and America and parts of Africa and Asia. She had, she said, placed a few calls and then let the network take over, passing on her inquiries to friends of friends of friends.

'Most of it irrelevant,' she went on. 'Repetitive. Not a popular man.'

'And that's throwing roses at it,' I said.

'Mm. Heard he was thrown out of his first job.'

'When he was curate? What do you mean "thrown out"? Did someone catch him being too friendly with the choir boys, or what?'

'Never any rumour like that about him. Cold fish. Vicar decided he was no go as a priest, found him the school job.'

'And I don't understand that one, either. By all accounts, he hated children. Why send him to a prep school?'

'Thirty years ago. Discipline still rigid. Brading good at discipline.'

'I'll just bet he was! So why did he decide to leave? Or was it not his decision?'

'Something happened. Don't know what. People are close-mouthed. Police need to dig there.'

There was a sudden cacophony of barking, almost covering the voice behind me. 'Where are the police supposed to dig?'

'Alan!' I didn't jump up to greet him. A person of my years, with my joints, doesn't jump. But I got to my feet as quickly as I could, and gave him a big hug. 'It feels like years,' I murmured in his ear. His only reply was an extra squeeze, which left me breathless and content.

'Had lunch?' asked Jane.

'No, and breakfast was a long time ago. Thank you *very* much, Jane.'

'Jane's been regaling me with what she's learned. So far, it seems nobody liked our dead dean very much.'

'No. But mere dislike, even when raised to a pretty high pitch, is not usually a motive for murder. Not this sort of murder. Money, ambition, sex, revenge – those are the usual things that set people off.'

'And the greatest of these is money.'

Alan swallowed a mouthful of chicken salad and sighed. 'Very often, yes. Tragically small amounts, sometimes. I was once in charge of a case where a woman murdered her elderly aunt for the sake of a fifty-pound legacy.'

'Did Brading leave any money?' I asked instantly.

'The Gloucester people looked into that, of course. There wasn't a lot, and it all went to his wife.'

'Aha!' I said, but without much conviction.

'Your heart wasn't in that, and for good reason. Mrs Brading is independently wealthy.'

'Thought you knew that,' said Jane reprovingly. 'Common knowledge. Why he married her.'

'I had been wondering about that. From all I've heard, he wasn't much interested in women. Nor, I must add, in men, from a sexual standpoint at any rate.'

'Cold fish,' Jane repeated. 'Knew he'd never make enough money as a priest to live decently. A scandal, what the Church pays its people. Had to marry money or take a different path in life.'

'So the money angle is pretty well washed out.' I took a deep breath. 'Alan, you'd better finish your lunch. I have a story to tell, and it's going to take away your appetite.'

He ate rapidly while we let Jane finish her

narrative. 'Nothing much to tell. Same attitudes everywhere. Respected as a priest, but not as a man. Made no allowances. Follow the rules or else. Followed them himself, expected everyone else to do as he did.'

'He followed all the rules, it seems to me, except one of the two most important ones,' I said. '"Love thy neighbour as thyself."'

'Don't think the man knew much about love. Old Testament all the way.'

'You know, I'll undoubtedly be barred from the Pearly Gates for saying so, but I'm so devoutly glad there is now no chance for that man to become our bishop. And honestly, Alan, saving your presence, but I still can't imagine how he ever made it to the shortlist.'

Alan downed a last bit of bread and sat back. 'Political pressure. There was enough opposition that I'm quite sure he wouldn't have been selected in the end. You know I can't tell you what went on in the meetings, but I think I'm allowed to say that Dean Brading was controversial. To say the least. But you said you had a story to tell.'

'Yes, and if the dean had lived, I would hope that someone would have told it to the world. They might not have, though, out of respect for the victim's feelings. Although he might never have known, poor man.' I told them about the Worthman family, as briefly and unemotionally as I could manage it.

'Whew!' said Alan when I'd finished. 'It's almost unbelievable that the man could have been that callous. I have every sympathy for the husband and father involved. To lose them both, and in such a terrible way . . . I'll have to call Derek, though, you know.'

'Yes, I do know. The Gloucestershire police will have to check it out. Maybe they can get the man into rehab and dry him out, though I'm not sure that's what he wants.'

'Probably not. He wants oblivion, permanently.'

Jane spoke for the first time. 'Heard the story, not all the details. Vile. Used to be a good man. Knew his mother. Gone now, thank God.' She wiped away a tear, and then glared at us, daring us to notice her shocking surrender to sentimentality.

'Anyway, Alan, that absolutely hateful story got me to thinking. What if we're looking in the wrong direction? What if Brading's murder has nothing to do with his being named as a candidate for bishop? What if it's a purely personal motive, like David Worthman's? He couldn't act on his hatred, unless everyone who knows him is wrong about his perpetual drunkenness. But what if there's someone else who could – and did?'

Alan sighed mightily. 'You just widened the scope of the investigation by several thousand possible suspects, you realize.'

'Almost everyone who's ever known the man, in short. Yes, I know. But maybe Jonathan or Walter will have come up with something. Has anyone heard from them?'

'Home tomorrow,' said Jane. 'Coming here first, maybe even tonight if traffic isn't too bad.'

'Good. Shall we convene tomorrow for breakfast? Our house this time; Alan scrambles a mean egg.'

Next morning, I woke up early, to Watson's great delight, and took him for a long walk. I was hungry for the sights and sounds of my adopted home. If anything, I love England more than ever, now that I'm a part of it. I have friends and family, cats and a dog, a husband I adore, and a seventeenth-century house which requires constant maintenance, constant care, and which I love almost as much as I love Alan. I'll never quite belong here in the same way that Alan does. My ancestors are buried thousands of miles away, not here in some country churchyard that's existed for half a millennium, at least. I don't quite speak the language; Americanisms still creep in, and now and then I'm baffled by some English expression. I still look American, somehow, and everyone I meet seems to know my origins, even though when my American friends visit here they all say I talk exactly like an Englishwoman.

But there is something deep within me that responds to the English air, the English way of doing things, the very colour of the sky and shape of the clouds. This, in some indefinable way, has always been my home, was my home before I was born. This is my place.

Watson and I came home across the Close, and there stood the Cathedral, the great, looming grey presence that has become another member of my family, a benevolent great-grandfather, perhaps – still, silent, watchful, protective. There were, in World War Two, brigades of men ready around the clock to protect the Cathedral from enemy action. They would have died to save it.

As I stood gazing up at the far pinnacles, I thought I, too, would be ready to die for it.

Watson gave his head a shake to rattle his collar and tags, and remind me it was breakfast time. 'Yes, mutt, you're very good at bringing me down to earth, aren't you?'

He trotted ahead, lest I had forgotten where his food bowl was.

Passing through the gate into our street, I saw two vehicles parked inches from each other. One was Bob Finch's disreputable old truck, falling apart but still serviceable for carrying garden tools. I could hear Bob whistling tunelessly as he worked in my back garden. The other, squeezed between Bob's car and the gate, was a highly polished, sleek Jaguar that had to be Jonathan's.

Lovely! They were here!

Watson was waiting impatiently by the front door, so I let him in and followed him to the voices in the kitchen.

'There you are, woman! We thought you and Watson had been abducted.'

'No, we managed to avoid both the sinister Chinaman and the tall, distinguished but menacing man wearing the ribbon of some foreign order. By the skin of our teeth, I might add, and only through the valour of Watson, here, who is slowly dying of starvation.'

'Here, pooch,' said Walter, handing him half a sausage. 'Reward for a hero.'

'No more of that, now,' I said sternly, filling his bowl with his own food. With an almost visible shrug he went to it, wolfed it down, and then returned confidently to the table. I poured myself a cup of coffee and sat down between Jonathan and Jane. 'Anything left for me?'

'Eggs and bacon coming right up,' said my resident cook. 'And I popped bread in the toaster when I heard you open the door. I must keep my American happy with hot toast.'

'You bet. So, have you all reported in, or did you save any tidbits for me?'

'We saved it all for you,' said Walter, 'though I've really nothing to tell. There were only three people in the whole village who remembered their long-ago curate at all, and their memories were vague in the extreme. It was thirty years ago, after all, and he didn't seem to have made much of an impression. One old cove said he didn't like him, couldn't understand a word of his sermons, and his wife thought she remembered him being cross with some of the children. No details at all, I'm sorry to say.'

'Then I suppose I'm going to be the star of this show,' said Jonathan, 'because I did find out something at the school. Something that's not nice at all, I'm afraid.'

Alan had just set a plate of perfectly scrambled eggs in front of me, with a lovely slice of sizzling bacon. 'Jonathan, do you mind if I eat while you talk? I'm sorry, but I'm starving.'

'You may not be hungry when you've heard what I have to say,' he said grimly. 'Jane and Alan gave us a rough summary of what you all had learned. I have a story to tell that's something like your worst one, Dorothy.'

'It concerns a child, doesn't it?' I said with foreboding, putting down my fork.

'Yes, a child at the school Brading headed. I have to say that no one wanted to talk about it, and it took all my skills – the skills you taught me, Alan – to dig it out. I couldn't get a name. Everyone claimed they didn't remember.'

'They remembered,' said Alan. 'But you can't get behind that excuse. It's the one lie you can't dislodge except with scare tactics. You can use those with suspects, but not with witnesses. Go ahead, Jonathan.'

'He was just ten, the boy. He was small and slender, no good at games. A nerd, we'd call him now, and I suppose the boys did then. That, and worse. He was bullied, at first emotionally and then physically. He went to the headmaster.'

'Stop,' I said. 'I don't think I need to hear any more. Brading did nothing about it.'

'I'm afraid I have to go on, Dorothy, because it's worse than that. Brading, according to reports from the other boys, told the boy he needed to stand up for himself, give as good as he got, start acting like a man instead of – well, I gathered he used some pretty strong language.

'Those boys are grown now, many of them with children of their own. The one who told me the most was the abused boy's one friend at the school. He tried his best to comfort him, to make the others stop, but he was only ten himself, and outnumbered.'

Jonathan took a deep breath. 'The boy hanged himself. Bedsheets tied to a window frame.'

Twenty-Seven

We sat and listened to the kitchen clock ticking merrily away. Watson whined and came to sit on my feet. I gave him my almost untouched plate.

Alan cleared his throat. 'It was hushed up, of course.'

'Of course. The other parents, the school governors, Brading – all of them conspired to pretend nothing had happened. The police were never called in. Brading told the boy's parents there had been a terrible accident, the boy choked to death. The mother, who had never been strong, had a complete breakdown. The boy was their only child.'

'And Brading?'

'Brading,' said Jonathan, speaking the word as though it left a bad taste in his mouth, 'Brading was then calling himself Stephen Owen. It was part of his name, so technically it wasn't a lie. I suppose he thought the role of schoolmaster beneath his dignity, or unsuitable for a priest, or something. When he started making it known that he was interested in a position in a church, he reverted back to Andrew Brading, so that, just in case word somehow got out about the school disaster, he could further distance himself from it.

'The boys had done very well for themselves in their further education. The parents were well pleased with the excellent discipline they had acquired, and the sound doctrine they had been

288

taught. Someone influential recommended him for the position at Upper Longwood.' Jonathan shrugged.

'The Teflon priest,' I said. I got blank stares. 'An American president, years ago, became known as the Teflon president, because nothing seemed to stick to him.'

'Yes, well, in the end something stuck to Brading.' Alan sighed deeply. 'You and I will have to go to the authorities with this, Jonathan. You got no hint of a name?'

'None. Nor of where the parents are now, though I gathered the mother never recovered and had to be institutionalized.'

'The father will have to be found. There's your hatred motive, Dorothy. Almost exactly the same as the poor man in Chelton. And if this one hasn't turned to drugs or alcohol to numb the pain, he may be our murderer. Dorothy, what is it?'

'I . . . excuse me, everyone. I'm not feeling very well.'

I went to our bedroom and closed the door.

I lay on the bed, remembering fragments. Something Jane had said about a member of the commission. An encounter in Birmingham. Jonathan's story.

I thought about what had started this train of events, the search for a bishop, for a holy man to lead his people, and the horrors that had ensued.

But no, that wasn't the beginning. It all began long ago, probably with a boy deprived of love, a boy who grew up to be a rigid, unforgiving clergyman, a man who knew everything about the law and nothing about mercy or grace.

Alan came into the room. 'Headache, love?'

'Heartache.' I sat up on one elbow. 'Where are the rest?'

'They went back to Jane's. They're worried about you, and so am I.'

I nodded and licked my dry lips. 'Alan, will you go with me to Birmingham? As soon as we can?'

He looked at me searchingly. 'You're on to something, aren't you?'

'I think so. Will you go with me?'

'To the ends of the earth, darling. When shall we go?'

'Now. This minute.'

'Why in such a hurry?'

'I don't know. I just feel – oh, Alan, please would you just call Mr Robinson and ask if we can come to see him, right away?'

I had to work to keep my voice steady. Alan gave me another close look and pulled out his phone.

I washed my face and ran a comb through my hair and was ready to go. Alan ended the call. 'His wife says he was called out to an emergency, but should be home by the time we get there. I'll get the car out and tell Jane we're leaving.'

'Why?'

'The animals, darling.'

'Oh, of course. I'm sorry, I'm . . .' I waved my hand vaguely.

The traffic was no worse than usual, I suppose, but I pushed the car every inch of the way. My shoulders grew stiff with anxiety; the headache Alan had suspected began to develop in earnest.

'Do you want to tell me about it, love?' he asked once.

'Not till I'm sure. Well, I am sure, really, but . . .'

He didn't press me. We said very little for the rest of the trip.

Alan found the Robinsons' house without difficulty, and I inwardly cursed the stiffness that kept me from running to the door. Alan helped me out of the car and held my elbow firmly as we went up the path. My head was pounding.

Mr Robinson answered the door, and the look on his face brought my tears to the surface. 'We're too late, aren't we?'

'I never suspected a thing,' said Mr Robinson. 'Brian was so distraught for so long, I saw no change. I blame myself greatly, and I shall have no qualms at all about declaring this a suicide while of unsound mind.'

'I should have worked it out earlier, too. All the clues were there. I just didn't put it together.'

'I still haven't,' said Alan. 'Why don't you tell us, Dorothy?'

Mrs Robinson had slipped out to make tea. She put a cup in front of me as I assembled my thoughts.

'All right,' I said at last. 'I'm Brian Rawles. I've just opened the morning paper. Maybe I'm sitting at my wife's bedside, my wife who will never be sane and whole again. I read, idly, about some priests who have been named as candidates for a bishopric in some obscure diocese. A name jumps out at me. Andrew Stephen Owen Brading.

'I'm still a churchgoer, despite everything. My rector, Mr Robinson, has been a great help to me, but nothing can penetrate my despair. I've heard

291

of Andrew Brading, dean of a cathedral not far away. I had never, until now, seen his full name. Is it possible that this is the Stephen Owen who caused my son's suicide, who destroyed my life?

'I kiss my wife, though she doesn't know it, and go hurriedly to get a day off work. I take a train to Chelton. The trains are slow, the schedules awkward. With every delay I become more impatient, more frenzied. I get out of the train at Chelton and walk to the cathedral, with no thought in my mind but to find the dean and find out for sure if it's the same man.'

My mouth was dry. I sipped some tea.

'I go to the church. I find the dean. He's just leaving. There doesn't seem to be anyone else around. He doesn't want to talk to me; says he's been away all day and is eager to get home; I should make an appointment. I think I recognize him, but I'm not sure, so I ask him straight out: was he ever headmaster at Stony Estcott? Yes, he says, and tries to push past me. I lose it. I yell at him, tell him I'm the father of the boy who killed himself. I can see he barely remembers the matter! I don't know what happens next – I'm so full of anger and hate – but then I see that he's lying there on the floor. He's hit his head on the desk. He's unconscious. I'm still furious. I leave him to his own devices and go to the railway station to go home. And the next day I learn that he has died.'

Mrs Robinson filled my cup with fresh tea and pushed it toward me. I picked it up with shaking hands and drank.

'I didn't want to tell you, Alan. I really, really didn't want to tell you.'

292

He covered my hand with his own.

'He will meet justice now, Mrs Martin,' said Mr Robinson. 'Perfect justice tempered with perfect mercy. I think he truly didn't want to live, hasn't wanted to for quite a time. It was his wife's death yesterday that tipped the balance. I had barely heard about it when I heard of his suicide. He left a note, you know, and you're quite right. It was an accident, but it was he who struck the blow that proved fatal in the end.'

'Did he say anything about Mr Lovelace?' asked Alan.

'Not a word.'

'Then perhaps Lovelace really did kill himself. We may never know for sure.'

'So many deaths, so many tragedies, and all so unnecessary.' I fished in my purse for two more ibuprofen, with little hope that they'd take away the pain in my head, or in my soul.

Kenneth Allenby came to see me a day or two later. I was sitting petting the cats and staring into space when Alan showed him into the parlour. He sat down opposite me. 'How are you, Dorothy?'

'I'm all right. I'm fine.'

'Now, you wouldn't lie to a priest, would you?' He handed me the box of tissues.

'It's just . . . I keep thinking I should have figured it out much sooner. There were so many things I overlooked, so many things I missed, looking in the wrong direction. Maybe he'd still be alive if I . . .' I blew my nose.

'If you were superhuman? If you knew everything? There's only One who knows everything, and He's sorted it all by now. It's not your responsibility. It's his.'

'But I'm supposed to be able to solve puzzles. I'm good at it.'

'Yes. But not perfect. And you weren't meant to be. Humility is a virtue, you know.'

'I keep trying to learn that. But, oh, Dean, I keep thinking of the damage that man did! And to think that he might have been our bishop! I get cold every time I think of it.'

'But God didn't let it happen, did he? And before you ask me if I think a murderer can be an instrument of God, don't. I don't know the answer to that any more than you do. I only know that things do, ultimately, work out for the best, even if "ultimately" may not be in this life.'

A year passed. It was a time of reflection, a time of healing. The Crown Appointments Commission got itself back together, recovered its equanimity, and proceeded to its business with a good deal less disharmony. They had, I liked to think, taken a lesson from seeing what unbridled strife could bring to pass.

One fine July day, Alan, Jane, and I made the trip to London. The Allenbys had gone ahead, since Kenneth had a role to play in the ceremony. The tourists were gawking, wondering if some royal occasion was going on at Westminster Abbey. We made our way through the crowd, presented our tickets at the west door, and were shown to our seats. Glorious music began, the stately procession entered, and we sat enthralled to watch the consecration of the new Bishop of Shrebury.

294